THE MIDWIVES *of* LARK LANE

BOOKS BY PAM HOWES

Fast Movin' Train

The Lark Lane Series

The Factory Girls of Lark Lane

The Shop Girls of Lark Lane

The Nurses of Lark Lane

The Mersey Trilogy

The Lost Daughter of Liverpool

The Forgotten Family of Liverpool

The Liverpool Girl

The Rock n Roll Romance series

Three Steps to Heaven

Til I Kissed You

Always on My Mind

That'll Be the Day

Not Fade Away

The Fairground series

Cathy's Clown

The Cheshire Set series

Hungry Eyes

Short stories

It's Only Words

THE MIDWIVES *of* LARK LANE

PAM HOWES

bookouture

Published by Bookouture in 2019

An imprint of Storyfire Ltd.
Carmelite House
50 Victoria Embankment
London EC4Y 0DZ

www.bookouture.com

ISBN: 978-1-78681-768-6
eBook ISBN: 978-1-78681-767-9

Dedicated to the memories of Scott Engel 1943–2019 and John Maus 1943–2011, who, along with drummer Gary Leeds, were the founder members of the fabulous Walker Brothers trio. Thanks for the wonderful music and the fond memories. May the sun always shine for you, Scott and John. Xxx

Prologue

Aigburth June 1960

Cathy Lomax eyed her reflection in the full-length mirror. She smoothed the cream silk fabric down and did a little twirl. The dress looked good, and not at all home-made. Her gran had done her proud. The dress was long and floaty, with loose Grecian-style sleeves and criss-cross ties down the front. She couldn't believe her wedding day was here at last and she was marrying her fiancé Gianni Romano after waiting so long. They'd been engaged a few years and their daughter Lucy was almost eighteen months old. Granny had told her that wearing white wasn't really appropriate, but there was no reason why she couldn't have a lovely wedding dress, no matter what the colour.

Cathy wasn't too bothered; her lifestyle was hardly conventional. Not many girls had a handsome, professional motorbike rider as a future husband. Gianni had rejoined his father's fair when it reopened in April after the winter break. Cathy and Lucy had stayed in Liverpool, first spending some time with Cathy's mam and three boisterous younger step-siblings before moving in with Granny Lomax at her peaceful bungalow. The last couple of years had been different and nothing like the ones she'd planned for herself after her longed-for nursing career had been put on hold when she'd found herself unexpectedly pregnant.

Cathy hoped that one day she would be able to resume her training. Still, things had turned out pretty well, although she was always waiting, heart in mouth, for a telephone call, or a knock at the door, that would tell her Gianni had been injured, or even worse… She shook herself and pushed those thoughts away.

Today, she and Gianni were sharing their wedding day with her mam Alice and her husband-to-be, Johnny Harrison. As soon as her mam's divorce from Jack Dawson, who was serving time in prison, had been granted, Johnny had asked Alice to marry him. Cathy had suggested, jokingly at first, that they should have a joint wedding. But the more they talked about it, the more they liked the idea. The vicar of St Michael's had known the family for many years and was delighted to conduct a joint ceremony for their early-June wedding.

Granny Lomax popped her head around the door. 'You ready, Cath? The car will be here in a minute.' She stepped into the room. Her lilac flower-trimmed hat was the exact same shade as her smart new dress and jacket. She picked up a circlet of pink rosebuds from the bed, popped them on top of Cathy's glossy dark hair and handed her the matching bouquet.

Cathy smiled as Granny's eyes filled. She looked away and fiddled with the silk bow that tied the bouquet together, while Granny composed herself and dabbed at her tears with a lace hanky.

'Oh, love, you look beautiful. I do wish my Terry were here to give you away. He'd be so proud.'

'I wish my dad was still here too,' Cathy said, a sob catching her throat. 'I spent so little time with him before he died.'

Granny smiled and patted her arm 'I daresay I will make a good enough job of it. I certainly intend to do my best and he'd be proud of us both.'

'He would, and we'll be fine,' Cathy said. 'Thank you so much for letting me and Lucy stay with you for the last few months. I know it's not been easy, having a toddler around, but I don't think

I could have coped much longer at Mam's. It was like a madhouse, most of the time.'

Granny laughed. 'Poor Alice, she certainly has her hands full. It'll be much easier for her when Johnny moves in permanently.'

Cathy raised an eyebrow. 'It will, although he's there most of the time now and they're really good when he's around. It's great that Mam was granted a divorce quicker than normal because of her circumstances, rather than having to wait years.'

Granny pursed her lips. 'Best all round. Those children never really knew their father anyway. They're better off without him.'

'They are.' Cathy shuddered at the thought of her evil stepfather.

'Here's the car,' Granny said as a horn tooted outside. 'I hope little Lucy's all right.'

'She'll be fine, Gran,' Cathy said. Her ex nursing colleagues had picked Lucy up earlier and were taking her to the church, all dressed up in her new outfit. 'They all love her to bits and will spoil her rotten.'

*

Gianni fiddled with the collar of his new cream shirt. His stepmother Maria moved his hand away and straightened his tie for the second time. She fastened a carnation into his buttonhole and stepped back.

'Do I look okay?' Gianni, who spent most of his days in jeans and a leather jacket, asked.

'You look very smart,' Maria assured him. 'The brown suit was the right choice.'

'Thanks for helping. I would have got it all wrong.'

'That's what stepmums are for,' Maria said softly. She hugged him and he blinked rapidly. His dad, Luca, rubbed his arm and broke his thoughts. 'You ready, son? You'll do Cathy proud.'

'As I'll ever be, Dad,' Gianni said as Maria went to answer a knock at the door.

They were staying at the Adelphi Hotel in the city centre where the wedding reception would later be taking place. The porter announced that the car was waiting by the main entrance to take them to the church. They followed him down the long, carpeted corridor, past the room where staff bustled in and out, preparing for the wedding reception later. His dad had booked the honeymoon suite for him and Cathy; he and Maria would look after Lucy in their own room tonight.

*

Alice took a deep breath as her next-door neighbour Millie finished pinning up her hair. Her younger daughters were sitting on the bed, smartly dressed and ready to go, their long dark hair fashioned into glossy ringlets. Sandra and Rosie were joint bridesmaids and looked pretty in their pale pink satin dresses, with cream sashes, that Millie had bought from Lewis's with her staff discount. She'd had quite a job fastening their hair up in rags to create the desired effect. But it had been worth all the squeals and grumbles. Their cream headdresses finished the outfits off beautifully. Alice's little son Rodney was next door at Millie's with Johnny and Millie's husband Jimmy, who were responsible for making sure his new outfit stayed clean.

'Right, Alice,' Millie said. 'Let's get your outfit on and then we're ready for when the cars come. You'll go in the first one with the girls and I'll get in the next one with the boys and we'll see you at the church. Jimmy will be waiting to walk you to the altar and give you away.' Millie lifted Alice's pale blue silk, slim-fitting dress from the wardrobe and helped her into it. She fastened up the zip at the back and handed her the little bolero jacket edged in a slightly darker shade of blue, which complemented the dress perfectly. 'Something new and something blue,' she said and dug into her pocket. 'And here's my silver bracelet for something borrowed.' Millie fastened it around Alice's slender wrist and smiled.

'I just need something old now,' Alice said. 'That's me, I guess. I can't believe it's the third time I'm doing this.'

'Third time lucky, eh, gel,' Millie said. 'Fingers crossed.'

'God, I hope so, Millie, I really do.'

'Oh, there's the doorbell. Now let's get you out of here before Johnny claps eyes on you. No bad luck needed today. Let's start this marriage as you mean to go on. Come on, girls,' she said to Sandra and Rosie. 'Your flower baskets and your mam's bouquet are on the table in the dining room.'

*

Gianni and his family arrived at the church in plenty of time and walked inside. The pews were filling fast and he nodded to friends and neighbours of Alice's who he recognised from the streets around the Lark Lane area. He spotted his friend and best man Davy in the front pew and Davy's wife Debbie sitting in the row behind him and went straight over to them. Cathy's friends from the hospital, Karen, Ellie and Jean, were sitting on the pew behind Debbie with his old mates, Nigel and Colin. Jean held his daughter Lucy on her knee; she was all dressed up in a pretty dress, her dark hair falling in soft curls around her chubby little face. He stopped to tickle her under the chin and she gave him a grin and held out her arms. He gave her a quick cuddle, then handed her back to Jean.

'Oh, *you* look nice and smart,' Debbie said as he drew level and dropped a kiss on her cheek. 'Almost as handsome as my Davy.'

'Thanks, Debs, so do you.' Gianni admired her pale green linen suit that looked lovely with her striking auburn hair, the first thing you noticed about Debbie. He shook Davy's hand and handed over two ring boxes. 'Red box is Cathy's and the black one's mine.'

Davy shoved them into his jacket pockets, muttering, 'Left Cathy's, right Gianni's.'

'You nervous?' Debbie leaned forward and asked, as Gianni sat down next to Davy in the front pew.

'A bit,' Gianni admitted. 'I can't believe it's happening at last. Ah, here's Johnny.' He waved as Johnny hurried up the aisle. 'Jimmy's his best man but he's walking Alice up the aisle,' he told Davy.

Johnny puffed out his cheeks as he reached the front pew where Gianni was nervously tapping his foot. They both turned as the congregation fell silent. The organist stopped playing background music and struck up with 'Here Comes the Bride'.

Gianni caught his breath as Cathy, a vision of loveliness, glided up the aisle on her granny's arm. Alice, following, was a picture of happiness and pride as Jimmy escorted her, followed by Sandra and Rosie and little Rodney, smart in his navy velvet pageboy outfit, his dark hair neatly brushed. Gianni's heart soared. Cathy was his only true love, and she'd soon be his. Not that she wasn't already, but to wake up next to her tomorrow as her husband, and every day after for the rest of his life, would be a dream come true.

*

Cathy's heart leapt as she looked at Gianni, his brown eyes shining with love. She stopped by his side and handed her bouquet to Sandra, who, cheeks flushed with importance, glanced smugly at Rosie and stuck out her tongue. Alice joined Johnny and handed her bouquet to Rosie, shooting Sandra a warning *behave yourself* look.

Gianni's hand crept out and stroked Cathy's hand and her stomach flipped at the simple touch. She took a deep breath and turned her attention to the vicar as he welcomed everyone to his church. She couldn't wait to be alone with Gianni tonight. It was ages since they'd had undisturbed time together. She turned her attention back to what the vicar was saying, pushing thoughts of lying naked in Gianni's arms to one side.

*

Gianni rummaged in his inside jacket pocket and pulled out a sheet of paper. He got to his feet and tapped a wine goblet to get the guests' attention. Even though they had invited only close friends and the extended family, there were enough of them to make quite a noise. Alice had told him she didn't feel confident enough to make the speech that traditionally the bride's father would have made, so Gianni had agreed to speak on Alice's behalf too. She had written down a few words she wanted him to say and he'd added them to his speech. Not that he was good with formality either, but he'd tried to make it amusing and hoped the guests would think it was too. He cleared his throat as a silence fell on the room; all eyes turned in his direction.

He felt Cathy's hand on his back, caressing him gently, and took a deep breath. He thanked Cathy's mam for entrusting her daughter to him. On behalf of Alice, he thanked Granny Lomax for giving Cathy away; Maria and his dad for standing by him and helping with the cost of the wedding; their guests, for their well-wishes and many gifts and cards. He thanked Sandra and Rosie, who giggled and squirmed in their seats, for being beautiful bridesmaids; and Rodney for being a good pageboy. He cracked a few jokes, and then turned to Cathy.

'And last but not least, I'd like to thank the wonderful girl beside me, for agreeing to become my wife, *and* for giving me our beautiful daughter, Lucy.' He took Cathy's hand and looked into her eyes as everyone clapped. Then he handed the reins to Jimmy, who made his best man speech for Alice and Johnny, before encouraging Davy to do his best man honours for Gianni and Cathy. Both couples got to their feet as a loud cheer rang around the room, accompanied by a few bawdy comments about wedding nights, and were toasted by their guests.

*

Cathy took her daughter from Jean and gave her a cuddle. She sat down with her friends while the hotel staff cleared tables. Evening guests began arriving and the room quickly filled. People

Cathy hadn't seen for ages, from Lewis's department store, where she'd worked after leaving school, nursing colleagues from the hospital where she'd begun her training, Gianni's friends from the company where he'd served his apprenticeship before joining the fair. So many people to catch up with and share their special day. The evening guests took seats around the room while others replenished their drinks at the bar. The lights dimmed and Gianni's friends, who'd brought along a record player and some records, asked the bride and groom to prepare for the first dance. Cathy handed Lucy back to Jean and reached for Gianni's outstretched hand.

He led her to the middle of the floor and took her in his arms as Tab Hunter's 'Young Love' filled the room. They were joined by Alice and Johnny. Cathy caught her breath and looked into Gianni's eyes as everyone clapped. Her stomach flipped and her legs felt like jelly.

'I asked him to play this,' Gianni said.

'Oh, I can't believe you remembered,' she whispered, thinking back to that first night in the Rumblin' Tum coffee bar when he'd held her close, looked into her eyes, and they'd danced to this song.

'How could I ever forget the night I fell in love with you?' he whispered back.

She buried her head in his chest and he held her tight as they danced. Cathy felt like she might burst with happiness. What a wonderful, but very different future they had to look forward to.

Chapter One

June 1960

As Luca's car drove over the rutted field and bumped towards the fairground, Cathy held her breath as she was thrown against Gianni, who held her hand. Maria turned from the front passenger seat to smile at them. They'd enjoyed a few days in New Brighton with Lucy for a short honeymoon and then had travelled to Leeds, after stopping off at Lucerne Street to say goodbye to her mam and family. She'd been sad to leave them all, but she would see them later in the year when the fair pitched up in Liverpool. She felt so excited at the prospect of her and Gianni living together at last. They'd waited such a long time. As the car pulled up alongside a shiny silver caravan, Gianni turned to Cathy and hugged her. She passed a sleeping Lucy across to Maria, and Gianni helped her out of the car and slipped his arm around her waist.

Luca also clambered out from the driver's seat and ceremoniously handed a set of caravan keys to her. 'Your new home, Mrs Romano,' he announced with a theatrical bow, a benevolent smile on his face as he gestured to the caravan that gleamed in the bright sunlight.

Cathy threw her arms around his neck. 'Thank you so much,' she said, tears of joy springing to her eyes.

'May you both be very happy.' Luca grinned as congratulations rang out and a loud cheer went up from the crowd of fairground workers, who'd gathered around the newlyweds, clapping and whistling.

'What a lovely welcome,' Gianni said, beaming. 'Ready?' He took the keys from Cathy and unlocked the door. He swept her into his arms to more cheers, and carried her up the few steps.

'You'll put your back out.' She grinned as he lowered her to the floor. She gasped and looked around, mouth agape. The red and cream interior looked warm and colourful; everything matched, including the cushions and curtains. Red upholstered benches formed an L-shaped seating area around a cream Formica-topped table. 'It's lovely,' she said. 'And much more spacious than I was expecting.'

Gianni nodded. 'The table folds down, so there's plenty of floor space for Lucy to play with her toys.'

Wood-panelled walls lined the living area and were finished with sparkling glass tops, etched with vines and flowers. The light from the sun shining through the small windows reflected and bounced little rainbows around the room. A wood-burning stove stood in an alcove, and a corner shelf above housed a small television set. Cathy glanced around the kitchen area, complete with sink, cooker and a compact fridge. She opened and closed cupboard doors and turned on the taps. 'Where does the water actually come from? Is there a bathroom? Where do I wash our clothes?'

Gianni laughed as her questions tumbled over one another. 'The water comes from tanks called jacks; they're stored below the wagon. I have to fill them as soon as we park up somewhere. You need to be careful not to waste water as it's a job and a half to do. Most people do their washing at the launderette, I think. You'll have to ask Maria about that.' He led her down a narrow corridor and slid back a door. 'Bathroom; it'll be a bit of a tight squeeze, but just enough room to share.'

Cathy looked at the tiny washbasin and toilet crammed in with the smallest shower cubicle she'd ever seen. They'd be lucky to get one in there, never mind the pair of them.

'We're fortunate to have that, you know,' Gianni said as he led her further down the corridor. 'Most of the caravans don't have a bathroom. The workers make do with strip washes or showers at the swimming baths. Anyway, this'll put a smile on your face.' He opened a door and gestured to the bedroom. 'Maria's done it all out with fancy stuff that she thought you'd like.'

Cathy smiled broadly as she walked into the room. 'It's beautiful. Maria has good taste.' A cream lace panel at the window gave privacy. Pink velvet curtains, tied back with silky tassels, matched the quilted bedcover. She sat down on the double bed, which was surrounded by built-in cupboards and had a neat bedside table either side.

'And next door is a lovely room for Lucy,' Gianni said.

Lucy's room was furnished with a little bed, a chest of drawers and a pink rug on the floor. 'It's very pretty,' Cathy said.

'The seating in the living area converts to a double bed,' Gianni told her. 'Lucy can have our room when she's older and if and when we have another baby, we'll put it in hers and we can sleep in the lounge. Right, let's go over to Dad and Maria's and claim our daughter. No doubt someone has waltzed off with her. You okay, love? You're a bit quiet.'

'Yeah, I'm fine. Just feeling tired. Erm, where can I bath Lucy?'

'Ah, now I've seen kids dunked outside when the weather's fine. We'll get her a little bath; like the one you use at Granny Lomax's.'

'Okay.' Cathy nodded, wondering how long it would take her to adjust to caravan living. 'It'll be a bit like a holiday in a way, but it's for life.'

Gianni frowned and pulled her close. 'Well that's okay, isn't it? You said it's what you wanted. To be in our own place at last.'

'Oh it is,' she reassured him. 'But don't forget *you've* had plenty of time to get used to this way of life and you haven't had a toddler under your feet either. It'll take a bit of adjusting, for all of us, I mean.'

'It will, but we'll be fine,' Gianni reassured her. 'I'm bloody starving. Maria promised us dinner tonight. We can relax and enjoy ourselves with a drink and a meal outside.'

Cathy smiled. 'Mmm, I'm looking forward to it. I love Maria's cooking and I'm so hungry I could eat a horse.'

*

Following a couple of relaxing hours of sitting around the campfire, and stuffed to bursting with Maria's delicious spaghetti bolognese, Gianni hoisted a sleepy Lucy onto his hip and slung his spare arm around Cathy's shoulders as they made their way back to the caravan. The warm evening air was still and silent, apart from a large owl hooting on an overhead branch, its chunky outline highlighted by the full moon.

As Gianni pointed the owl out to Cathy, the slim figure of a dark-haired young woman, wearing a long floaty skirt and strappy top, sashayed towards them, holding the hand of a tall youth with blond hair. She stopped and stared for a moment and then her face broke into a wary smile. She yanked on the youth's arm and he stopped too.

'Eloisa,' Gianni greeted her. 'How are you?' He felt Cathy stiffen beside him and pulled her closer.

The half-smile left Eloisa's face but she nodded at Cathy. 'When did you two arrive, or should I say, three?'

'We got back earlier,' Gianni said. 'Maria was expecting you to join us for supper.' Eloisa was Maria's only daughter, his stepsister.

Eloisa pouted. 'I left her a note to say I was going out with Ronnie. We've been to the pictures to see *Carry On Constable*.'

'Any good?'

'Yeah, it was quite funny.' She stood up on tiptoe and pecked Gianni on the cheek. 'So, how did the wedding go? I suppose I should congratulate you.'

'Thanks. The wedding was great. Wasn't it, Cathy?'

'Yes, we had a lovely day.' Cathy chewed her lip.

Gianni sensed she felt awkward. 'Right, we've gotta get this little one to bed. Catch up with you tomorrow.' He hurried Cathy away, conscious of Eloisa's eyes staring at his back.

'Sorry about that,' he apologised.

'Not your fault,' Cathy said. 'We can't really avoid her.'

'More's the pity.'

In the caravan Cathy took Lucy from him. 'I'll get her ready for bed while you make us a cuppa.'

Gianni put the kettle on and sat with his feet up, thoughts in a whirl. Eloisa was the only blot on his otherwise happy landscape. When he and Cathy had split up over two years ago, he'd had a one-night stand with Eloisa, who'd then accused him of fathering her expected baby. Luca and Maria had insisted the pair marry, but then Eloisa finally admitted the truth: Gianni's cousin Alessandro was the father. After a fall, Eloisa had lost her baby and Alessandro had been sent home to Italy. A few weeks prior to that a letter had arrived from Cathy for Gianni but had been intercepted by his cousin.

When Gianni finally got his hands on the letter, he'd learned that Cathy was also pregnant, and travelling the country looking for him. He'd set off to find her, just in time for Lucy's premature December birth. Cathy and Lucy were his world. He'd never let them go again. But he knew deep down that Eloisa hadn't forgiven him for leaving in such a hurry and without a word of goodbye. And now that he'd brought his family on his travels he'd wager a bet that she wouldn't make life too easy for them.

*

Cathy was awakened the following morning by people shouting and dogs barking close by. She groaned and reached for the bedside clock. Seven thirty. Gianni was still sleeping, snoring gently beside her. She could hear Lucy singing in her room along the corridor and smiled. She opened the bedroom door quietly, used the bathroom and then crept into the kitchen. They might just get a brew in peace before Lucy started shouting for attention.

Maria had thoughtfully stocked the cupboards and fridge with groceries and Cathy made two mugs of tea. She carried them into the bedroom just as Gianni was rousing himself. 'Good morning. It's a lovely day,' she said, handing him a mug as he sat up and leaned back against the padded headboard. 'Maybe we could have a little walk this afternoon if you're not needed on the site.'

He shook his head. 'Sorry, love, I won't have time. We open at six tonight and we've got loads to do today. The rides need finishing setting up. You and Lucy could have a little wander around though; see if you can find some shops, and just across the way is a small swing park. She might enjoy that.'

Cathy shrugged. 'Okay. I'll get something nice for tea. A play in the park will keep Lucy occupied.'

By midday Cathy was back from the shops with fresh fish and new potatoes for tea, and a whole afternoon stretching ahead with not much to do, but it was a chance for her to put her feet up and read while Lucy had her afternoon nap. She'd bought a *Woman's Weekly* magazine from the newsagent's and had popped into a little bookshop and picked up a couple of books. She'd heard Gianni mention he fancied reading Harper Lee's *To Kill a Mockingbird* and she'd found a Mills and Boon medical romance for herself. No doubt the story would be nothing like real hospital life, but it might give her a taste of past times, if nothing else.

She unpacked her shopping bags while Maria took Lucy over to her caravan for a sandwich and drink. She'd told Cathy to come and eat as soon as she'd put her shopping away.

Lucy was sitting on a picnic rug by Maria's caravan steps, tucking in, when Cathy joined her.

'I feel like I should be offering to help out over there.' Cathy gestured with her thumb to what looked like a war zone. 'There's stuff all over the place and they're running around like mad things.'

Maria smiled. 'They all know what goes where and it's easier to just let them get on with it. By six tonight you won't recognise the place.' She handed Cathy a plate and a mug. 'Sit down and have five minutes.'

'Thank you.' Cathy took a welcome sip of tea. 'We had a nice stroll, Lucy enjoyed the swing park, but I don't know what I'll do for the rest of the day. I feel like a spare part. I'm not used to just sitting around. I've always been busy either working, taking my turn running the family home while Mam was at work or helping my granny.'

Maria nodded. 'Maybe we can find you a little job to do in time, but for today just take it easy.'

The fairground was in full swing by eight o'clock and Cathy knew it would be pointless trying to get Lucy into bed. The noise was horrendous. It was a good job Lucy had managed a slightly longer afternoon nap than usual, Cathy thought. Bright lights on the rides flashed on and off and even with curtains drawn Lucy's bedroom was lit up all the time. Excited squeals from the girls on the waltzer and ghost train echoed through the air and Eddie Cochran's 'Three Steps to Heaven' blasted from the tannoy speakers, quickly followed by Brenda Lee's 'Sweet Nothin's'. It was a warm night and with the door and windows open the smell of diesel fumes and fried onions filled the caravan, along with the sickly sweet aroma of candyfloss and toffee apples.

Cathy gagged and wrinkled her nose as she sat with her feet up on one of the bench seats, trying to read her hospital romance. She could hear the roar of the motorbikes and the punters cheering. She supposed she should go and watch Gianni performing, but couldn't bring herself to move – and she'd have to take Lucy, who might be a bit frightened by all the noise. Besides, the wall of death ride terrified her.

Gianni had hurried in earlier and wolfed down the fried plaice and new potatoes she'd made for tea. He'd taken a quick shower, thrown on his show outfit, given her a hug and a kiss and dashed away, looking very handsome in his red satin shirt and black leather trousers. Everyone was working, Maria in her fortune-telling tent, Eloisa on her hook-a-duck stall and Luca on the bikes with Gianni. Cathy felt nothing short of useless. But what job could she do? And who would look after Lucy if she *did* work here?

After another half an hour of non-stop noise, her head banging, she closed the sitting room doors and windows and took two aspirins with a glass of water. Lucy was crying now with tiredness and Cathy picked her up and took her to the bedroom to get her ready for bed. Everywhere in the caravan smelled of fried food and it was stiflingly warm. Cathy wafted the stuffy air with her *Woman's Weekly* and closed the window to try to shut out the noise and smells.

'Let's get you a drink of milk,' she said to Lucy. 'And what about a nice biscuit?' She carried her back to the airless sitting room and laid her on the bench seat, putting a cushion behind her head. She filled Lucy's cup with milk and helped her hold it. Lucy took a few sips and then pushed the cup away. She shook her head at the biscuit. 'Want Granny Alice,' she whimpered. 'No like that noise.'

'Neither does Mammy,' Cathy said quietly. What she'd give right now to be sitting in Granny Lomax's peaceful lounge watching the TV, or even her mam and Johnny's slightly chaotic sitting room with all the kids in bed. There was no chance that Lucy would be asleep when Gianni got in just after ten, and that was far too late a bedtime for a toddler. She sighed and swept Lucy's fringe out of her eyes. Maybe it would get quieter when the novelty of the fair being in town had worn off a little.

*

By the following Sunday morning, the big packing, dismantling and clearing of the site was under way, ready for the move to another part of Yorkshire. Maria brought some boxes and old newspapers across for Cathy to pack her pots and pans and ornaments away.

'Are you okay, Cathy? You look a bit pale.'

Cathy shrugged. 'I'm just very tired. I'm not sleeping and neither is Lucy. She's all out of routine, very late to bed, restless all night and then up really early. Gianni sleeps like a log and doesn't even realise I've been up half the night trying to keep her quiet while he gets some sleep.'

Maria patted her shoulder. 'You'll soon get used to it. Let Lucy run about outside during the day. Fresh air will tire her out. There's plenty of people around to keep an eye on her.'

Cathy nodded, knowing that was something she wouldn't do. There were all sorts of strangers coming and going, as well as dogs roaming the site and a rushing stream in a dip behind the big rides. It didn't feel a very safe place to let a toddler play out on her own.

'I'll make sandwiches for the hired hands about twelve. Come over to my van for a bite to eat. You'll get a good sleep tonight as the fair is closed and we won't be on the road until eight in the morning. See you in a while.' Maria left with a flurry of colourful skirts and a toss of her long curly hair.

Cathy packed away their few belongings in the boxes and changed into a light blue cotton shift dress and white sandals. She took Lucy to the swing park for half an hour and then went back to Maria's caravan.

Gianni was already there with his dad and Uncle Marco, Luca's brother. They were sitting in front of the caravan on a picnic rug and Eloisa was sitting a bit too close to Gianni for Cathy's liking. Lucy squealed, 'Daddeeee,' and he jumped up to catch her as she ran towards him. He held out an arm to Cathy, who strolled up to him, giving Eloisa a stare as dark as the one Eloisa was shooting in her direction. Gianni wrapped his free arm around Cathy and dropped a kiss on her lips. 'Let's sit on the steps,' he suggested. 'You look a bit pale, love. Are you okay?'

She nodded. 'Everybody keeps asking me that, but I'm just really tired.'

'Try and have a lie-down later, see if you can persuade Lucy to lie with you.'

'I will.'

'At least we can get an early night and spend a bit of time together,' he said, winking at her.

After they'd made love and Gianni had fallen asleep, Cathy tossed and turned all night. At six am she shot out of bed and into the bathroom, where she dropped onto her knees over the toilet bowl, retching for all she was worth. She flushed the toilet, swilled her mouth and face and slumped onto the floor again, her back leaning against the tiny wall-space between the sink and toilet. She held her head in her hands and took some deep breaths.

The bathroom door slid aside and Gianni popped his head in. 'You okay? Heard you throwing up. Come on; let me get you a drink of water.' He helped her to her feet and into the sitting room. 'Go and sit down,' he ordered, running water into a glass. He handed it to Cathy, who took a couple of mouthfuls.

'Do you think it's something you ate?' he asked, looking worried.

She shrugged and took another sip. 'Maybe. Or just the heat and smells and being overtired. It's all catching up with me. You go back to bed for an hour, love. You've got a lot of loading to do soon. I'll stay here in case I need the bathroom in a hurry again.'

'Okay.' He nodded. 'If you're sure.'

By the time the fair left Leeds for York later that morning, Cathy felt a bit better and she and Lucy, along with Maria, followed the procession of wagons and trailers in Luca's car. Gianni was driving as Luca was behind the wheel of the trailer that housed the wall of death ride. It was another warm day and the slight breeze blowing in through the open windows was very welcoming.

Chapter Two

Walton Gaol July 1960

Jack Dawson stretched out on his bunk and yawned. He broke wind loudly, scratched his balls and rolled over on to his side. He smirked as his companion in the bunk above him yelled, 'Dirty, stinking swine.'

Jack was totally fed up with his life, stuck in a small, cockroach-ridden cell for most of the day, with the thickest Scouser on the planet. He reached under his pillow and pulled out a surprise letter he'd received last week from Lorraine, an old girlfriend. She'd told him that his ex-wife Alice had remarried and wondered if he knew. He didn't, because no one had bothered to tell him. But thank God for that. At least when he got out he'd have his freedom and no kids to support. *Let the new husband take on the responsibility for them all*, Jack thought. *More fool him.*

He wished he'd never got involved with Alice and her eldest brat in the first place. Even at the age of five Cathy had been a snobby little cow, always turning her nose up at his vague attempts to be her stepfather. Then the other three kids had come along after he'd specifically told Alice he didn't want any. He hated becoming a father. Knee-deep in dirty nappies, puke and screaming brats was not his idea of fun. Alice could hardly blame him for going elsewhere when all she had to offer were droopy tits, a flabby stomach and a bloody headache, most of the time.

He'd felt trapped for years and blamed Cathy for everything that had gone wrong in his life. She'd accused him of touching her – and this after giving him the come-on, cheeky little tart. She'd flaunted herself in front of him and then made out he was to blame when he'd made a pass. Then she'd cried rape when he tried to show her a bit of loving *his* way. Her biker boyfriend had beaten him up and injured his tackle so badly with a well-aimed boot that he'd spent a week in hospital. Alice had kicked him out and, homeless, with his faith in women at an all-time low, he'd met barmaid Lorraine. She'd put a roof over his head and food in his belly. But that relationship also ended after he'd been arrested for raping Cathy's mate in the hospital grounds. Stupid girl shouldn't have got in the way. He'd been after Cathy but the little blonde nurse had come by first and he'd taken what he could and then cleared off.

Yes, his downfall was all Cathy's fault. And one day he'd get his own back. Two years into his sentence, he'd got at least another five to do. He'd been told that he might be moved from Walton to another prison in a year or two. He'd no idea where or when, but lived in hope that it wouldn't be too long and would get him away from the snoring pillock in the bunk above. But knowing his luck it would take forever. He slid out of bed and limped over to the table under the window. His wooden foot was rubbing against the stump of his lower leg today and causing him pain. He'd lost half his foot in a wartime shooting accident and ended up having the rest removed when infection set into the bone, causing him horrendous pain and an addiction to painkillers and alcohol.

Jack switched on his transistor radio, turning the volume up as high as it would go. 'Jerusalem' blasted out from the tinny little speaker. Sunday service; he grinned. That'd wake the bastard up good and proper. He lay back down on his bunk, hands behind his head, and stared at the peeling paint on the pale green wall in front of him. The guards would be hammering on the door soon and then they'd both be up and emptying the stinking slop bucket before going downstairs to the canteen for the usual tasteless grey porridge and burnt toast. He thought about the short time he'd spent at Lorraine's place; the Sunday fry-ups she'd spoiled him with, following an energetic early-morning session. He felt his balls tingling at the memory and groaned, drawing his knees up to his chest. He needed a woman's touch like he'd never needed it before.

*

Gianni wiped his oily hands down the front of his faded denim jeans and glanced up to the top of the wall of death barrel, where Luca was talking to Lenny, one of the fairground hands.

'Want a sandwich, Dad?' Gianni yelled above the roar of a bike engine as his Uncle Marco rode around the top of the walls, rehearsing his part of the routine he did with Luca.

'Be with you in a minute, son,' Luca yelled back. 'You go on ahead. Tell Maria I'm on my way.'

Gianni strolled across the park to his caravan, where Cathy was sitting on the steps, twiddling her long hair between her fingers. Lucy was playing on the grass with her dollies.

'You okay, love?' Gianni dropped a kiss on Cathy's lips.

She smiled up at him, looped her hair behind her ears and blew down the front of her loose top. 'I'm too warm,' she grumbled. 'I wish it would rain for a while to cool everywhere down.'

Gianni squinted up at the cloudless blue sky, from where the sun beat down relentlessly. 'Not much chance of that. Anyway, rain puts the punters off and we need the money.'

Cathy sighed and got to her feet. 'Maria's waving.' She waved back. 'I guess lunch is ready.' She pulled Lucy to her feet. 'Go and scrub your hands, mucky daddy, and we'll see you over at your dad's place.'

*

Gianni watched her walk away, his head on one side. Cathy didn't seem very happy and he wondered why. The caravan probably wasn't an ideal place to bring up a family and he knew she would have preferred a more conventional way of life, but that wasn't an option. There was no way he was going back to Liverpool, living in a house and doing the nine-to-five slog each day. Besides, he'd rented out the terraced house that he'd inherited from his mother to Davy and Debs and the couple were well settled with their young son Jonathon. He wouldn't have the heart to ask them to leave now.

He sighed and went indoors. He rubbed soap into his hands, rinsing them clean under the tap. The water spluttered and came to a stop. The bloody jacks were empty. As if he didn't have enough to do today; full blown rehearsals with his dad later and then the show tonight. But he'd have to make time to fill them or there'd be no water for showers later. And that would be something for Cathy to pull a face at. He'd told her to be careful and not to waste the water. Might as well as talk to a brick wall. He pulled the door closed behind him, ran down the steps and walked towards his dad and Maria's caravan.

*

Cathy told Lucy to sit down on the picnic rug that Maria had put on the grass. She parked herself on a chair beside a small table that was set with glasses and assorted plates and cutlery.

Maria brought out a big platter of sandwiches and a freshly baked quiche, cut into slices. Eloisa followed her mother, carrying a bowl of salad. She put it down on the table and glared at Cathy, who looked away.

Cathy could sense the girl's jealousy over Gianni. Well tough, he was hers. She saw Eloisa's eyes light up and a smile spread across her face. Cathy didn't turn around. There was no need; Gianni was on his way. The only time Eloisa came to life and looked happy was in his company. Lucy clapped her hands and ran to him, squealing a welcome. Gianni picked her up and swung her round and round. She giggled and grabbed his hair.

'Luca said I can do a routine with you,' Eloisa announced as Gianni put Lucy down and went to sit on the seat next to Cathy. Then she smirked and walked away, wiggling her backside in tight white shorts, before he had a chance to reply.

He groaned. 'Sorry, love,' he muttered to Cathy. 'I'll have a word with Dad later. No way did that idea come from me, honestly.'

'I know.' Cathy sighed and stroked his arm.

'Thing is, it's all the rage now, girls on bikes,' he said.

'Not at this fair!' Maria pursed her lips. 'She's not doing it. I won't allow it.' She swept away with a swish of skirts, her face red with anger.

Raised voices sounded from the caravan, and then Eloisa stomped down the steps, shot Gianni a look that could kill and ran off towards the rides.

Gianni grinned. 'When Maria has a go at Dad, that'll be the end of it,' he said to Cathy.

*

Back at the caravan Maria was giving Luca a dressing-down. He turned as Eloisa approached. 'Why the hell do you tell lies?' he snapped. 'You are *not* riding and I never said you could.'

'You said you'd think about it,' Eloisa snapped back.

'You always mither me when I'm at my busiest,' he said. 'I wasn't aware of what you were asking with all the noise. Anyway, no, you can't ride, and that's the end of it.' He stormed off in the direction of the wall of death barrel, Gianni on his heels. Cathy got up to help Maria tidy the table.

'And *you* needn't look so smug,' Eloisa yelled at Cathy. 'It was me Gianni wanted to marry, not you. If I hadn't lost our baby he would have done too.'

'It wasn't Gianni's baby,' Cathy said quietly, 'and you know it.'

'It might have been, but we'll never know now, will we.'

'Eloisa!' Maria shook her head as Eloisa ran off. 'I'm so sorry Cathy. Don't let her comments upset you. She knows full well it wasn't Gianni's baby.'

Cathy half-smiled and picked up Lucy, who was sucking her thumb and looking worried. 'I think I'll put this little one down for a nap and maybe have a quiet hour to myself. I'm struggling in this heat.'

'You have a nap too, my love,' Maria said and gave Cathy a hug. 'You look wiped out.'

*

Cathy lay on the bed and stared up at the ceiling. Through the open window she could hear loud voices and the hum of generators, along with a couple of the hands singing. It was too hot to close the window and she couldn't sleep, even though she felt really tired. Eloisa's comment about Gianni marrying her sat heavy in her heart. She hated the girl and wished she'd leave the fair. But there was no chance of that. It was all Eloisa knew and there was nowhere else for her to go. She didn't trust her one little bit around Gianni, the way she flaunted herself, constantly making eyes at him. Ah well, all she could do was put her trust in him. She didn't think for one minute that he'd ever let her down. But just knowing that he'd been intimate with Eloisa on any level made her feel sick, and the girl would never let her forget it. She turned on her side and closed her eyes, willing herself to drift off while Lucy napped.

A sudden wave of nausea washed over her and she shot off the bed and into the bathroom, where she vomited up her recently consumed lunch. She wiped her face with a damp flannel and brushed her teeth, gagging at the minty flavour of the toothpaste. When she turned the tap to rinse out her mouth, it spluttered but nothing came out; she couldn't even brush her teeth properly.

Feeling cross and unwell, she went to fetch the glass of water from her nightstand.

After rinsing out her mouth, she gripped the edge of the wash-basin and stared at her pale reflection in the small mirror fixed to the wall. She took a deep, calming breath and went back into the bedroom. Her handbag was in the wardrobe and she rooted inside it, found her diary and did a quick date check. It was early days, but her period was definitely late, over a week in fact. Coupled with the nausea and spells of sickness, the feeling tired all the time, she was in no doubt that she was pregnant again. She'd felt just the same with Lucy. No doubt this was a honeymoon baby. She didn't know whether to laugh or cry. Gianni would be thrilled to bits, but the thought of looking after another child in this caravan didn't exactly make her feel like jumping for joy.

Gianni's face lit up with a big smile when Cathy broke the news to him in bed that night that she suspected she was pregnant. He kissed her and held her tight.

'Oh, that's wonderful,' he said. 'I might get a son this time.'

'You might,' Cathy agreed. 'I need to see a doctor soon to confirm it, but all the signs are there. Don't say anything to anyone just yet until we know for sure.'

'I won't. But there's a doctors' surgery on the road leading into the park. Maybe you could make an appointment there.'

'I'll see.' Cathy cuddled up closer to him as a germ of an idea came into her mind. When the fair was ready to move on from York in a couple of weeks' time, she might suggest that she and Lucy travel back to Liverpool by train. She'd prefer to see her own doctor in Aigburth and not only that, she was feeling really homesick too and wanted to see her mam and her family and friends.

A break spent with them all would do her good and that would bring them up to August. If the fair headed for Liverpool in September she could rejoin them for a few weeks before they packed up for the winter months. Gianni would then be with her for a good while. She'd leave it a few days and then tell him how she felt and what she wanted to do. Cathy didn't really want to leave Gianni with Eloisa on the prowl, but knew she could trust him.

*

Gianni puffed out his cheeks and nodded his head slowly. The fair was packing up to move on again, this time to Thirsk, and Cathy had just announced that she wanted to go back to Liverpool for a few weeks and why.

'Right,' he began. 'I understand you wanting to be with your family for a while and see your own doctor, but you're not going on the train by yourself. You'd never manage, lugging a case and Lucy in her pushchair. We don't want any accidents. Once everything is sorted here and they're all packed up, I'll ask Dad to lend me his car and I'll take you home. Someone can tow our caravan up to Thirsk. I'll stay overnight with you in Liverpool and then drive back up north. I know you want to keep it quiet for now, but can I tell Maria and Dad why you're going home? I mean, they're bound to think it's a bit odd so soon.'

'Okay,' Cathy agreed. 'But make sure they don't say anything to Eloisa. I'll take Lucy for a little walk now out from under everyone's feet and I'll call my mam from the phone box and let her know to expect me.'

Chapter Three

Aigburth September 1960

Cathy stretched her arms above her head and yawned. It was early Sunday morning and Lucy was curled up beside her, still fast asleep. It was lovely to be tucked up in the spare room at her granny's bungalow. She was missing Gianni but he'd called her before the show most nights and she'd reassured him they were both doing fine. Sliding out of bed, she walked into the bathroom. The smell of toast made her stomach rumble and she heard the rattle of crockery coming from the kitchen.

Granny was already up and no doubt ready for early Sunday morning service at St Michael's church. She smoothed her nightie down over her already visible baby bump and smiled. She was only three months but was already bigger than she'd been with Lucy. Gianni might get his wish; this could be a boy. She strolled into the kitchen and sat down at the little table.

'Morning, my love,' Granny greeted her. She placed the loaded toast rack on the table alongside a dish of butter and a pot of strawberry jam. 'Do you want a poached egg?'

Cathy shook her head. Her tummy was still a bit iffy in the morning – mind you it was iffy any time of day – but it was getting better as time went on. 'I'll just have the toast thanks, Gran. Are you going to church?'

'I am. If I put the leg of lamb in the oven on a low light will you keep an eye on it for me? I won't stay for coffee at the church hall, then we won't be eating too late. I know you want to go and see your mam this afternoon.'

'You can stay and have your coffee. I know you love a natter with your friends, don't miss out just because I'm here,' Cathy said. 'I'll get the veg ready and put the potatoes in with the lamb. I don't need to be at Mam's any earlier than four anyway. I'll pop in and see Debs and Davy while I'm over that way too. It's lovely catching up with everyone. I'm hoping I can get a phone call in with my nursing pals later as well when they come off duty. I'm going to try and meet up with them this week.'

'Well, don't be doing too much running around. The doctor told you to rest, then your blood pressure stays down.'

Cathy laughed. 'I'm fine. I think it was high last week because I'd been so worked up about everything. How am I going to manage two little ones in a caravan and going back to all that noise again?'

At the doctors' surgery, when she'd had her pregnancy confirmed, her blood pressure had been high, something that had not happened with her first pregnancy. It was a bit of a concern, but Cathy knew from her nursing days that anxiety could shoot a patient's blood pressure through the roof, so she wasn't unduly worried.

She'd try not to think of the realities of next year on the road with the fair, and instead concentrate on resting and winding down while she could. In Liverpool, she'd stayed for a week at her mam's place and was now at Granny Lomax's for a week. So far it was working out perfectly.

Cathy smiled as Debbie's son Jonathon invited Lucy to play with his wooden bricks. The pair were busy building a wall with the coloured blocks while Debbie and Cathy caught up on each other's news. Debbie handed Cathy a mug of coffee and sat down beside her on the sofa in the sitting room.

'So how long are you going to stay in Liverpool?' Debbie asked.

Cathy shrugged. 'Well, at least until the fair arrives at the end of September. To be honest, I don't particularly want to go back, but I'm really missing Gianni and so is Lucy. And I can't stay with Mam and Granny forever. Not once I have two little ones to look after. It wouldn't be fair. Mam and Johnny have got enough with the other kids to look after.'

Debbie chewed her lip. 'You don't think Gianni will want his house back, do you? We love living here, but if we have to find somewhere else, will you ask him to give us plenty of notice?'

'Oh, Debs. No, of course he won't want it back. He loves his fairground lifestyle. Our new caravan is beautiful and I feel that I'm being ungrateful towards Luca and Maria after they went to so much trouble and expense to buy it for us, when I say I'd rather live in a house. I don't think I'll ever be able to persuade Gianni to live under a normal roof again. It's caravan life or nothing, apart from the winter months, when we'll stay with Mam or Granny. I'll just have to get used to it.'

Debbie smiled. 'Sounds fun to me, travelling all over the place. Like a permanent holiday.'

Cathy choked on her tea. 'If only. It's noisy and smelly and I get bored to tears with nothing to do. It takes five minutes to clean and tidy the caravan and then I've got all day to twiddle my thumbs. And then there's Eloisa always giving me the evil eye and she fancies Gianni like mad. Doesn't even hide it.'

'Cheeky cow!' Debbie exclaimed. 'I'd have scratched her eyes out. Do you think she'll try it on with him again now you're out of sight?'

'I doubt it. He ignores her. She caused him enough trouble last time he got involved. She gets on his nerves.' Cathy sighed and looked at the clock on the mantelpiece. 'I'd better get over to my mam's,' she said. 'She's doing a salad for tea so I'd better go and help. Sorry my visit was short. I'll catch up with you in the week when I'm staying at Mam's for a few days. Maybe we could take these two for a stroll around Seffy Park?'

'Sounds like a good plan.'

Cathy squeezed into her jeans and took a deep breath to do up the zip. Blimey, she was piling weight on now the morning sickness was easing off. The jeans had fitted fine a couple of weeks ago. This baby was going to be a big one.

She planned to leave Lucy with her mam for the afternoon and go over to the Liverpool Royal Hospital to spend a bit of time with her nursing friends, who had a few hours off between shifts. She couldn't wait to see them all again for the first time since her wedding day in June. 'See you later, Mam,' she called as she let herself out at the front door.

'Enjoy yourself, chuck,' Alice called back. 'I won't come to the door because my hands are covered in flour and I've got Lucy standing on a chair helping me to make pastry.'

'Okay. Bye Lucy-Lu,' Cathy called and set off down the street, swinging her handbag. It was a lovely day, much cooler than the summer had been, but bright and dry. She called into the bakery on Lark Lane and bought a Victoria sponge cake to share with her friends, then hurried to catch the bus on Aigburth Drive.

Ellie and Karen were waiting for her in the foyer at the nurses' home and greeted her warmly. 'You go on up to Ellie's room and I'll go and grab us three mugs of tea from the canteen. Jean's been delayed with a delivery and will join us later if she can,' Karen said.

'See if you can get some small plates and a knife.' Cathy held up a square white box. 'Cake.'

'Oh yum. Will do.' Karen dashed off and Ellie led the way, past Cathy's old ground-floor room and the telephone in the hallway and up the back stairs to the first floor.

'Take a pew.' Ellie gestured to the single bed in her neat and tidy room. Cathy sank down with a sigh.

'Please excuse me doing this, but I can't breathe.' She popped the button on her jeans, lowered the zip slightly and let out a relieved breath. 'I need to get a bigger size. These are killing me. Think I'll pop down to Blacklers while I'm out.'

'Here, try this for now.' Ellie produced an elastic band from her bedside drawer. She threaded it through the buttonhole, secured it and looped it around the metal button of Cathy's jeans. 'There you go, but don't forget to do your zip up before you leave here. At least you'll be a bit more comfortable for the next few hours. Don't squeeze into clothes that are too small. It's not good for you or Gianni Junior in there.' She laughed. 'Bound to be a boy this time, it looks quite big for just over three months.'

'That's what I thought.' Cathy nodded. 'Gianni would be over the moon with a son.'

'I'm sure,' Ellie said as a banging noise at the door startled them both. Ellie opened it a fraction and saw Karen lifting her foot to kick at the bottom of the door again, her hands carrying a laden tray preventing her from knocking.

'Sorry, couldn't knock properly. It's time women evolved to have three hands.' She waltzed into the room and placed the tray on top of the chest of drawers under the window.

Cathy cut the cake and shared it out, leaving some for Jean for later, and the threesome caught up with their news. Both Karen and Ellie were about to finish their state registered nurse courses and would be training as midwives soon. Jean was already halfway through her midwifery training.

'This is what I miss about my nursing life,' Cathy said. 'Having you all for company. I do envy you so much. I really want to come back and finish my training and then do midwifery. Hopefully when this baby arrives, they'll have moved on and changed the rules about married nurses working here.'

Karen nodded. 'That's in the pipeline. But how would you manage? You've still got the problem of who minds the kids and the fairground lifestyle. You're never in one place long enough to do anything.'

Cathy half-smiled and took a sip of tea. 'I'm hoping that when we have two children, Gianni will give up the fair and settle down with us as a family.'

'And pigs might fly,' Ellie said, raising an eyebrow.

Karen nodded her agreement. 'I don't mean to be harsh, Cathy, but you could have brought Lucy up with your mam's help and not got married. Then you could have finished your training. But now see, you're expecting again and that's double the trouble. I know the rules are unfair, but I think nursing is something you're going to have to forget about until the kids grow up and then you can see what sort of regulations are in force.'

Cathy pulled a face. 'I guess you're right.'

Karen nodded. 'You know I am. You've got what we haven't; a gorgeous hunk of a husband that worships the ground you walk on. A beautiful daughter, as well as a new baby on the way. You should go back to Gianni and stay with him, forget about all this for now. Count your blessings, Cathy.'

On the way back from the hospital Cathy caught a bus into the city and popped into Blacklers, where she bought a pair of black maternity slacks and a couple of loose tops. Mindful of what Karen had said about going back to Gianni and the fairground, she decided to take a train from Lime Street station to Aigburth so she could call into the ticket office and ask about trains to Carlisle, where the fair was destined to pitch up next week.

The man she spoke to told her the journey took just over a couple of hours and she would need to change at Preston. She could purchase her ticket on the day she decided to travel. She thanked him and waited on the platform for the Aigburth train, her mind in a whirl. Should she do it, just turn up in Carlisle and surprise him? She'd see what her mam and Johnny thought about the idea tonight.

'If you feel you've had a long enough rest and are up to it then yes, go back to the fair,' Alice said when Cathy broached the subject later that night. 'But not on the train. Tell Gianni that's what you want to do when he next rings you and let him come here for you. You'll struggle with all your bags and Lucy. Lifting heavy things isn't good at any stage in a pregnancy.'

'But he's in Carlisle, Mam. It's a long way to ask him to come back here for me. The fair will be here next month. Maybe I should just wait. It was something Karen said today that made me realise where I should be.' Cathy took a deep breath, feeling troubled. 'But my head's all over the place. I felt sad when I was in the nurses' home and that I'd had to give it all up. Karen and Ellie are nearly ready to start their midwifery training. Then I think of Gianni and how we should be together. But I know how boring it is just sitting around waiting for him to finish work. All I do is read or play with Lucy. I feel totally useless.'

Alice rolled her eyes. 'I'd give my right arm to just sit and read or play with Roddy. Are there no other young mothers on the site?'

Cathy shook her head. 'None at all. A couple of the hired hands have teenagers who work alongside them on the stalls, but no, there's just me. The only one anywhere near my age is Eloisa and there's not a chance we could ever be friends.'

Alice shrugged. 'I don't know what to suggest, love. It's such a shame, because if things were different you could be living across the street.'

'No chance of that happening either, Mam.' Cathy got to her feet. 'I'd better go on up to bed. I'll have a think.'

*

Cathy rolled onto her side and picked up the alarm clock. The luminous hands told her it was only three am. She frowned, wondering what had caused her to wake up. As she rolled back to the middle of the bed she flinched as a cramping pain wrapped itself around her lower stomach and back. 'Ouch!' she muttered and drew her legs up to relieve it. But the pain was quickly replaced by another. Cathy wriggled up the bed to a sitting position. She pushed back the bedcovers and slowly swung her legs over the edge, glad that she was on her own – Lucy had crept into bed with Rosie earlier – and slipped her feet into her slippers. Might be a full bladder giving her the twinges.

She made her way slowly to the bathroom across the landing. She tried to straighten up, but another pain was beginning and she leaned forward, clutching her stomach. She bit her lip to stop herself crying out and waking the household. Then she felt dampness between her legs and checked herself to see what was happening. Even in the low light, she could see her hand came away dark; she was bleeding.

'Mam,' she cried out, going back onto the landing and tapping on Alice's bedroom door. Within seconds Alice opened the door, her eyes blinking in the bright light from the landing bulb.

'What is it?' she asked, joining Cathy and closing the bedroom door behind her.

'Mam, I think I'm losing the baby,' Cathy said, choking on a sob. 'I woke up with cramp-like pains and I'm bleeding. What shall I do?'

'Oh lord,' Alice said, putting her arms around Cathy. 'Can you make it back to the bedroom?'

Between them they shuffled into Cathy's room and Alice helped her onto the bed. 'I'll just go and get you a pad from the cupboard.' Alice hurried to the bathroom and came back with a packet of sanitary towels. 'Put one on,' she instructed. 'Is the bleeding heavy?'

'Yes and I can feel more coming now,' Cathy cried.

'I'll phone for an ambulance. They might be able to do something to stop it at the hospital. Just lie as still as you can.' Alice shot out of the room. She was back within minutes. 'They're on the way. Just let me tell Johnny what's happening and throw some clothes on and I'll come with you. Don't worry about Lucy, he'll see to her.'

Cathy clung to her mam's hand as the ambulance sped up Lark Lane and onto the main road. With bells clanging and lights flashing, they were at the Royal in no time.

Cathy was carried inside on a stretcher, groaning in pain as the cramps grew stronger. Alice hurried alongside the attendants as they handed Cathy over to two nurses, who rushed her into a cubicle. Alice took a seat in the corridor, calling out to Cathy that she was just nearby. She waited for someone to tell her what was happening.

From where she was sitting, Alice could hear her daughter crying out as her pains got stronger. Then there was silence, followed by the nurses comforting a sobbing Cathy. One of the nurses appeared at Alice's side and touched her shoulder.

'I'm so sorry,' she began.

Alice looked up as a sob caught in her throat. 'Can I see her?'

The nurse nodded. 'We've just called the doctor. Cathy will need a procedure called a dilation and curettage.'

Alice nodded. She'd heard of the D & C procedure.

'It's just to make sure everything is clear and nothing is left behind that may cause problems later,' the nurse explained. 'You go in and see her and then we'll get her ready for theatre.'

Alice popped her head around the cubicle curtains. Cathy was lying facing the wall, her body shuddering with sobs. 'Sweetheart.' Alice put her hand on her daughter's shoulder. 'I'm so sorry.'

Cathy rolled to face her. 'Was it something I did? Is it God's will because I'm never satisfied, no matter how lucky people tell me I am with everything I've got? Gianni will be so upset, Mam. Will you tell him when he rings tomorrow? Tell him I'm so, so sorry.'

'I will. And it's nothing to do with God. Let's just get you sorted out and back home. We'll worry about Gianni tomorrow. You'll be in here for a few days while things settle down. It was nothing you did, Cathy. These things happen for some reason or other. Nobody knows why.'

By the following afternoon Cathy was coming to terms with losing her baby. The D & C procedure had been successful. She'd lost a fair amount of blood but had been given some back in a transfusion. The doctor had visited her this morning on the gynaecological ward and told her that there was no reason she couldn't carry another baby to full term and that no one knew why these things happened. She should have no future problems as far as he could tell. He wished her well and told her she could go home after another couple of days of bed rest.

Ellie and Karen had come to visit her after the staff nurse got a message to them. They'd given her hugs and sympathy and brought flowers. Jean came in on her way home that evening.

'I'm so sorry, Cathy,' she began, tears filling her eyes. 'I was half-hoping you'd be one of my deliveries in time. Has anyone got word to Gianni?'

'Yes, Mam came in at seven and she'd spoken to him. He was really upset and wants to come and see me. She told him to wait until the weekend when I'm home and not to come rushing all that way or he'll be having an accident. He's going to ring her again in the morning.'

Jean nodded and stroked Cathy's arm. 'You need to get some rest if you intend going back with him to the fairground.'

Cathy sighed. 'All I've been thinking while I'm lying here is thank goodness I was at Mam's and not the back of beyond in the caravan. That's something to be thankful for, if nothing else. At least Mam knew what to do. Can you imagine being stuck on a field with no phone and no nearby hospital with just strangers to look after me? Gianni would have gone into a right panic. Then there's Lucy to worry about. At least I know she's being taken good care of while I'm in Liverpool.'

'There's a lot to be said for having family around you at a time like this,' Jean said. 'And Alice is a good auxiliary nurse and would know how to respond right away.' Jean got to her feet. 'I'll pop in tomorrow. Get some sleep now.'

The pair said goodbye and Cathy watched her walk briskly up the ward, smart in her midwife's uniform. She closed her eyes to the bustle of the ward, an overwhelming sadness washing over her for the loss of the baby she would never hold or name, and willed sleep to come.

*

By the time Gianni arrived on the Saturday, Cathy was tucked up in the front room on the sofa bed. Her mam had insisted she rest and had been feeding her up on liver and onions, which she wasn't keen on, but she knew that, along with iron tablets, it would help her iron levels get back to normal after her blood loss.

Gianni knelt beside the sofa bed and put his arms around her, hugging her gently. Her eyes filled as she looked into his. He looked so sad. 'I'm sorry,' she whispered.

'Nothing to be sorry about,' he said, his voice breaking. 'Maria said things like this happen and sometimes for no reason.'

'There may have been something wrong with him. He might not have survived his birth. Maybe it's better this way,' Cathy said quietly.

'Did they tell you it was a boy then?' He choked on a sob.

'Oh, no, they wouldn't be able to tell. It was too soon. But I always thought it would be a boy. I wanted to give you a son.'

He nodded. 'I know you did. One day, when we're ready, maybe?'

She smiled. 'We'll see.' She stroked his cheek and reached up to kiss him.

He held her for a minute. 'Cathy, I've been thinking. If you'd been where the fair's pitched when you started losing our baby it would have been a nightmare. It's way out of the city on a recreation ground. I'd never have got you to a hospital in time.'

Gianni looked straight into her eyes. 'I can't stop thinking about what could have happened to you and the baby. I really think you should stay on in Liverpool with your family. I miss you more than words can say, but it's safer for you and Lucy to stay here.'

Cathy felt her eyes filling with tears of love for her wonderful husband.

Gianni gave her a little squeeze. 'We can be together when I'm in a nearby town and for all the winter months too. I know you were bored stiff at the fair. You need to follow your dreams like we always said you should. Finish your nurse training while I get the fair out of my system for a while longer. Be that nurse you always wanted to be. Make us all proud of you. Do it for Lucy and our little lost boy. And then one day soon, we'll be together for always.'

*

'It's good to have you home, my love,' Granny Lomax said, giving Cathy a big hug. Johnny had been to pick her up for tea and the family was packed into the back sitting room at Lucerne Street. 'And look at the size of this one.' She patted Lucy, who hung back shyly, on the head. 'I think I might have a little something in my bag for you,' she said encouragingly. Lucy's face lit up as Granny rummaged, pulled out a parcel and handed it to the little girl.

Lucy tore at the wrapping paper and squealed with excitement as she pulled out a dolly dressed in a pink knitted outfit.

'Oh, isn't she lovely. What do you say?' Cathy prompted.

'Fank you,' Lucy said, beaming.

'Come and have a seat and Cathy will pour you a cuppa,' Alice said. 'Get off that chair, Roddy, let Granny sit down. How are you feeling today?'

'I'm better for seeing my two girls,' Granny said, smiling. 'I'm okay, thanks, Alice. I get a bit weary at times and I've slowed down a lot, but the doctor at the hospital said the pills he prescribed should help. I'm not totally convinced it's my heart, but they gave me a good examining and said I don't need to go back for six months. I'll see how I get on and take it from there. Having these two around will do me the world of good.'

Alice laughed. 'It'll do us all good. Tell Granny your plans, Cathy, while I bring the food through. I've made a cold buffet seeing as we don't have enough chairs to all sit around the table. A buffet is easier to eat off our knees.'

As Alice went into the kitchen Cathy told Granny her future plans and Granny's face lit up.

'I'm sure Alice and I can manage to look after Lucy between us,' she said. 'And it won't be too long before Gianni is home for the winter to help too.'

Cathy nodded. 'Debs has offered to help me on the odd day as well. Lucy and Jonathon are similar in age and get on just fine, so they'll be company for each other. It all just depends on me getting a training place again. I'm seeing my nursing friends later this week, so I'll have a bit more information by then. The sooner I can start the better really and then I can make up for lost time. I'd like to do the same as Jean and train to be a midwife once the state registration course is finished. I know that's what Ellie and Karen plan to do as well, eventually.'

Granny smiled. 'Well, let's keep our fingers crossed then that they will let you back on the course.'

Chapter Four

Aigburth June 1963

Cathy whispered, 'See you later' to her mother and slipped quietly out by the front door while four-year-old Lucy's back was turned. Her daughter was currently occupied with choosing a biscuit from the barrel and would no doubt kick off as soon as she realised Cathy had left her behind; but hopefully Granny Alice would pacify her. Hurrying down the front path, Cathy waved at Debbie, who was wiping down the windowsill of her house across the road. 'Catch up with you later, Debs,' she called and hurried up Lucerne Street and out onto Lark Lane, where she stopped off at the post office to send an airmail card and letter to her Uncle Brian and his wife in America, congratulating them on the birth of their second son in three years. Brian getting married had come as a surprise to his family back in Liverpool, but a very nice one all the same.

After exchanging pleasantries with Mrs Jones behind the counter, Cathy ran to catch the bus on Aigburth Road. She was on her way into the city to meet up with Jean, Karen and Ellie, to celebrate the end of Karen and Ellie's midwifery training with afternoon tea at the Kardomah Café. Although Jean had qualified twelve months earlier, she'd insisted on joining her friends today to help celebrate their achievements.

Cathy couldn't believe she'd only got six months left to do before she also qualified as a midwife. From the point when Gianni had suggested she restart her training, and she and Lucy had moved into the spare bedroom in Granny Lomax's bungalow on Linnet Lane, the time had absolutely flown by. She'd been very lucky with all the help she'd received in looking after Lucy over the last few years. It had been a struggle at times, combining working, studying and being mother, daughter, granddaughter and wife, as well as big sister to her three half-siblings. She hated the time she was apart from Gianni, but was proud of the fact that she'd worked hard, succeeded in fulfilling her lifelong dreams and was now a state registered nurse and over halfway to becoming a midwife.

She stuck her hand out as the bus approached, jumped on board and found a seat downstairs. The cheerful conductor collected her fare and walked away down the aisle, whistling Cliff Richard's 'Summer Holiday'. Cathy tucked her hair behind her ears and smiled to herself, wondering if she and Gianni might manage a week away this year. Summer was always a busy time with the fair, so the most they'd probably get would be a few days together when it visited Sefton Park for a week in the middle of next month. Even that would be better than nothing though.

Lucy would be five in December and was due to start school in September, which would make life easier all round. Debbie had also been helping her out, but was now pregnant with her second child, and although Granny Lomax had coped well enough, she was getting a bit too old to be doing the bulk of the child-minding; and her mam was still working a couple of days a week at the Royal as an auxiliary nurse. It was a joy to see her mam so happy and Johnny was a great stepdad to the kids, who loved him. After the awful father they'd had in Jack it was so nice for them to have someone who took little Roddy out to play football and was quite happy to turn a skipping rope handle for Rosie and Sandra out in the back garden.

Johnny, along with Millie's husband Jimmy, ran a property renovations business and they worked all over Liverpool, doing up old houses. For the first time in her life, her mam was enjoying having a nice home with all the mod cons and new furniture.

Cathy jumped off the bus near Lime Street station. She was a bit early, so she decided to have a quick wander around the shops and headed over to Ranelagh Street and into Lewis's store. She smiled as she spotted Millie in her smart navy uniform with her blond hair pinned up in a neat chignon, walking around with a clipboard, talking to the girls on the various cosmetic counters. Millie was the supervisor over cosmetics now and Cathy thought back to the days before she started her nursing career, when she herself had worked on the Max Factor counter with Debbie. Cathy's mam had been the floor supervisor in those days but had always wanted to be a nurse too and when Cathy discovered her mam could get a place as a trainee auxiliary, Alice had taken the opportunity. She loved her job on the children's ward.

'Millie,' Cathy called as Millie spun around and smiled at the sight of her.

'Hiya, love. Have you got a day off then? You look nice and summery.' Millie admired Cathy's blue and white flower-patterned shift dress and white kitten-heeled court shoes.

'Yes.' Cathy nodded. 'Mam's got Lucy for a few hours. I'm meeting friends for a bite to eat. Bit of a celebration really for Karen and Ellie. They've just qualified as midwives.'

'Oh, how lovely. You haven't got much longer to go to your finals now, have you?'

'Six months. I can't believe it. It's absolutely flown.'

Millie laughed. 'Well you had a good start didn't you, love? Delivering your little brother at home when you were only fifteen.'

Cathy rolled her eyes and thought back to the day seven years ago when her mam had gone into labour with Roddy. Just before he made an appearance, the young nurse accompanying the midwife had slipped on ice in the back garden and broken her leg. While everyone was rushing around helping her, Cathy had successfully delivered the baby herself. It was an event she would never forget and had strengthened her longing to become a nurse.

'I certainly did.' She grinned. That young nurse had been Jean, now one of her best friends.

'When's Gianni back up this way?'

'Next month. I can't wait to see him again. That's the only thing I don't like about my life right now; the fact that we can't be together all the time. But there's no way he'd leave his dad to manage the fair alone now his Uncle Marco has gone back to Italy, and he knows I can't handle that lifestyle. So we have to meet in the middle and make the best of a bad job, for now, anyway.'

Millie nodded. 'Just like Sadie. She couldn't handle fairground living either.'

Cathy sighed. Gianni's mother had left Luca when Gianni was a baby, even though she'd never divorced him or stopped loving him. It was only after her tragic death that Gianni had found his father. Much as she hated being apart from him, Cathy knew she'd never force Gianni to choose between them. It made the time they did spend together even more precious.

'Are you staying at your mam's tonight?' Millie asked.

'Yes,' Cathy replied. 'Not sure what time I'll be home though. We're having afternoon tea and then a bit of a wander around town.'

'I'll pop in and see your mam later for a brew,' Millie said. 'Might catch up with you then. Enjoy your afternoon off. Makes a nice change from working.'

'It does.' Cathy waved goodbye and strolled back outside the store. She looked across at the Adelphi Hotel and swallowed a lump that had risen in her throat. Her mam and dad's one-night honeymoon had been in the hotel before he was sent off to fight in World War Two. Cathy knew she'd been conceived that night because her dad had been away for the next five years. She vaguely remembered spending time with him before his untimely death, but she'd never really known him. Framed photos at Granny Lomax's showed he'd been a nice-looking young man, smart in his soldier's uniform and dark-haired and blue-eyed, just like Cathy.

She turned onto Bold Street and strolled down towards the Kardomah, swinging her white handbag and enjoying the warm sun on her bare arms.

*

Jack looked up as the clinking of keys sounded and the cell door clanged open. A large man with ginger hair and a neat beard strolled in, accompanied by the prison warder, who pointed to the top bunk and told the man that was his. Jack swung his legs off the bed and slowly got to his feet. His lower leg was hurting like hell and he had taken a couple of his prescribed tablets earlier. He wouldn't be allowed any more until later, but he could do with them now. That was the problem with being banged up; there was no alcohol to take the edge off his pain.

He'd been on his own for the last couple of nights as the thick Scouser had been given parole and sent home with conditions. Jack had relished the peace and quiet but had known it would be short-lived. The warder left the cell and locked the door behind him.

Jack nodded at the new bloke, who nodded back. 'The name's Jack,' he ventured, but didn't hold out his hand, as the bloke didn't look the hand-shake type.

'Andy,' the man responded in a strong Glaswegian accent. 'What time do they serve afternoon tea in this establishment?' His mouth twitched and Jack realised he was joking.

He laughed. 'Six on the dot. But we get a brew and a biscuit in about half an hour. There's a cupboard over there for your stuff. Bottom shelf, mine's on the top. Welcome to Walton Palace.'

'How long have you been here?' Andy asked, putting his meagre belongings and a spare set of prison-issue clothing on his allocated shelf.

'Too bloody long,' Jack said. 'I've another five years to go. And you?'

Andy winked and rummaged in his backpack again, pulling out a box of playing cards. 'New sentence. Fifteen years this time... but not if I have my way,' he added, lowering his voice. 'Let's just see, shall we? Fancy a game of cards?'

Jack smiled and invited Andy to sit down on his bunk. He pulled the small table across from underneath the barred window and Andy proceeded to deal the cards.

'We'll play for fags,' Andy said as Jack sat down beside him. 'I've a full pack with me.'

'I've two left,' Jack said.

'I noticed you limping. Problem with your leg?'

Jack explained about his wartime injury and Andy nodded sympathetically. 'I lost a few mates overseas. I managed to come back in one piece to find my wife had buggered off with a Yank. You married, Jack?'

'Divorced. Thank God.'

'That bad, was it? Waste of time, women. They screw you over and will never take the blame for anything.'

'You can say that again,' Jack agreed, thinking how he was going to enjoy Andy's company much better than he'd enjoyed his time with the thick Scouser. At least having a decent cellmate would help the next few years go by a bit quicker.

*

A young girl in a black-and-white waitressing outfit greeted her warmly as she entered the coffee shop.

'Table for four, please,' Cathy said. 'Could we have one by the window? My friends will be joining me shortly.'

'Of course, Madam.' The waitress led the way over to the big window that looked out onto Bold Street. Cathy sat down on a chair closest to the window and peered around. The Kardomah was always a special place to have tea. She'd been with Granny occasionally on her birthday. The high ceilings gave a grand feel to the room and the tall leather seating in an orange-red contrasted boldly with the highly polished black wooden tables.

Through the window she spotted her three brightly dressed friends crossing the street. Almost as though she knew she was being spied on, Jean looked across, her red hair blowing in the gentle breeze coming up from the Mersey. She waved and pointed and Ellie and Karen looked over and waved too. Cathy grinned as they hurried into the café and joined her at the table. There were hugs and shrieks of delight as the girls took their seats and the waitress brought the menus over.

'You three look lovely,' Cathy said, admiring their summer dresses in various pastel patterns on white backgrounds. Their neatly styled hair, Ellie's blond and wavy and Karen's as dark and straight as Cathy's, hung freely to their shoulders, free from the usual confines of white caps and kirby grips.

'It's so nice to get dressed up like proper ladies,' Jean said with a grin. 'It's such a treat to be off hospital premises for a few hours.'

The foursome ordered assorted sandwiches and chocolate cake, with pots of tea, and caught up with each other's news.

'Where will you be living now you've qualified?' Cathy asked, moving the menus to one side as two waitresses brought over a tea trolley laden with their order and placed everything on the table. 'Thank you.' She smiled as the two girls left with the empty trolley.

'We're not sure, yet,' Karen replied. 'We've talked about renting a flat or house between us, Jean as well now she's not seeing Nigel any more.'

'That sounds like a great idea,' Cathy said as Ellie nodded her agreement. 'Well, until you all decide to stroll down the aisle.'

Karen laughed. 'All in good time. Anyway, I'll need to find a fella I fancy enough to commit to, first.'

'I don't think marriage is for me,' Ellie admitted shyly. 'What happened to me has kind of put me off blokes for life. I don't trust anybody. Well except for your Gianni, of course.'

Cathy took a deep breath and nodded. Ellie's rape by Jack Dawson had affected her friend badly. He was still in Walton Gaol and could rot in there forever as far as she was concerned. He'd never been in contact, not even to ask how his kids were doing. She pushed the thoughts of him out of her mind, picked up the teapot and filled their cups. 'You don't need to have a man in your life to be a success, Ellie.' Cathy touched her hand as Ellie smiled. 'I mean, it's 1963 and we gels can do what we like, right? What about you, Jean, anyone in mind?'

Jean shook her head. 'Not at the moment. Nigel was a bit too clingy and just didn't seem to get that I don't want to be married or even engaged. Like you said, it's not the be all and end all for me like it is for a lot of women. I'm glad to have a break from him to be honest. But I've got some plans going through my head that might help us all in time.'

'Tell Cathy,' Karen urged, reaching for a salmon sandwich. 'I know she's got a roof over her and Lucy's heads at the moment, but for the future, well, you never know.'

Cathy stared open-mouthed as Jean spoke of her plans. 'It's early days of course, but if we could find a house in Liverpool that's big enough for us all to comfortably share, we could live in half of it and turn the rest over to providing a sort of private maternity home with top-rate care.'

Jean paused for breath and looked around at her friends. 'Also, we could help the young unmarried girls we look after to make a choice for themselves about keeping their babies. Far too many are having them ripped out of their arms and adopted without a say in the matter. They often have no choice other than to go back to parents who are in the main more concerned about what the bloody neighbours think than about how their poor daughters are feeling. Just imagine, Cathy, if you and Gianni hadn't got back together and your mam had insisted you put Lucy up for adoption.'

Cathy swallowed hard, remembering the awful time when she'd dumped Gianni because she was terrified of losing him while he was riding the bikes, and then discovered Lucy was on the way. 'I couldn't have survived that,' she admitted. 'I was also very fortunate to have all of you on my side as well as a supportive mam and granny. So many girls don't have anyone. I think it's a wonderful idea, Jean.'

They all nodded their agreement. 'We'd be the family those girls don't have,' Ellie said. 'They'd learn from us how to take care of their babies and if they can't go home then we'd help them to find suitable accommodation and jobs so that they could provide for themselves. We'd be giving them time to adjust to being a mother.'

Jean sighed loudly. 'Our main problem is finding a big enough place and getting some help to finance it all.'

'How would that work?' Cathy asked. 'I mean if a mother-to-be wanted private care, she would be willing to pay, surely.'

'Yes, she would, and the more patients we got that were after something a bit more special than a big hospital ward the better. It would help us to finance the other side of things. We may qualify for some help from the council and the NHS. It needs a lot of plotting and planning. But I think it's a worthwhile project, don't you?'

Cathy nodded. 'I do, definitely. And when my training is over and done with, you'll have another midwife to join the team. If you want me of course.'

'It goes without saying.' Karen raised her rosebud-patterned china cup. 'Here's to the future.'

'The future,' they all said, gently clinking cups together.

'All we need now is a suitable place,' Cathy mused. 'There are hundreds of big houses in and around Liverpool. My stepdad

Johnny does up old houses with his brother Jimmy. I'll ask him to keep an eye out for something that will be just right for us.'

On her way home and true to her word, Cathy called on Debbie, who let her in and led the way to the back room.

'Sit yourself down and I'll pour you a cuppa,' Debbie said.

In spite of feeling awash with tea, Cathy joined Debbie at the table for a catch-up. 'How are you doing?'

'Feeling fat and whale-like again,' Debbie complained, rubbing her huge tummy. 'Sorry, Cathy. I shouldn't be complaining. I know you'd have given your right arm to have got this far with Gianni Junior.'

Cathy smiled. 'I would, but don't worry about having a grumble. That's some bump you've got there.'

'Can't wait for next month. I hope you are on duty when I go into labour.'

'So do I. But if not, it will be one of my friends that you know, so you will be fine, and I'll be on the ward anyway most days so I'll see plenty of you.'

Debbie smiled. 'Davy's just got a new job. He starts next week. So hopefully he'll like it, and it's much better money than Lewis's too.'

'Oh brilliant. Where?'

'At Littlewoods Pools. Floor manager in the pool-checking department. He'll be managing a lot of people, and it will be a change from selling tellies and washing machines. We've got some decent money saved and Davy will be able to get a better mortgage now and it means I don't need to worry about going to work when this baby arrives. Well, at least until it's ready for school anyway. When Gianni next calls you, will you ask him to ring Davy here? There's something we'd like to ask him about the house.'

'Of course I will, Debs. I'm really pleased for you both.'

'That will be great,' Debbie said. 'We love what Johnny's done to your mam's place, the extension and everything. It's fabulous. We'd like to do that too eventually. I love living on this street and it would be nice to have a bit more space with this little fella coming soon.'

Cathy grinned. 'Or little lady.'

Debbie grimaced. 'I'd love a girl, but knowing my luck!'

Chapter Five

June 1963

Jack fidgeted uncomfortably as the white van bumped and rocked its way over the rutted surface of the diverted road. He stared at Andy, sitting on the opposite bench seat. His fellow prisoner didn't meet his eyes, keeping his gaze fixed to the floor. He wondered why. For the time he'd shared a cell with the tall, thick-set Glaswegian, Jack had felt they had got along reasonably well. Although half the time he struggled to understand what the bloke was saying. He spoke fast in his strong accent and every sentence was peppered with swearwords. Still, anything was better than the dense Scouser he'd shared with when he was first sentenced.

Today, Friday, was the long-awaited transfer from Walton Gaol to Armley Gaol in Leeds and he and Andy were being transferred together. Jack wasn't bothered about being moved away from his native Liverpool as no one ever came to visit him anyway. He wondered if he and Andy would share a cell in the new place; highly unlikely, seeing as not much ever went in his favour. Knowing *his* luck, he'd no doubt get lumbered with some psycho, sheep-shagging, Yorkshire pillock.

He glanced at the prison officer he was handcuffed to. The man sat ramrod-straight beside him. He was a young fellow, well, younger than him at any rate; tall, but of slight build. If they'd been alone Jack knew he could have overpowered him. But they weren't alone. Andy's accompanying officer was built like a brick house and the officer driving the van was of a similar build.

God, he could murder a cigarette and no doubt Andy felt the same. He had that tetchy air about him that Jack recognised as him needing a fag time. Andy slowly raised his eyes to Jack's and half-smiled. Jack smiled back. He had fags with him, but they were stashed away in a small rucksack with the rest of his meagre belongings that had been placed out of his reach.

Andy began to whistle and tap his feet slowly as the van veered across to the right-hand side of the road and came to a sudden and unexpected stop. Jack fell sideways against his officer and was immediately pushed back into a sitting position.

The officer handcuffed to Andy shouted through to the driver, 'What the hell is going on? Why have you stopped? Shut the fuck up,' he snarled at Andy as his whistling became louder.

Jack recognised the tune and smirked as Andy burst into Elvis Presley's 'It's Now or Never' at the top of his voice, almost drowning out the sound of the loud gunshot that reverberated through the van. Andy sang louder still, adding his own words to the song, 'It's now or never, come rescue me,' throwing back his head as he emphasised the word rescue, rolling his r's.

'Shit, what the fuck was that?' The officer peered through the small window into the front of the van, where the driver was slumped over the wheel; his brains were splattered across the dashboard and what was left of the windscreen.

Jack saw the look of horror in the officer's eyes as the van's back doors were flung wide open and pandemonium broke out.

'Boys, what took you so long?' Andy called gleefully as two men clambered into the van, the tallest of the pair waving a shotgun at the white-faced officers, the second man swinging a bunch of keys from an index finger. Both wore face-distorting stocking masks and had black woollen hats pulled low, covering their hair.

Jack shrank back against the seat, feeling his bowels turn to liquid. He hoped he wouldn't shit himself. He couldn't afford to look a prat in front of these men, who were obviously hardened criminals. If they'd shot the other officers, he was certain they'd have no qualms about shooting him too in case he blabbed. Andy was doing time for armed robbery; these two were probably the partners in crime who had reportedly got away and had been lying low for a few years.

The taller man poked Andy's officer in the ribs with the gun and spoke, his accent as thick as Andy's. 'Which key for the cuffs?'

The officer pointed and Andy was freed. The man then ordered his officer to lie face-down on the bench seat and handcuffed his spare wrist to his other behind his back as Andy lumbered to his feet.

Then the man freed Jack and ordered his officer, who Jack could feel trembling by his side, to lie face-down too. He handcuffed him and then yanked Jack to his feet, steadying him as he wobbled.

'Let's get out of here,' Andy yelled as Jack reached for his rucksack.

They stumbled out of the van and the man with the keys locked it. Jack could see a large black car parked a few yards up the road and felt himself being dragged along towards it by Andy. He struggled to keep upright, his bad leg giving way.

Andy turned to yell at the man with the shotgun, who was busy blasting through each van tyre. 'Come on; let's get out of here before some fucker comes to see what all the noise is about.' The man finished his job and legged it towards them.

'Well done, lads. That diversion worked perfectly.' Andy slapped shoulders all round. He turned to Jack who had been bundled into the car alongside him. 'Right, you've got two choices, Jackie boy,' he began.

Jack felt sick. This was it; they were giving him the choice of death now, or later. The shorter man fired up the engine and the car shot forward, jerking Jack almost out of his seat.

Andy pulled him back and continued. 'You can come up to Scotland with us, or make your own way to freedom. We can drop you off shortly, if that's what you choose.'

Stunned by the events of the last few minutes, Jack sat back and closed his eyes, tasting freedom. He didn't have a clue where they were, but he'd find out soon enough. All the years he'd been stuck in Walton he'd dreamed of escape and what he'd do to that little bitch Cathy if their paths ever crossed again, never once believing that his freedom was merely weeks away. He didn't need to think. He'd do his own thing, make his way back to Liverpool and look for her.

Andy and his cronies dropped him off, having made him promise to keep his trap shut if he ever got picked up. With twenty Woodbines, a box of matches and the gift of a roll of notes in his pocket totalling forty quid, the world was his oyster. The money would keep him in food, beer and fags, for a good while anyway. All he had to do was go into hiding for a week or two while his hair and facial hair grew and the initial search for him and Andy had quietened down. The thought of living rough didn't faze him. He'd already done it – he'd had no choice when Alice chucked him out of their home – and anything was better than prison life.

He'd need a change of clothes soon enough, so a quick eyeballing of washing lines was a must, and an eye out for a disused shed on an allotment to provide him with shelter. Andy's mates had told him he that wasn't too far from the city of York, so if he could locate the railway line that ran from York to Liverpool or even Manchester, there was bound to be an allotment or two running close to the tracks. In his experience, many allotments were situated near railways. He lit a cigarette, hoisted his rucksack onto his shoulder and set off at as brisk a trot as his wooden foot would allow.

*

Cathy drank the last mouthful of tea, rinsed her mug at the kitchen sink and placed it on the draining board. She smoothed her pale blue cotton nurse's dress down and put on her navy coat, shoving a small carrot from the vegetable basket into her pocket. She and Lucy were to stay at her mam's this weekend to give Granny a bit of a break. She could hear the sound of voices on the stairs and popped her head around the kitchen door.

'Shh,' she whispered as her teenage sisters Sandra and Rosie burst into the back sitting room. 'Why are you two up so early on a Sunday?' She shook her head. Typical. It took forever to get them moving on a school day.

'We're going to Seffy Park today,' Sandra announced, looping a strand of hair behind her ears. 'Johnny says he'll treat us to ice-creams if we help Mam with the chores this morning.'

Cathy smiled. Her sisters were growing up to be pretty girls with their long dark hair, big blue eyes and slender figures. 'Well you won't be going until after dinner,' she said. 'It's only half past six. Go back to bed and don't wake Roddy and Lucy up. Let Mam and Johnny have a lie-in. They deserve it. Right, I'm off to work. It's my early shift today and I have to walk part of the way because it's too early for the bus.' She peered out of the window at the start of a bright day. 'Still, at least it's not raining. Enjoy your afternoon out.' She gave them both a hug, picked up her bag and set off to walk into the city.

It was a very pleasant morning and she waved at Sandra's friend Ben as he wobbled on his bicycle down Lark Lane, heavy bag, loaded with Sunday papers, slung over his shoulder. Charlie the milkman, who was delivering pints to nearby houses, also waved to her. His black-and-white horse neighed and flicked his tail as Cathy stroked his velvety nose. He nudged her pocket and Cathy laughed and gave him the carrot. 'How did you know?' she said. 'You're such a clever boy, Captain.'

'Ah, you spoil him.' Charlie grinned. 'He's got used to you having a surprise in your pocket for him now. Off to save a life or two, then?' he said as he lifted a crate of empties back on to the cart.

'Let's hope it's not that sort of day, Charlie. I'm on maternity and it's usually quite happy on there. More celebrations than sadness, although we do get the odd time…' She tailed off, thinking back to last week's stillbirth and the heartbroken young parents. Those times were just so hard to deal with.

Charlie nodded. 'Well enjoy it, whatever the day brings. We'll see you again.' Whistling, he led Captain away, the milk cart trundling along behind, bottles jingling in their crates.

Cathy strolled along swinging her bag, enjoying the peace and quiet before everyone got up, some to attend early-morning church services, others to watch amateur football matches on the recreation ground. Halfway into the centre she stopped at a bus stop where several members of Liverpool Royal staff were waiting for the first bus of the morning. She exchanged pleasantries with a couple of ward cleaners and kitchen staff who she'd known since she'd first started working at the hospital.

'Morning, chuck. 'ow's yer mam and Johnny doing?' Doris, one of the cleaners, asked.

'Oh, she's fine, thank you,' Cathy replied. 'They're very happy.'

'Nothing less than she deserves after everything that bugger Jack Dawson put 'er through.'

'Aye,' Queenie, one of the kitchen staff piped up. 'Third time lucky for Alice, bless her.'

Cathy smiled and thanked them. She wondered if Jack knew her mam had remarried and that his three children now had a wonderful stepfather. Maybe the prison authorities had told him. No one else would bother, she was sure. He'd know he was divorced; surely he'd had to sign the papers. Hopefully, when the time came for his release he'd have no need at all to come anywhere near Aigburth and the family. He'd never wanted to know the kids when he lived with them, so knowing he was off the hook now, he would hopefully scarper to somewhere far, far away. Cathy held on to that pleasing thought as she boarded the bus and by the time it pulled up outside the hospital gates she'd put all thoughts of Jack out of her mind.

She hurried up the corridor to the lifts that would take her up to Maternity Ward B. Ellie and Karen were on early duty today as well, and Jean was just coming off a night shift. She was in the middle of the handover as Cathy fastened her apron and clipped her white cap to her pinned-up hair. She fixed her fob watch to the front of her apron and proudly stretched the red elasticated belt around her waist. Red was the colour of a second-year midwifery student. She went into Sister's office, where staff midwife Jean was going through the patient list with Karen and Ellie and Sister Mason, Cathy's favourite sister, who had also just come on duty.

'It was total chaos last night,' Jean announced. 'We didn't even get a break. Two bouncing baby boys delivered within an hour of each other. Both they and mums are doing well. We also had a little pre-termer of twenty-six weeks. She survived for a couple of hours but sadly her lungs were underdeveloped and she didn't make it. Mum's in a private side room and her hubby has stayed with her. They're only youngsters. Poor kids, such a sad time for them. We'll probably discharge her tomorrow when she's had a good rest. It will only cause her further distress to stay in here with all the babies around her. Doctor will be on the ward to check her over later. We've a couple of labours on the go at the moment – one is five centimetres and the other is almost fully dilated, so she's ready to go into delivery.'

Jean took a deep breath. 'And that, my dears, is where I'm going to love you and leave you. I'm starving as well as shattered. Breakfast in the staff canteen and then bed for me. You'll all be finished by the time I'm back in tonight, but I'll catch up in the morning. My last shift tonight for a few weeks; two days off and then earlies next. Thank the Lord.'

'See you tomorrow, Jean,' they chorused as the breakfast wagon was trundled into the ward by Joe Banks, one of the kitchen porters.

'Breakfast and a brew and then we'll get stuck in. No visit from Matron today. I love Sundays for that very reason,' Sister Mason said, a twinkle in her eye. 'But you didn't hear me say that!'

*

Alice lay back on the grass and watched Johnny playing rounders with Rodney, Lucy and Rosie. Sandra had disappeared, saying she was going to the ladies' in the Palm House café. More likely to eye up the lads that hung around the Palm House on a Sunday afternoon, Alice thought, just like Cathy and her friend Debs had done a few years back. The kids were growing up fast, and Johnny was so good with them. Nothing was too much trouble.

She couldn't believe her luck that she'd met such a loving and kind man as Johnny Harrison and that not only did he want *her* but he was also willing to take on her family too. Little Lucy adored him – he was a perfect grandpa to her and a great father to her younger ones too. Before they'd married, Johnny had confessed to Alice that he was unable to father any children due to problems caused by mumps as a child. He'd told her that to have a ready-made family was just the job for him and he would always treat her children as his own.

After being widowed so young and then marrying that waste of time Jack Dawson, Alice was in seventh heaven with her new man and had never felt so loved and lucky in her life. Rosie and Rodney now called Johnny Dad, and she felt safe with him. It was a good place to be in after the trauma of the last few years.

*

Cathy wrapped the red-faced baby boy in a white sheet and handed him to Sally, his exhausted but beaming mother. 'Well done. He's a little belter.' The baby had a mop of dark hair and he opened his big blue eyes and glared at the young girl who was gazing proudly down at her swaddled bundle. Cathy always felt a little twinge of sadness for herself when she delivered a baby, mixed with joy for the new parents. That feeling would probably never go away.

'He looks a bit cross,' Sally said, tears streaming down her cheeks. She wiped them away with the back of her hand.

Ellie handed her a tissue and smiled. 'He was getting a bit too comfortable in there,' she said. 'He's just objecting to being disturbed.'

'Two weeks overdue.' Sally sighed. 'Thought he'd never come. Wait until your daddy sees you. He'll be that proud, he'll be signing you up for Everton before you can walk.' She gave a yell and screwed up her face. 'Ouch!'

'Have we got a name?' Cathy asked, squeezing her hand to distract her from the pain as Ellie took charge of delivering the placenta.

'We have,' Sally gasped, squeezing back. 'We chose Adam, after Adam Faith, for a boy. So he's being called Adam and David, after my dad.' Her lips trembled. 'Such a shame he'll never know him. Dad was killed in the war not long after he married Mam.'

'I'm sure he'll be watching over you and will be very proud,' Cathy said, feeling choked as she thought about her own dad and how proud he would be of Lucy. She swallowed the lump in her throat and smiled. 'Right, I'll go and ring your mother-in-law and then she can get word to your husband. Congratulations, Sally. You did really well.'

Cathy and Ellie queued up in the staff canteen for their roast dinners. Sunday was always traditional fare, with the best Yorkshire puddings in Liverpool. As Mavis the server loaded their plates with slices of beef Cathy's mouth watered with anticipation. They were late today; it was almost two o'clock. Mavis offered them two puddings each. 'You might as well,' she said. 'You're probably the last pair to come down for your dinner.'

Cathy nodded her thanks and helped herself to vegetables and gravy. She and Ellie sat at a table in the window that overlooked the back of the nurses' home. Cathy looked across and half-smiled. The window directly opposite had been her room when she'd started her training and lived on the premises. It was the room she'd smuggled Gianni into by suggesting he climb onto the dustbins beneath. It was that secret night of passion that had led to Lucy's conception. She felt her cheeks heating as she speared a roast potato and sliced it in two.

Ellie raised an eyebrow as she followed Cathy's gaze and noted her pink cheeks. She grinned. 'I can read you like a book,' she said. 'Bet no one else has smuggled a boyfriend in that way.'

'I bet they have,' Cathy said, laughing. 'I won't have been the first and most certainly not the last.'

'Well the current occupant definitely won't be getting up to the tricks you and Gianni got up to. It's Maude Parker and you know what she's like. Thinks all men are heathens. Mind you, she's not entirely wrong there.'

Cathy nodded. 'She's a decent enough nurse.' Maude Parker's bark was worse than her bite and she kept herself to herself, even though others had tried to encourage her into joining them in the communal sitting room to watch the telly at night.

'I guess so,' Ellie agreed. 'Glad I don't work with her though. She's miserable with staff and creates an atmosphere, so I've been told.'

The pair tucked into their dinners and as they finished, Mavis brought over a tray with their laden dishes – two each – of apple pie and custard and mugs of steaming hot tea.

'Thank you, Mavis, you spoil us,' Cathy said as Mavis collected their empty plates.

'You both work hard, you need looking after,' Mavis said as she headed back to the counter.

Cathy finished her pudding and sat back in her chair. She blew out her cheeks. 'I'm well and truly stuffed,' she said.

'Me too.' Ellie sighed. 'Well we won't need any tea tonight.' She pushed back on her chair, the legs scraping the floor tiles beneath. 'Shall we go back upstairs?'

'I could go to sleep,' Cathy sighed. 'I don't know about going back to work.'

Chapter Six

Sandra lay on her bed in the room she shared with Rosie, listening to the end of *Pick of the Pops* on the little transistor radio Mam and Johnny had bought her last Christmas. Rosie was having tea with a friend, so she had the room to herself. She loved listening to the charts and all the hit records, singing along to all the songs she knew. Gerry and the Pacemakers were number one this week with 'I Like It'. They'd just knocked 'From Me to You' by her favourite group the Beatles off the top spot.

She couldn't wait to be fifteen in September because Mam had said she could go to the Cavern Club in the city when she was older. All the groups played there and some of her friends had already seen the Beatles more than once. Sandra felt she was missing out by not being allowed to go into the city at night with her school pals. It wasn't fair. And if she didn't get a move on with this growing-up business, someone would steal her almost-boyfriend Ben Jarvis right from under her nose. Ben lived on Bickerton Street, which ran parallel with Lucerne Street, and his mam used to mind her little brother Roddy before he started school, so their mams were friendly.

Ben was a few months older than Sandra, already fifteen. They went to the same school and youth club and he had a paper round that gave him a bit of spending money to go out. He went to a café called the Rumblin' Tum that Cathy said she used to go to with Gianni a few years ago and another place called the Jacaranda in the city. Ben had told her that lots of beat groups were forming and playing in all these places and she was desperate to get out and see them. Mam had told her there was plenty of time for all that nonsense and she needed to concentrate at school this year so she could get her O levels and decide on what she wanted to do for the future.

Sandra knew exactly what she wanted to do. She planned to follow in her sister's footsteps and train to be a nurse. She felt confident that she'd get the results she'd need to get into nursing school right away and not have to work first like Cathy had done. Sandra knew she was lucky to have a good stepdad who supported them all. Her own dad was a horrible man; he'd always shouted at her and Rosie and made them cry. He was nasty to her mam and Cathy too. She was glad he was in prison because he couldn't hurt any of them any more.

She jumped as she heard her name being called. 'Coming, Mam,' she yelled back and turned off the radio. Damn it, she'd miss the end of the programme now, but she knew better than to argue with her mam. She placed the radio on the bedside table, jumped to her feet and ran down the stairs.

'Ah, there you are,' Alice said, peering out from the kitchen. 'Fetch me that washing in off the line, love. It's starting to spit with rain and I'm just buttering bread for our tea. Just drop it into the basket and then fold it when you bring it inside. I'll iron the clothes tonight.'

Sandra picked up the laundry basket and peg bag and dashed outside as heavy spots of rain started to fall. She quickly unpegged everything as Millie from next door, bringing in her own washing, called over the fence. 'Tell your mam and Johnny we'll see them later. We'll be round at seven for the *London Palladium*.'

'Will do,' Sandra called back. She used to love Sunday nights because her mam and Johnny and Millie and Jimmy got together to watch the best show of the week and they'd have a drink indoors and always treated the kids to a bottle of dandelion and burdock and packets of crisps. But now she was older she'd rather go out with her pals. Her mam had mentioned earlier that Frank Ifield was on the show tonight as the star and he was such a square compared to the Beatles.

*

Cathy lay back in the bath and closed her eyes, relaxing in the pine-scented Radox steam. Her aching muscles were easing already. Lucy and Roddy were in bed and the rest of her family was watching telly in the front room with Jimmy and Millie. She mustn't fall asleep. There was a Babycham waiting for her downstairs and she was looking forward to it. Gianni had phoned just after she got in and it was good to hear his voice. He was currently pitched up somewhere in Yorkshire, she couldn't remember where he'd said, and would be back in Liverpool in just a few weeks. She couldn't wait to see him again. He'd told her he was missing her and Lucy and was looking forward to spending time with them both. They'd go and stay with him in the caravan while the fair was pitched up on Sefton Park. It would only be for a week, but it was better than nothing.

Climbing out of the bath, she yanked out the plug and towelled herself dry. She pulled on fresh underwear, jeans and a T-shirt, fastened her damp hair into a ponytail and dumped her dirty uniform in the laundry basket. She ran downstairs on bare feet, slipping into the front room, where her drink was waiting on the coffee table alongside a small dish of salted peanuts. Her mam and Millie were gazing dewy-eyed at Frank Ifield as he yodelled his way through his latest hit. She smiled and sat down on a chair under the window. Jimmy and Johnny were nowhere to be seen and she wondered where they'd sloped off to. Maybe the pub – but no, they would have taken Mam and Millie with them. She picked up her drink and took a sip. They'd tell her once Frank had finished his singing, no doubt.

As the final song came to an end and the Palladium audience cheered and clapped, her mam turned to Cathy and smiled. 'Oh, he's so good. What a lovely voice and such a nice smile. Did you enjoy your bath, chuck?'

'I did thanks. I feel all relaxed now. It's been a long and busy day. Where are the men?'

'They've just popped out in Jimmy's car for a few minutes to look at a house on Woodlands Road. It's going up for sale as the owners have passed away and the family want to sell it. None of the family wants to live in it as it's too big and it needs a lot of updating to make it modern again. The couple that lived there had six children. One son they lost in the war, another now lives in Australia, so it makes sense to get rid of it and split the money from the sale. Johnny and Jimmy won't be looking inside it tonight but they just wanted to have a nosy round the grounds and to see what they can through the windows. It's bigger than anything they've taken on before, but the pair of them went out of here all excited, so we're waiting for the verdict.'

Cathy frowned. 'Well what will they do with it if it's too big for one family?'

'No idea, love,' Millie said. 'They've just sprung it on us. They met one of the sons in the off-licence earlier when they went to get our drinks, and knowing they're in the trade, he told them about it. A lot of big houses get divided up into flats now, so that might be an option. Anyway, they won't be long, so we'll find out soon enough.'

Johnny and Jimmy were talking excitedly when they came back and sat down on the sofa. Johnny picked up the drink he'd left on the coffee table and took a sip. He pulled a face. 'Bit flat that. I'll top us up, Jimmy.' He went out to the kitchen and brought in a fresh bottle of brown ale.

'What was the house like then?' Alice asked, once they were all settled again.

'Not bad,' Jimmy said. 'We'd have our work cut out if we bought it, but there's a lot of scope there. Plenty of upstairs windows, which means lots of bedrooms, and nice big rooms downstairs. There's loads of garden and a big driveway. Would make a nice block of flats, or a doctors' or dentists' surgery. Or even a nice private nursery for kiddies. Of course the other option is a big family home, like it's always been, but it'd be costly to run if you were also supporting a big family to fill it. The couple that owned it were teachers – well he was a headmaster and she taught piano and gave singing lessons from the house. They also had a couple of injured ex-soldiers lodging during the war. They lived a comfortable lifestyle in spite of having a big family. But as the son we spoke to told us, none of them could afford to keep it running and buy out their siblings' shares as well. So it's got to be sold. We'll have a think about it and do some figures as soon as we are given a price. Then it's a case of seeing the bank manager.'

Cathy's ears had pricked up at the mention of a doctors' surgery. She wondered if the house would be suitable for the venture that Jean, Karen and Ellie had talked about. It was certainly worth mentioning to them tomorrow when she went into work. Mind you, none of them had money to even think about that at the moment, but still. She looked across at her mam, who'd gone a bit quiet, and wondered why. Maybe worrying about the amount of money the pair would need to borrow for the house purchase and the work needed on it. Mam had just got used to not having to scrimp and scrape every day. Ah well, Johnny and Jimmy seemed to have good business heads on them and must know what they were doing.

*

Maria shook her head as Eloisa slunk out of the caravan. She watched as her daughter ran into Ronnie's outstretched arms. The lad pulled her close for a kiss and squeezed her backside.

'Eloisa!' Maria called. 'Quick as you can with those flyers, girl. When you get back I want you in here, helping me. No sloping off.' She tutted as Eloisa rolled her eyes and grabbed Ronnie by the hand. The pair hurried away, swinging the bag of flyers between them.

Maria went back indoors and poured a coffee from the pot on the stove. She sat down as Luca hurried into the kitchen, his dark hair, now flecked with silver, glistening from his recent shower.

'Has she gone?' He helped himself to coffee and leaned against the sink to drink it.

'Yes, thank the Lord.'

'Did you tell her one flyer on each tree and lamp-post around the recreation ground, and to hand the others out to as many people as she could?'

'Of course. She's not completely useless, you know.'

'Really?' Luca raised an eyebrow. 'She does a good job of pretending she is. It's time she settled down, found a nice lad. Ronnie's not the brightest button in the box, but he's better than nothing. She seems to like him and he her.'

Maria frowned and shook her head. 'Ronnie's not the one for my Eloisa.' She sighed and muttered under her breath. 'Such a pity it didn't work out for her and your son.'

Luca heard her mutterings and shook his head. 'Well Gianni *definitely* wasn't the one. Oil and water, those two. Thank God for Cathy. That girl's been the making of my boy.' He drained his cup and reached for his jacket. 'Right, I'm off. The more we get done today, the better. I want a good opening day tomorrow. The nice weather looks like it is holding; should be a great weekend.'

*

Luca strolled around the recreation ground, checking the various rides and making sure the operators and hired hands knew which duties they were assigned to. He nodded at Lenny, who was busy erecting the Ferris wheel with his gang of helpers.

'You okay, Len?' he called as the burly Cockney wiped his sweaty brow with the hem of his baggy T-shirt and leaned against the framework of the wheel.

'Not bad, boss, but we really could use some extra hands.'

Luca nodded. 'Hopefully the flyers Eloisa's handing out will bring in some enquiries.' He and Maria had sat up late, adding a few words to the printed flyers asking for casual labourers. 'We can but hope.'

'Where's Ronnie?' Lenny asked.

'With Eloisa. I'll send him to you as soon as they get back.'

'Not that he's much use,' Lenny said. 'But he's better than nowt.'

Luca laughed and made his way to the wall of death ride where Gianni, Luca's younger brother Marco and a couple of the hands were almost finished. Luca felt a familiar thrill of anticipation course through his veins at the thought of the first test ride. No matter how many times he did it, the feeling never left him.

'Hey, Dad,' Gianni called from the top of the barrel. 'You ready to roll?'

Luca smiled. He could see in his son's twinkling brown eyes that he felt the same.

'Maria's waving at me,' he called back. 'Give me two minutes while I see what she wants.'

*

Alice was up early on the Monday morning, long before anyone else woke up. She sat at the table in the little back dining room, her hands wrapped around a mug of tea. She was on early shift at the hospital today and so was Cathy. But she needed half an hour on her own to get her thoughts in order. Johnny had talked excitedly into the night after their guests had left and they'd gone up to bed. He was really keen to buy the house and she would support him as much as she could.

But if he and Jimmy used their homes as collateral against the purchase, she was worried. She'd been in danger of losing her home in times past and didn't think she could deal with all that worry again. And not only that, when it had been mentioned that ex-soldiers had lodged there her stomach had flipped over. Jack had taken lodgings after his wartime injury, in a big house on Woodlands Road. What's the betting it was the same one? But then again, why would that matter? He was out of her life now and it was of no consequence. All the same, it had made her feel a bit strange for a while afterwards. She looked up as Cathy hurried into the room, fastening up the buttons of her blue uniform dress.

'Sit down, love, and have a cuppa,' Alice said.

'Thanks, Mam. It'll have to be a quickie. I need to get Lucy up and ready to take to Granny Lomax's. I'll make a couple of slices of toast and then she can eat some on the walk round. Granny will give her a proper breakfast when we get there.'

Johnny hurried downstairs followed by the kids, who were all talking at once – well, Rosie and Sandra were.

'Put some extra bread on the grill, Cathy. Sandra, make sure Rodney has his tie and shoelaces fastened properly before you drop him off at school,' Alice instructed above the noise. 'Sit down, son; I'll get you some cornflakes.'

'I'll drop Roddy off,' Johnny offered as Sandra smiled secretly.

'What you smiling at?' Rosie asked loudly, sitting down at the table.

'Tell you later,' Sandra whispered, kicking Rosie's shins under the table and helping herself to toast from the plate Cathy brought through.

'Save a piece for Lucy,' Cathy called as she ran up the stairs to get her little daughter ready.

Leaving her brood eating breakfast, Alice followed Cathy up the stairs and dashed into the bathroom. She took a deep breath, brushed her hair, pinning it up into her usual French pleat, and pulled on her pale-green uniform dress that was hanging behind the door. She opened her compact and dabbed Crème Puff powder on her face. A slick of lippy and she was ready.

Cathy was leading Lucy downstairs as Alice dashed out of the bathroom. 'Are we ready?'

'Just about,' Cathy replied. 'I'll get her a quick drink of orange juice and her toast.' She and Alice said goodbye to Johnny and the kids and left with Lucy.

Granny Lomax was waiting for them at the gate of her white bungalow on nearby Linnet Lane. Cathy gave the elderly lady a hug and a kiss on the cheek. 'I'll be back about three thirty,' she said. 'Be a good girl for Granny, Lucy.'

'She always is,' Granny said, a warm smile lighting up her lined face. She put her hand to her mouth and coughed violently, her shoulders shaking. 'Oh, dearie me.' She patted her chest and caught her breath. 'George next door is having his grandson today, so they can play nicely in the garden together. See you both later. Don't work too hard.'

'We'll try not to,' Cathy said. 'I'll stay at Mam's again tonight so that you can get a full night's sleep and not have Lucy waking you too early.

Granny nodded. 'Okay, love. I'd be worried about disturbing you both as well.'

They said their goodbyes, Lucy waving until Cathy and Alice turned the corner.

'Granny looked a bit pale today, don't you think?' Cathy said. 'Hope she's okay.'

'Probably a bit tired,' Alice said, 'But yes, she was a bit paler than usual. Might have had a rough night with that cough. It's still troubling her. She was coughing at Easter and it's nearly July now. Has she seen a doctor, do you know?'

Cathy shrugged as they reached the bus stop. 'I doubt it. She said it's nothing that a bottle from the chemist won't get rid of. But I don't like the sound of it and I wonder just how many bottles from the chemist she's taken now. I'll speak to her later when I go back to pick up Lucy. Might be a good idea to see if Ben's mother will look after Lucy for a while so that Granny can get herself right. I'll nip round tonight and see if she's got a free child-minding place.' She stuck out her hand as the bus approached their stop.

*

Sandra hung back on Lark Lane as Rosie ran on ahead and caught up with her friend. She waited until the pair were far enough in front not to notice her and then ducked down a nearby alleyway. With Johnny taking Rodney to school, she could hang around and wait for Ben. He was always late; by the time he'd finished his paper round and gone back home for his breakfast, he never had much time. She took a peep around the corner and saw him coming out of the top of Bickerton Street. Good, he was on his own. She stepped from the alleyway and bent down to fiddle with her shoe as he drew alongside her.

'Oh hi, Sandra,' he said. 'Didn't see you there.' He held out his hand to help her up from the floor and kept hold of it when she wobbled slightly.

'Hi, Ben. How are you?'

'I'm fine thanks. No Rosie today?'

'She's gone on ahead with her friend,' Sandra replied, stepping along beside him as he set off up the road. He'd let go of her hand now but turned and smiled, keeping pace with her.

'Well that's good. Means we can chat in peace. Did you listen to *Pick of the Pops* yesterday? That Gerry fella has knocked the Beatles from number one. But they're not a patch on the Beatles.'

Sandra nodded. 'I know. I was quite surprised actually.'

'Me too. I mean they're okay and I've seen them at the Cavern, but there's nobody as good as the Beatles as far as I'm concerned.'

Sandra would have gone along with anything Ben said, whether she agreed or not. She was thrilled just being in his company. She was jerked out of her daydreams when a harsh voice yelled his name from across the road. Her heart sank when he turned to see who was calling him and waved at the girl with brassy blond hair and a spotty face. Janet Smyth lumbered across the road. Her face red from exertion, she glared at Sandra, who glared back.

'Youse goin' the youth club tomorra, Ben?' she asked, her Scouse accent strong.

Ben shrugged. 'Might be. Depends.'

'On what?'

'On whether Sandra is allowed out. We're going together.' Ben reached for Sandra's hand and squeezed it.

She squeezed his back. That was the first she'd heard about them going to the youth club together and she wondered if he meant it, or whether it was an excuse to get rid of Janet.

Janet stared at Sandra with a look that would surely kill. 'Are youse two going out together then?'

Ben nodded and squeezed Sandra's hand again. Sandra gave the girl a half-smile and got daggers in exchange.

'Right, well I'll see youse around.' Janet stomped off up the street as Ben breathed a sigh of relief.

'Thank God for that,' he muttered, pulling Sandra along with him. 'She bought it.'

Sandra stopped walking and removed her hand from his. 'Bought what?'

'She believed we're going out together. You saved my neck there, gel. Thanks for that.'

Sandra stared at him. She didn't know whether to laugh or burst into tears, but then he continued, 'But if you *can* get out tomorrow night, I would love it if we could go to the youth club together. That's if you want to, of course.'

Sandra smiled. 'I'd love to.' Her plan of hanging around waiting for him had worked. With her sister out of the way, and his mates not with him, he'd finally asked her on a sort of date. Now all she had to do was convince her mam it was a good idea.

Chapter Seven

The morning shift was busy as always and Cathy didn't get a chance to tell Jean about the house on Woodlands Road before she left the ward after her night shift. But Cathy managed to tell her there was something she needed to speak to her about and that she would call her tonight from home. Jean said to leave it until after seven as she was having a good sleep and then going to get her hair trimmed and do a bit of shopping.

'I'll leave it until after I've put Lucy to bed,' Cathy said as Jean made to leave the ward. 'Gives you time to have your tea as well without being disturbed. Be near the phone about seven thirty then.' The wall phone that the live-in nurses used was in the corridor opposite Cathy's old room.

'Will do,' Jean said. 'Hope it's not too busy for you. Good luck with the twins, they'll arrive in the next couple of hours, you mark my words. Jenny is going to need a shoulder to cry on.' She left the ward with a wave of her hand and Cathy went back into the office to await her duty instructions.

Ellie was given temperature, blood pressure and urine sample checks duties and Cathy was told to accompany Karen, who smiled and picked up the notes for Jennifer Moore, the patient who would soon be delivering twins. She was a nineteen-year-old unmarried mother whose parents had brought her in and left her with clear instructions that the babies were to be placed into foster care and then adopted at the first opportunity. Jennifer's history was sad: her boyfriend Billy, to whom she'd been engaged, had been killed on his way home from work, just days after they'd found out Jennifer was pregnant. They'd planned to marry, she'd told Karen and Cathy, but she was left to break the news to her parents alone. She was heartbroken from her loss and her parents' firm decision that she must give up her baby, and there'd been further upset when two heartbeats were detected five months into her pregnancy. Jennifer had been sent from her Wirral home to stay with a straight-laced maiden aunt in Liverpool for the rest of her time, but the aunt had been no help in supporting her. She'd agreed with Jennifer's parents that they should stick to their guns, and more so when twins were confirmed.

'Young Jenny is the sort of girl we could be helping if we had the private maternity home,' Karen whispered as they hurried down the ward towards Jennifer's side room.

Cathy nodded. 'I know. And I've got something to tell you on that score at break.'

Karen's eyes lit up. 'Oh, sounds interesting.'

'I hope so,' Cathy said, opening the door to Jennifer's room as the girl let out a groan.

'Come on, Jenny, let's take a look at how far you've progressed since you were last checked,' Karen said, smiling kindly at the girl, who looked worried to death.

Cathy helped Jennifer into a more comfortable position and supported her from behind while Karen examined her. The poor girl was huge and struggled to even move up the bed by herself.

'Oooh,' Karen said. 'Almost fully dilated. I think it's time to get you into the delivery suite, my love. Now don't worry,' she added as a look of panic crossed Jennifer's face. 'Nurse Romano and I won't leave your side until it's all over and your babies are safely delivered.'

Cathy squeezed Jennifer's hand while Karen went to fetch a wheelchair to take her down to the delivery suite. 'You'll be just fine,' she told her in what she hoped was a reassuring tone. Poor

Jennifer would never be fine again once her babies had been delivered. How cruel her parents were to deprive her of them after tragically losing her Billy. How Cathy wished she had a spare room she could offer Jennifer until she got on her feet. Their planned maternity home couldn't come soon enough, she thought as Karen came back in the room with a wheelchair. Cathy gathered up Jennifer's few belongings and put them in a bag that was on the bedside chair. 'I've put your Agatha Christie book in there as well,' she told Jennifer as Karen helped her onto the chair. Cathy handed her the bag and followed them down the ward and out onto the corridor after first collecting Jennifer's paperwork from Sister's office. By the time they'd got Jennifer in the very slow lift and up two floors to delivery she'd started to have contractions every few minutes and was crying out with pain.

'Oh no, I've just wet myself,' Jennifer howled, clutching Cathy's hand. 'How embarrassing.'

'No, you haven't,' Cathy reassured her. 'It's your waters breaking and don't worry about it, you've got a pad on. Now come on, let's get you on to the delivery trolley.' Between them they helped Jennifer on to the low padded trolley and then cranked it up to a suitable height. Cathy pulled the waiting steel trolley of sterilised instruments to one side and wheeled the gas and air tank closer.

Karen unhooked a rubber mask from the tank and handed it to Jennifer. 'Now take some deep breaths and try and relax and we'll have those babies out in no time.' She took Jennifer's blood pressure and then placed a stethoscope on her tummy and listened in, moving the stethoscope around. She looked at Cathy, frowned and gave a slight shake of her head.

Cathy took a metal, trumpet-shaped pinard off the trolley and placed the wide horn on Jennifer's tummy, her own ear placed to the smaller flat end. She pressed gently but firmly and listened, biting her lower lip as she realised what Karen was shaking her head at. No matter where she positioned the instrument, there was only one solid regular heartbeat and nothing else – or was that a very faint beat, or just the echo of the other one? It was hard to tell. She looked at Karen for instructions.

'Go to the desk and tell Sister we need help and to call both the obstetrician and paediatrician,' Karen whispered. Jennifer was moaning softly as she breathed in the gas and air.

Cathy nodded and dashed out of the room to go to the reception area on the corridor, the swing doors almost knocking her off her feet as one caught the back of her shoe heel. She was almost catapulted into the arms of a young doctor making his way towards the doors.

'Steady on, Nurse,' he teased as she caught her breath. 'Where's the fire?'

'Oh, Doctor Morley, I was just going to ask Sister to call you and the paediatrician. We have a problem, or we think we do. Twins, but we can only detect one heartbeat.'

'I just got a call from the sister on your ward to say you'd brought the patient up here,' Doctor Morley said. 'I was on my way up anyway to see someone else, so that's good timing. Twins, eh? It's possible they've shifted position now labour's started, with one hiding behind the other. It does happen. You pop along and ask Sister to make the call and I'll see what's happening in there.'

Cathy dashed away as the obstetrician went into the delivery room. He greeted Karen and picked up Jennifer's notes, scanning through Jean's neat entry from earlier. 'Hmm, both heartbeats were heard at seven this morning with nothing unusual detected.' He reached for the pinard from the trolley and placed it on Jennifer's tummy, moving it around as she moaned with the pain of another contraction. His brow creased and he spoke softly. 'How dilated was Jennifer when you last examined her?'

'She's fully dilated,' Karen said. 'But she's not attempted to push yet, even though her contractions are strong and regular.'

He nodded and palpated Jennifer's tummy. 'We have one facing in the right direction, but who appears to be stuck, and the other one is breeched. I'm going to suggest an emergency Caesarean. One baby is in a distressed situation and I'm afraid we don't have the luxury of time to let nature take its course. Best all round for Mum and babies. I'll ring theatre now and warn them we're on our way. I'll leave you to explain to Jennifer what's happening. I'll ask the desk to send a porter to take the trolley and you two can accompany her. I'll go and get scrubbed up and meet you up there.'

He dashed out of the door as Cathy hurried back inside.

'Sister is trying to contact the paediatrician on duty. He's on the children's ward, she thinks,' Cathy said. Karen nodded and told her quietly what was happening. Then she spoke to Jennifer. The gas and air had made her relaxed and if she heard or understood what Karen was saying to her she didn't respond, but when Cathy took her hand and squeezed it gently, she squeezed back. The porter arrived within minutes and between them they transported Jennifer into theatre.

Doctor Morley was ready and waiting with the anaesthetist. Cathy and Karen put on gowns, gloves and face masks and stood back to let them take over, handing instruments as they were called for. It was only seconds before Jennifer was sound asleep, her blood pressure stable and her abdomen swabbed with iodine. A deep cut was made and Cathy said a silent prayer and looked up to the ceiling as the paediatrician, gowned and masked, dashed into the theatre. A faint little wail sounded and a dark-haired baby boy was handed to Cathy. She rushed him over to a side table, where soft white towels and cotton sheets sat. Along with the paediatrician she rubbed him gently with a towel; he was tiny, perfectly formed, and had the right number of toes and fingers.

The paediatrician examined him and nodded that he was fine. 'A tad small but he's a fighter,' he said, smiling, handing the baby over to Cathy.

Cathy swaddled the tiny boy in a sheet and held him close as he opened his blue eyes and stared at her, unblinking. Tufts of hair stood up on his head where she'd rubbed him, like a miniature quiff. He was a bit bigger than Lucy had been at birth, although he still needed his weight to be confirmed. Karen rushed over with the second baby, another boy, but much tinier and not moving. Cathy held her breath as the paediatrician gently tried to resuscitate him. 'Sorry,' he whispered eventually and shook his head. Karen nodded and wrapped the lifeless little body in a sheet, blinking rapidly while Cathy tried hard to stop tears rolling down her cheeks. At least she and Gianni had been spared this heartbreaking scenario.

Doctor Morley finished seeing to Jennifer, stitched up her abdomen and then joined them at the table. 'Poor little chap,' he said, shaking his head sadly. 'Looks perfect on the outside, doesn't he? We need to let Mum know when she's had a bit more recovery time. She'll need extra-careful handling. We'll pop her in a side room for now. Maybe one of you can stay with her and as soon as she comes round, give me a shout.'

Karen sighed. 'What do you think happened there?'

The paediatrician explained, 'I doubt his lungs were fully developed, plus they are non-identical twins, and that usually means separate placentas, which could mean his wasn't as well developed.'

'His placenta was in a bit of a bad way,' Doctor Morley agreed. 'I'm actually surprised he survived in the womb as long as he did. If he'd been a single baby he might have made it, but sadly he didn't really stand a chance. I'll get a porter to collect him and take him to the morgue for now. Jennifer may want to see him when she wakes up. Put a little shroud on him. There are some on a shelf in that cupboard over there.' He pointed to the back of the room where a floor-to-ceiling cupboard stood. 'Can one of you do him the honour? He'll need labelling too. Poor little soul doesn't even have a name so "Baby Moore" will have to do for now. I'll write out birth and death certificates and they can be given to Jennifer later. Poor young lass. I'm sure you two will do your best for her. See you both later.'

Doctor Morley dashed away, followed by the paediatrician, who looked sad as he thanked them both. Cathy felt her eyes filling as she held on tightly to Jennifer's surviving baby. No matter how many times the staff saw this happen, it was still a shock to everyone concerned. Surely now Jennifer's parents would have a change of heart and let her keep her son? She hoped so, but they'd have to wait and see.

The sister in charge of the delivery suite came into theatre and smiled kindly. She took over and told them to go to the canteen for a break and she would look after Jennifer and her baby until they came back. 'Take an extra five minutes, girls,' she said. 'Losing a new baby is always a very sad time for both parents and staff alike. I can see this has really upset you both.'

In the busy canteen Karen found a table and Cathy went and got two mugs of tea and a plate of toast. Not that either of them felt like eating, but they needed something to give them a bit of energy to help them get them through the rest of the morning. Cathy carried the tray across to Karen.

'Looks like we've missed Ellie with going to theatre,' Karen said. 'We'll catch up at dinnertime.'

Cathy took a sip of tea and sighed. 'Poor Jenny. I know she wasn't keeping the twins, but even so. To know one didn't survive will really upset her. She's had enough loss for a nineteen-year-old. I wish there was some way we could help her to keep that baby, somewhere she could go to for a few weeks while she gets on her feet.'

Karen nodded. 'That's why Jean's maternity home idea is a good one. There'll be hundreds more Jennys in Liverpool needing help over the next few years.'

'Ah, well, that's what I wanted to tell you,' Cathy said, remembering. 'Sadly, it'll be too late for Jenny, but…' She told Karen about the house on Woodlands Road and Johnny and Jimmy's plans.

Karen's face lit up. 'Wow. It sounds as though the house may be just right.'

'I'm going to call Jean tonight and let her know about it. Hopefully they'll have been to look inside the house by tomorrow, and then they'll know how much work needs doing. They may let us look around as well if they make an offer to buy it. We'll be able to tell them what we want and then see about getting some council or NHS funding to run it. They might agree to let us rent it from them. I doubt we'd be able to buy it, but maybe we could raise money to pay half and rent half. We'll need to make a lot of notes and then have a meeting at my mam's place with Jimmy and Johnny and take it from there.'

Karen smiled. 'It sounds just the job. I bet my dad would help out financially and Ellie and Jean's dads too if they saw we were really serious about making a go of this.'

Cathy nodded. 'With a bit of luck it might not be such a pipe dream after all.'

'Hopefully not. Right, let's go back up to Jenny. I'm not looking forward to it.'

The delivery suite sister was sitting with Jennifer when the pair arrived back upstairs and the young girl's heartbroken sobs could be heard as soon as they entered the corridor. Her surviving baby boy was in a little plastic crib at the foot of the bed.

Sister got to her feet and ushered them back out into the corridor. She spoke in a soft voice. 'Baby Moore has taken an ounce of diluted dried milk formula, which he had no trouble polishing off. He's changed and settled for a while now. Jennifer knows her second son didn't survive his birth. I've asked if I should call anyone for her, but she's declined. You two have spoken to her about her situation and you've got to know her better than I do, so I'll leave that to you. She may change her mind.'

She shook her head and sighed. 'Maybe try and persuade her to choose a name for baby though. I know he's being put up for adoption, but I do think it helps a mother if she can give her child an identity. It's just something to hold on to in her mind; because sure as eggs are eggs, over the coming years there will not be a day that goes by when she doesn't think of him. And it will be so much nicer to remember him with a name that she's chosen.'

Cathy and Karen slipped back into the room and took a seat either side of Jennifer's bed. Karen handed Jennifer a tissue and patted her hand. 'Is there anyone at all you'd like us to call for you, Jenny?'

Jennifer sniffed and shook her head. 'I've been racking my brains over what to do. The only person that might help me is Billy's older married sister Audrey. She lives in New Brighton. She's a really nice lady and loved her brother so much. She was heartbroken when he died. My parents forbade me to get in touch with her, so I've been unable even to write to her. She's not on the phone and she doesn't know about the baby. We were going to go and see her at the weekend of the same week Billy was killed. Once the funeral was over and I told Mum and Dad about the baby they said I was to have no further contact with any of his family. They didn't want them interfering, they said. They wouldn't even let me out of their sight to go and see Billy's parents and then of course they sent me away to my aunty's. I've had no money for train or bus fares to even do a secret visit back to the Wirral to see Billy's family. My baby is part of their family and I'm sure they'd help me. But how can I do it without mine finding out and putting a stop to it?'

Cathy smiled and patted Jennifer's hand. 'Don't you worry. We'll help you to do that,' she whispered. 'I'll go downstairs and get you some stationery from the hospital shop. Write to both Billy's sister and his parents this afternoon. I'll post the letters for you tonight on the way home from work. I'll write down the ward phone number for you to add to the letter, so they can ring to let us know if they want to come and visit you – we'll be taking you back down to the ward shortly. They won't clash with your own parents at visiting time because *they* won't come here until we tell them it's time for you to go home and they come to collect you. We can take it from there.'

Jennifer gave a watery smile. 'Will it work, do you think? My parents say that because I'm under twenty-one I have to do what they say, but now that I've seen my baby and he looks so much like Billy, I just can't let him go. And now I know the other one died, well…' Her lips trembled. 'I owe it to my Billy to look after him, don't I? He's our flesh and blood and I want to keep him. Thank you for saying you'll help me, Nurse Romano. It means such a lot.'

Cathy held back her own tears with difficulty. 'Have you thought of a name for baby, so that you can tell Billy's family?'

Jennifer nodded. Her blue eyes filled again as she said, 'William Peter, after his daddy; Billy junior. And our other baby I'm thinking of as Michael James. James is Billy's dad's name. I hope my Billy will look after his son in heaven as I will look after our Billy junior down here.'

Karen blinked rapidly and Cathy's eyes gave up the fight to hold back tears and they each gave Jennifer a gentle hug.

'That's just perfect,' Cathy whispered.

Chapter Eight

It was Cathy who took a phone call on the ward three days after the birth of Jennifer's baby, from a lady called Audrey Broome. She told Cathy she was responding to a letter she'd received from her late brother's fiancée Jennifer Moore. She asked if she could come and visit tomorrow. Cathy told her she was welcome any time and that she would let Jennifer know she was to expect a visitor. Audrey said she planned to get a ferry over from New Brighton and would book into the Adelphi Hotel for a few nights so that she could visit Jennifer more than once.

Cathy popped her head around the door of Jennifer's room. It had been decided that due to her circumstances, she was to keep her single room for the time being. She was lying on her bed reading while baby Billy snoozed in his little cot beside her. The pair oozed contentment and Cathy couldn't bear the thought that they would ever be parted. 'I've just taken a phone call from this young man's Aunty Audrey,' Cathy said, watching Jennifer's face light up with a delighted smile. 'She's coming to see you both tomorrow. Isn't that great news?'

'Really? She's coming here? Oh, Nurse Romano, that's wonderful. Thank you so, so much.'

'It's my pleasure. Now, how about I help you to take a bath and we'll wash your hair so that you're all bright and breezy for tomorrow.'

*

At seven o'clock that night Alice let in Jean, Karen and Ellie. 'Follow me, girls.' She showed them into the back room where Cathy was waiting with Johnny and Jimmy, who had pages of handwritten figures and some photographs waiting on the dining table.

'How do, girls, come and sit down,' Johnny invited. 'Cathy's talked to us about your private maternity home plans and we both think it's a smashing idea.'

'You do, really?' Jean gasped. 'Well, that's marvellous to know.'

Johnny nodded and continued. 'It's early days and we know financing needs to be figured out, but where there's a will there's always a way. We've put in an offer to buy the house anyway and it's been accepted. We've arranged for one of the sons to meet us there at half seven tonight to show us around again. So if you girls are happy to join us and use your imagination, we might be able to work out some internal plans that will suit your needs.'

'Yes please,' they all shouted at once, laughing.

'I can't believe it,' Jean said. 'Oh, I really hope we can make this happen.'

'Aye, well Cathy's told us about young Jennifer and her baby and I think there's a big need for somewhere like this to help young lasses like her. And there's them that are willing to pay for a bit of preferential care as well,' Jimmy said. 'We feel it's a very worthwhile project.'

'We think so,' Cathy said.

'And you might just find a place for me to work with you,' Alice said. 'Be just the job as it's so much closer than travelling to the Royal.'

'Mam, that would be great,' Cathy said. 'We'll need various levels of staff to give us a hand. You love working with children and we'll need help in the nursery with feeds and what have you.'

'You'll be more than welcome, Alice,' Jean said. 'In fact we'll bite your hand off now and say that you joining us is a given.'

Alice beamed. 'Right, well this calls for a quick celebration cuppa before you all go and look at the house.'

'We'll have one when we come back, chuck,' Johnny said, looking at his watch. 'We need to start walking over to Woodlands Road so we're not late. Come with us, Alice. See what you think.'

Alice smiled. 'I'll just make sure Sandra is around, then she can keep an eye on Roddy and Lucy. They're already asleep so they won't be a problem. Was she out the front when you came in, girls?'

'Sat on the front wall talking to Ben,' Karen said. 'Well more like staring into his eyes while he did all the talking. Young love, eh!'

Alice rolled her eyes and went to find her daughter. She ushered her indoors with Ben and told them to sit quietly in the front room while they all nipped out for a bit. 'Don't play records loud or you'll wake the little uns. Our Rosie is doing her homework upstairs. Hope you've done yours, young lady.'

'Yeah.' Sandra flicked her long hair back over her shoulders. 'Course I have. Finished it before I went to call for Ben.'

'Right, well, just behave then. No hanky-panky.'

'Mam!' Sandra exclaimed, blushing furiously as Ben tried to hide his smirk and Cathy popped her head around the door.

'She used to say that to me and Gianni,' Cathy said with a grin.

'Yes, and looked what happened there.' Alice folded her arms.

'Well it all worked out good in the end,' Cathy said, giving her mam a playful shove on the arm. 'Anyway, Ben, I need to pop round to see your mam soon. I'd like her to mind Lucy for me. Granny Lomax isn't very well. She could do with a rest.'

'Sorry to hear that, Cathy,' Ben said. 'I like your granny. She gave us chocolate cake when me and Sandra popped in to see her. I'm sure Mam'll be glad to help you with Lucy.'

'What's up with Granny?' Sandra asked, her face clouding. 'We all love her; she's been like a proper grandma to all of us and we haven't got another.'

'Her cough isn't getting any better,' Cathy told her. 'I'm going to make her go and see the doctor soon and I'll go with her. We'll get her sorted. Don't worry. She'll be fighting fit again in no time.'

'Of course she will. Tough as old boots is Granny,' Alice said. 'We'll see you in a bit, Sandra. Help yourselves to some pop and crisps from the kitchen.'

Johnny and Jimmy led the way across Lark Lane and down onto Aigburth Road and the girls following, all talking at once. They turned left into Woodlands Road and Johnny signalled for them to stop as they approached a large white, double-fronted house set well back from the road, fronted by a low brick wall and a tall hedge that afforded some privacy. The double wrought iron gates stood open, and a large shiny black car was parked on the drive.

'Barry's here already,' Johnny said as the door flew open and a smiling blond-haired man who looked a similar age to Alice, early forties, greeted them.

'Come on in,' he invited, holding the wide front door back for them all. 'Quite a party you've brought, Johnny.'

Johnny smiled and introduced them all as they trooped into the cavernous hallway. 'My wife, Alice. Her daughter Cathy, and the other lovely ladies are nurses and midwives from the Royal Hospital who have a few plans up their sleeves for this place.'

'Pleased to meet you all. Do tell, or are the plans a secret for now?'

Jean shook her head. 'Not really. But of course everything's in very early talking-it-through stages. We're hoping to make the house into a lovely private maternity home as well as our own home, if the council will grant us planning permission.'

'That sounds a grand idea to me,' Barry said. 'I'll keep out of the way while Jimmy and Johnny show you around. There's still a couple of old bench seats in the garden so I'll go and sit out there and have a ciggie. Just explore to your hearts' content, ladies.'

'Where would you like to start?' Johnny asked.

'The kitchen, I suppose,' Jean said. 'We'd be doing a lot of cooking so it needs to be a big one. You lead the way and we'll follow.'

The kitchen was wide and long with enough room to fit a couple of small tables and chair sets in for the staff to enjoy their meals while on duty. It needed refitting to bring it up to date, but the possibilities were endless. There was a utility room off at the end, big enough for a couple of domestic-sized washing machines and dryers like they had in the laundry at the hospital. The downstairs cloakroom housed a toilet and washbasin, both of which needed replacing. Behind the utility room was an area of garden that would be good for drying clothes on a fine day. The lounge at the front was enormous as well as light and airy. It had a large marble fireplace that would be cosy to curl up in front of and watch the telly on cold winter evenings. Johnny led them through to a large, light dining room with big windows, overlooking the garden. Another sitting room at the back with a sunroom attached made Jean smile. 'It's a perfect place for babies to sleep in their prams if the day is wet or too cold to put them outside.' Jean squinted through the windows and pointed at a building at the bottom of the garden. 'What's that down there?'

'It used to be a garage,' Jimmy said. 'But the owners had another one built at the side of the house. The old drive down to it has been grassed over and the garden all fenced in safely. I think their kids used the building as a playhouse. It has a little staircase and a room above to hide in. Great for hide-and-seek games. You'd be able to store a lot of stuff in there. Gardening equipment and what have you.'

Alice had been quiet as they looked around the house. It was definitely the one Jack had lodged in. She'd recognised it as soon as they walked down the drive. But not to worry. She wasn't going to let anything put a damper on this wonderful plan the girls were so enthusiastic about. And besides, Jack was well and truly locked away for a few more years and would have no reason to show his face again in Aigburth if he knew what was good for him.

Upstairs they wandered around the five large bedrooms. 'Some of these can be divided into two,' Jimmy said. 'Maybe that'd be better for your private mums. I reckon with a bit of shuffling around we can make eight bedrooms. We can add another bathroom up here as well. Perhaps put washbasins in the private single rooms like they do in seaside boarding houses. Makes a nice touch, I always think.'

Alice chewed her lip as she gazed around. It was all going to cost an awful lot of money and she wasn't sure how they'd find enough to do it; but she kept quiet as she seemed to be the only one worrying on that score. And where would the babies be delivered? They'd need a room solely for that purpose. And what if there was a problem? Mind you, an ambulance or doctor could be summoned right away in that case. These girls knew what they were doing, or they wouldn't have thought the idea up in the first place. There were a few private maternity homes in Liverpool, but nothing in their locality, so they'd be the first. She pushed any doubts away and tuned in to what Jean was saying to Johnny and Jimmy.

'We'll let you draw up the plans and I'll make enquiries with the council about getting the permission we need. We'll also be speaking to our dads to see if they can help financially.'

'We'll go and tell Barry we're done for the night then,' Johnny said. 'Now it's just a case of time, getting everything sorted and we'll see how it goes. I think this calls for more than a celebratory cuppa though. We'll call in the offie on the way back and get a bottle of sherry and some brown ale.'

*

Gianni smiled as he strolled back to the fairground from the telephone box on the edge of Saint George's Fields in York, where they were pitched for the next week. He'd just spoken to an excited

Cathy, who'd told him of a plan she and several other midwife colleagues were cooking up, along with her stepdad and Millie's husband Jimmy. They'd all been to look at a house last night. It sounded good, apart from the financial side of things being a bit iffy. But it was early days, so things might sort themselves out. She'd also told him that their friends Davy and Debbie wanted to buy *his* house and to give them a call. He'd do that tomorrow night as he'd need to make sure Davy was home from work first and it was a bit too early now. He'd be too busy later tonight with the fair. But if they *did* buy it he could invest some of his money from the sale into the midwives' venture. He wouldn't say anything to Cathy yet as he didn't want to let her down if things changed and they didn't buy the house after all. They'd have to wait and see. He couldn't wait to see her and Lucy again in a couple of weeks when the fair pitched up at Sefton Park. It had been a long time and he missed them both so much. His dad Luca greeted him with a pat on the back as he walked into the caravan home belonging to Luca and his wife Maria.

'How's my lovely granddaughter doing?' Luca asked. 'Being a good girl for her mama, I hope.'

'She has her moments,' Gianni said. 'But on the whole Cathy says she's doing fine. Can't wait to see her again.'

'Nor I,' said Maria, his stepmum. 'I miss her, I miss both of them. Not long now and they'll be joining us again. You boys get from under my feet while I start to unpack. Supper will be ready in an hour.' She shooed them outside, laughing as they protested.

*

Kneeling on the floor, Maria looped her long black hair back behind her ears, finished unpacking the last of the newspaper-wrapped china and glassware and sat back on her heels. It always seemed such a time-consuming chore. They might be caravan dwellers for most of the year, but she liked to keep her standards up and use the fancy stuff once they were settled, and the couple of hours spent unpacking was worth it in the long run. Mind you, Luca and Gianni were always so hungry when they came in that they wouldn't care what they ate their meals off. She looked up as her daughter Eloisa came indoors and plonked herself down on the bench seat near the dining table.

'Gianni and Luca are almost done setting up the wall of death and everyone else is helping with the other rides. Why are you in here idling when there's work to be done?' Maria asked. She got to her feet and smoothed her long cotton skirt over her knees.

'I just needed a break,' Eloisa said. 'We've not done too bad considering we're a man down since Bobby left us. Marco's helping with the dodgems and ghost train because Ronnie's hurt his hand and is about as much use as a chocolate teapot, so Lenny pulled him off erecting duties. He said the last thing we need is accidents.'

Maria nodded her agreement. Eloisa's boyfriend Ronnie was a bit too dopey at times. She often wondered what her daughter saw in the lad. 'Indeed. You can give out the flyers tomorrow in the town and take Ronnie with you. We'll get some extra casual help now we're in York. There are usually plenty of students looking for part-time work around this time of year.'

Chapter Nine

Cathy went straight to Jennifer's room when she reported for duty. She smiled as the girl cradled baby Billy in her arms. 'Are you ready to leave us?' Billy was ten days old and they were both due for discharge. Jennifer's wound had healed well and her stitches had been removed a couple of days earlier. Billy's sister Audrey was taking the pair to New Brighton to begin a new life with her and her husband George. There had been no hesitation on her part in offering Jennifer and Billy a permanent home. They had no children of their own and it was unlikely to happen now, Audrey had told Jennifer. So to have her younger brother's child growing up under their roof would be a joy to the couple.

Baby Billy's paternal grandparents had also been to visit and were overjoyed with their first grandchild. They'd been horrified when Jennifer related her tale, how her parents had insisted the baby be adopted. 'Over my dead body,' Billy's mother had said. 'He's our Billy's flesh and blood and he'll be brought up in our family.' A small funeral service was to be held at Audrey's local church for baby Michael James and he would be buried in a family grave alongside his family. Jennifer was so grateful that her tiny son wouldn't be shoved into a paupers' grave and at least this way there would be a place to visit on his birthday and take flowers. George and Audrey had a small bakery with a café attached and had offered Jennifer a part-time job as soon as she felt up to it. Between herself and Audrey they would look after Billy.

'I am ready and waiting,' Jennifer said. 'I can't thank you enough for all your help. Billy and I now have a future and a safe home that I could never have dreamed of a few months ago. And do you know what, Nurse Romano, considering my parents haven't even phoned here once to ask if I'm okay after my aunty let them know I'd been admitted, I don't feel I owe them anything. I know they think I'm supposed to be in here for two weeks, so they're not going to come looking for me for at least another four more days and I know none of the staff will call them. That's it now. I'm done with them. I will write to them eventually, but I won't be giving them an address and when I tell them Billy's parents are delighted with their grandson, I think they'll be too shamefaced to go calling on them for information. Billy's mam will soon see them off anyway. She's feisty and very angry with them after the way they've treated me.'

Cathy nodded. 'I'm not surprised. I'd feel the same if he were my grandson. I'm so glad it's all worked out for you.' She handed Jennifer a slip of paper. 'I've written my address down,' she whispered. 'Will you let me know that you're okay from time to time? We're not supposed to do this, but no one needs to know. I've got to go on duty now, so I wish you all the luck in the world. Don't forget to have Billy checked and weighed at the local clinic regularly and make sure you register with the doctor as soon as you can because you will need your post-natal check-up at six weeks. It's important for your health that you get it done. Take care of yourself and little Billy, Jenny; it's been lovely looking after you both.' Cathy gave her a hug, planted a kiss on the sleeping baby's brow and hurried from the room before she burst into tears. If she, Jean, Karen and Ellie could make a difference like this to just one young mum and her child's life, what a fulfilling job it would be to run their new maternity home. She really couldn't wait to take her final exams in just a few short months and then she would be ready to join them in their venture.

*

Jack swung the door open, stuck his head outside and took a quick look around. He was used to the allotment holders' routines, and knew they'd all be going home for the night about now. Voices faded as the old men called out their goodbyes to each other. He was bursting for a piss but didn't want to do another in the abandoned shed he was dossing in. It stank to high heaven as it was. But at least he'd got a roof over his head, and his bed of straw-filled sacks served him well. He nipped around the back and relieved himself. There was an old pub not far from the allotments and he'd been slipping in the bogs daily for a shit and a bit of a wash. Fortunately, the gents was out the back and he'd managed to find a way in from the small car park without having to go through the pub itself. The wooden hatch to the beer cellars was also around the back and Jack had noticed the doors were a bit worse for wear. Should be easy enough to break into and nick a few bottles of something if the opportunity ever arose.

His stomach rumbled and he hoped the little chippy down the lane was open tonight. He'd found a battered straw trilby in the shed, an old pair of gardening trousers that he tied up with the twine that was already threaded through the belt loops, and a much-patched jacket that was far too big, but covered his prison clothes well enough. He'd still not managed to find a decent outfit yet for fear of being spotted lurking in gardens. There always seemed to be an old biddy or two around. He scratched his head and the beard that had started to grow. It was itchy and he wouldn't be surprised if he'd got fleas. He'd chased away a manky old moggy that had been sleeping on the sacks. He felt dirty and knew he stank to high heaven and looked like a tramp. He could do with a visit to the swimming baths for a clean-up, but until his hair and beard grew a bit more he was stuck with lying low. A few more days of sleeping rough and he'd be on his way to a new life.

Hoping it was the usual blind-as-a-bat woman in the chippy; he lit a fag and set off to buy his tea.

*

Later that week, Jack read the headlines again. He and Andy were last week's front-page news. The greasy paper had been wrapped around his chips from last night's tea. The mugshot, taken years ago, didn't look much like him now. Short hair, chubbier cheeks and a full set of teeth. He'd lost weight in Walton, along with a bottom front tooth that some pillock had knocked out one night during an altercation, and now, with his longer hair and newly grown facial hair, he doubted anyone would recognise him from that photo. He needed to think up a name change and adopt an accent along with a new identity. He was good at mimicking, had got Andy's Glaswegian accent off to a T. And although the police were looking for a Scottish bloke, that's where the similarity ended. Andy was twice his size. No one was going to notice a little fellow with a twang that looked like he did. Today he planned to find some half-decent clothes and take a swim at the local baths. Changing rooms were a good source of jackets and shoes, as well as the contents of pockets. He smoked his last half-fag and set off for his usual morning ritual before the allotment holders turned up.

*

Alice dashed back into the house after taking Rodney to school. She'd got a day off today and planned to do a bit of shopping after a big clean-up. Cathy was also off and had taken Lucy to her minder and then was taking Granny Lomax for a chest X-ray, as advised by the doctor. The last few days had been hectic as Johnny and Jimmy finalised the purchase of the house on Woodlands Road. They'd pored over figures each night, working out how best to buy it. Both of their homes had been used to secure the mortgage on the property. Johnny had told her that if the girls couldn't go ahead with their plans to open the maternity home then he and Jimmy would turn the place into four self-contained flats. Meanwhile they would start to do repairs to the roof and take out the bathroom and kitchen fittings. Either way, they could make a start. Jimmy had assured her and Millie that they'd more than get their money back over the next few months, no matter what happened with the house. Alice hoped he was right.

She took off her jacket and hung it on the hall stand. In the back room, she gathered up a pile of newspapers from the floor by the side of Johnny's chair, mainly the *Echo*. With being so busy recently he'd had no time to read them all, so she put them on the table to sort through and made two piles, roughly folded and read ones for the fire and the neatly folded unread ones for later. The final paper she picked up caught her eye and as her legs buckled she sat down heavily on a dining chair. Two male mugshots dominated the headlines, along with the words

ESCAPED PRISONERS ON THE RUN.

As she read the report her stomach churned. Jack Dawson and another man were wanted for the murder of a prison officer who'd been shot dead while driving a van taking the pair to Armley Gaol in Leeds. The report said that there had been no sightings of them in Leeds or the surrounding areas but that they were believed to have made their way to Glasgow with two more men who were also on the run from a previous crime. It also stated that Dawson had family and contacts in Liverpool. Alice checked the date on the paper. It was from over a week ago. She didn't recall seeing anything on the news and if Jack was making his way here, he certainly hadn't been in touch with anyone she knew. And she was certain that if he'd tried to contact any friends from the Legion, where he'd worked, they would have let her know.

That poor man who'd been shot was from Liverpool – she was surprised that none of their neighbours or people in the shops had mentioned it to her. But then again, they'd all been so busy with work, the new house plans and Granny Lomax being ill that Alice hadn't really had time to stop and gossip with anyone. Maybe people *had* seen it and felt it best to keep out of her business now that she was married to Johnny.

Surely Jack wouldn't show his face around here? He wasn't that daft. She hoped he'd be caught soon, and in Scotland, as far away as possible. He was hateful but she would never have had him down as a murderer in a million years. She shuddered and dashed to lock and bolt the front door and then did the same with the back. In the front room she peered through the net curtains out onto the deserted street and then pulled the red velvet curtains across.

A sudden thought struck her. What if he still had a key that he'd kept hold of and had let himself in like he did when he attacked Cathy a few years ago, and was hiding upstairs? Then she shook herself. Johnny had fitted new doors back and front last year and new locks too. Now she was just being silly, scaring herself like that. She forced herself to go into the kitchen and put the kettle on. On the windowsill was a hammer that Johnny had used last night to knock a couple of picture hooks into the sitting room wall. He must have forgotten to put it back in his tool bag.

She needed the toilet but wasn't going to go to the outside one. She picked the hammer up, just in case, and crept upstairs to the bathroom. She opened the door and peered inside. Empty. She breathed a sigh of relief and dashed into the room, holding her breath as she locked the door and put the hammer down on the floor. The house was silent. 'You daft beggar, Alice, get a flipping grip,' she muttered as she washed her hands. But she still picked up the hammer as she crept into each bedroom and looked in the wardrobes and under the beds. 'Right, he's not here so get yourself downstairs and make a brew.' Cathy would be home soon and she may well bring Granny back with her.

As she was pouring the boiling water into the teapot she heard a rattling at the front door and nearly dropped the kettle. The door handle turned and then the bell rang. The letter box clattered and Cathy shouted through it, 'Mam, are you there?'

Alice dashed to take the bolts off and swung the door open, as bright a smile as she could muster fixed on her face.

'What's wrong with the door?' Cathy asked, leading a very fragile-looking Granny Lomax inside. 'Did you have the bolts on?'

'Er, I must have done,' Alice said, shaking her head at Cathy, indicating she didn't want to say any more.

Cathy nodded, looking puzzled. 'Come on, Granny, let's get you sitting down and I'll make you a nice cuppa.'

'There's tea in the pot,' Alice said. 'I've just this minute made it. And I've got some nice scones from the bakery, so sit yourselves down and I'll go and do the honours. Sit in the front room, it's less chaotic than the back. There's no toys to trip over in there.' As Cathy opened the door and exclaimed that the curtains were closed, Alice realised her mistake. Damn.

'Oh dear, I dashed out without opening them this morning,' she fibbed. 'Such a rush getting the kids up and out to school, you know how it is. Help Granny to a seat.' She dashed back to the kitchen.

Cathy appeared in the doorway as Alice, her hand shaking, poured the tea. Cathy took the pot from her, frowning. 'Mam, what's going on? I opened those front room curtains before I left the house earlier; you know I did because you asked me to do it when I went in to get something. You look pale and mithered and you're acting all weird.'

Alice took a deep breath. She went into the back sitting room and picked up the newspaper from the table. She showed Cathy the headlines, holding a finger to her lips and inclining her head towards the front room. 'No point in putting the wind up Granny. Hopefully he's miles away by now, but with him having robbed her once I'd hate her to be terrified by this news.'

Cathy's mouth dropped open and her hand shook as she read the headlines. 'Oh my God! So they think he's in Scotland?'

Alice nodded. 'Wouldn't you think the police would have come here to warn us though? Not a flipping word from them. We hardly had the telly on this last week, well not the news anyway. I only found this paper because I was tidying up. It was in the pile waiting to be read next to Johnny's chair.'

Cathy shook her head. 'Murder though. Oh my God. I can't believe that of Jack. Nasty piece though he is, I would never have thought him capable of murdering anyone.'

'Hmm,' Alice said, nodding slowly. 'Granny always blamed him for your dad's death in that accident. Maybe he *did* fiddle with the brakes on purpose, although the police said it was impossible to say what caused the crash because the bike was in such a bad state afterwards. And Jack would have never admitted it, even if he did do it deliberately. He always acted hurt when she had a go at him.'

'It does makes you think.' Cathy picked up a mug of tea and took it through to her granny. 'Won't be a minute, Mam's just buttering you a scone,' she told her and went back to join her mam. 'Do her a scone and then she can tell you what the hospital said about her chest. It's not great news, Mam, there's a shadow on her lung, but I'll let her tell you. Then I'll take her home and make sure she's safe.'

'All right love, I'm sorry to hear that.' Alice handed the buttered scone to Cathy on a small plate.

Cathy sighed. 'Thanks Mam, we can talk when I come home. I'm sure Jack will be well away by now, but I'm going to ring the police as soon as I get back here. I want some reassurance that they definitely know he's not in this area.'

*

'Did she settle all right?' Alice asked as Cathy came back into the house after taking Granny Lomax home.

'She did. And I checked to see that she had something in for her tea, and we called at the bakery for a loaf, so that should do her for today. I'll pop in tonight for an hour and keep her company, then I can make sure she locks up after me, now that we know about Jack. I'll be glad when we get a date for her to go into hospital. I really don't think it'll be too long before they find her a bed. I'd rather she was safe in there than on her own if Jack's on the prowl. I'm really worried that it's something serious. She's just not picking up at all, no matter what remedies she's taken.'

Alice nodded. 'She's not been right for a good while now. It's such a worry for you, love.'

'I know I should probably stay at the bungalow with her,' Cathy continued. 'But I'm worried about Lucy catching something, and me, for that matter. I'm handling newborn babies and I can't afford to pass on any nasty germs to them or their mothers.' She reached into the sideboard cupboard for the telephone directory. She looked up the number for the local police station and went into the hall to the telephone to make the call.

Alice hovered in the background wringing her hands as Cathy raised her voice, demanding answers to her not unreasonable questions. She heard her say goodbye and slam down the phone.

'They're about as much use a chocolate fireguard,' Cathy said angrily, coming back in and plonking herself down on a dining chair. 'Apparently they sent two officers round here a few days after Jack's escape to see if he'd been in contact, but there was no one home. I told the policeman I just spoke to that we are all at work during the day and couldn't they have tried again or at least phoned us so we could be on our guard. They didn't have our number, he said, but they do now, so no excuses.'

Cathy narrowed her eyes, looking furious. 'And apparently they are short of officers so that's why we didn't get a second visit. Bet if we'd robbed a bank or something, they'd be here in force. Anyway, he tried to reassure me that they are certain Jack is not in Liverpool as he was seen in the car with the other man and his accomplices. They are all from the Glasgow area so the police believe he will have teamed up with them. They're a notorious gang of robbers apparently, so no doubt they'll welcome him in with open arms,' Cathy finished.

Alice swallowed hard. 'Even so, we must be careful and not take any chances. Make sure you're not on your own if you walk home in the dark and always lock the doors both front and back if you're in by yourself. Better to be safe than sorry. I wouldn't trust him as far as I could throw him.'

'I know, Mam, and neither do I. Shall I tell Ellie or leave it? She obviously hasn't seen the paper or news or she would have said something by now.'

Alice blew out her cheeks. 'It was not being warned about the prowler in the hospital grounds that got Ellie raped by Jack. I would tell her so that she can be on her guard. Not that I think for one minute he would show his face back at the hospital at all; lightning doesn't strike twice in the same place, but even so, she needs to know he's escaped from prison and he's on the run. We don't know what's going through his deranged mind. Revenge for getting him sent down. Anything could tip him over the edge. We all need to be alert. I must tell Sandra and Rosie too. Just in case he's in Liverpool and hangs around their school looking for them. Roddy's a bit too young to understand and I don't want to frighten him.'

Cathy raised an eyebrow. 'Is it likely that he'd try and see the kids? He never bothered with them before. I doubt he'd want to see them now. But I suppose you should tell them, especially Sandra and Rosie as they will recognise him. But don't scare them, Mam.'

Chapter Ten

July 1963

Walking down the road, Jack rooted in his jacket pocket and pulled out the piece of paper a young woman had thrust into his hand a few days ago. She'd given him a knowing smile before tossing her long hair over her shoulders and sashaying over to a lad standing under the trees. Jack glanced at it again. It was a flyer for a fair. He was about to screw it up and chuck it over his shoulder when the name caught his eye: *Romano's Fair.* Wasn't Romano the name of the half-Italian biker lad Cathy had been seeing? He knew from Alice's late friend Sadie that she'd left his father because she didn't like the fairground lifestyle and the bike show he was involved with.

Jack tugged at his little beard and reread the bit added and handwritten in ink at the bottom of the flyer. The fair was looking for casual labourers to report for duty no later than tomorrow. He wondered what had happened between Cathy and the lad. Had they ended up together? There was no one he could ask. Alice wouldn't have had reason to tell him, and he'd lost contact with the few mates he'd had before his arrest. He'd done a bit of fairground work in his teens before he'd started training as a motor mechanic and before the war had begun.

Back in New Brighton, helping to man the waltzers, he'd had a great time. There were always screaming girls who'd begged him to stand on the little pivoting cars and give them an extra spin. It often guaranteed him an easy lay at the end of the night. He grinned as he felt his balls tingle at the pleasant but long-ago memory. He'd give it a shot. *Why not?* They might even provide accommodation on a short-term basis and there was always half-decent grub to be had at a fairground, even if it was only hot dogs and fried onions. 'Time to perfect that Scottish accent, Jack,' he muttered, shoved the flyer back into his jacket pocket, and then made his way to the swimming baths.

*

Cathy waited anxiously in the front bedroom, watching from the window, waiting for the ambulance to arrive outside her granny's bungalow. She'd called round on her way to her early shift to see how she was and, getting no response to her knock on the door, had let herself in with the key she kept in her handbag. She'd found Granny, still in bed and struggling for breath. After reassuring her she'd stay with her, Cathy immediately phoned for an ambulance and then called the ward to let them know what was happening and that she'd be in a bit later today. She'd hurriedly packed a few of Granny's nighties in an overnight bag, along with some underwear, toiletries and a towel. She'd helped Granny to the bathroom and then had her sit on a chair by the bed with her dressing gown and slippers on, ready for her short journey to the Liverpool Royal.

'It's here, Gran,' Cathy announced as the ambulance pulled up. 'Is there anything else you want to take in with you?'

Granny shook her head. 'I can't think right now,' she wheezed. 'You look after my purse and the bungalow, love. If I don't come back here there's a letter for you in the bureau in the hall.'

'Granny, don't say that. Of course you'll be coming back,' Cathy said, her eyes filling. 'I'll go and let the attendants in.' She dashed to the door, fighting back tears, and explained to the two men what the problem was.

They carried in a stretcher and a small tank of oxygen and laid them on the bed. They checked Granny's temperature, pulse and blood pressure and gave her some oxygen to stabilise her breathing before making her comfortable on the stretcher.

'Are you coming with us, Nurse?' the taller of the two men asked.

'Yes.' Cathy nodded. 'I was on my way in to work anyway. Thanks, it'll save me getting the bus and I can stay with her until she settles in.'

Cathy held her granny's frail hand as the ambulance sped towards the city. Granny's eyes were closed and her colour pale, her lips tinged with blue. Cathy's heart filled with love for the woman who'd always been by her side and supported her, no matter what. The thought of losing her was more than she could bear. She pushed the thought away and concentrated on thinking positively.

Granny Lomax was admitted to the women's medical ward and Cathy stayed with her until she was certain she was settled. Halfway through the morning, with her granny sleeping and Sister's reassurance she would call and let her know immediately if there was any change for the worse, she made her way over to Maternity with a heavy heart. The doctor would be in later to see Granny and the complete results of her recent X-ray and other tests that had been done at the same time would be with him.

Karen greeted her as she hung up her coat and hat in the ward cloakroom and fastened her apron around her waist. 'Sorry to hear about your gran, Cathy. Sister told us earlier why you'd be late in today.'

'Thanks. I'm afraid it's not looking good. But I'm trying to be positive. It's not easy though.'

Ellie popped her head around the cloakroom door. 'How is she?'

'Sleeping when I left her. She's on oxygen. Not much else I can do down there. I might as well as be up here working to take my mind off things.'

'We're a bit quiet this morning,' Ellie said. 'No current labourers, but we've got two going home and who knows what else the day will bring.'

'Right, well let's get to it,' Cathy said. 'Otherwise it'll be dinnertime and I won't have done a stroke of work.'

*

Jack fastened the leather belt around his waist. The faded denims were a bit on the snug side like the Teddy Boys wore, but didn't feel too bad. Not really his style but beggars couldn't be choosers and the red satin shirt looked good with them. Black Cuban-heeled boots and a leather flying jacket in dark brown finished the outfit. He felt clean for the first times in ages. He combed his hair into an elaborate quiff with a neat DA at the back to look the part. It was a bit longer than was customary for Teds, but it would do. It had been a good haul at the baths. He'd spotted the Ted and followed his movements until he was sure he was out of the way. On top of the diving board and without his Buddy Holly-style specs the lad was blind as a bat, and totally unaware that his changing cubicle was in the process of being robbed. On his way back from the chippy last night, washing left out on a line had provided a couple of T-shirts, socks and pairs of Y-fronts. With his new look he reckoned he could pass for half his age and was planning to knock at least ten years off his forty-three if asked. He'd spent last night reading aloud from a binned newspaper he'd found, trying out his new accent. It was softer than his cellmate Andy's, so he'd decided to say he was from Edinburgh. He'd worked with a guy from that neck of the woods at Garston bottle-washing plant not long after leaving school, before the fairground job, and reckoned he sounded similar.

He packed his few belongings into his rucksack and set off for a little café that was close to the recreation ground. A mug of strong tea and a couple of slices of toast should set him up nicely for the morning.

*

Eloisa stared at the man who was eyeballing her from across the recreation ground. He half-smiled and walked towards her. 'Can I help you?' she asked.

'Err, aye. Is the boss around?'

'Luca,' she yelled. 'Man wants to see you.' She pointed in the direction of the wall of death ride and turned her attention back to setting up her hook-a-duck stall. She glanced back over her shoulder. He was still staring at her. She liked his leather flying jacket and slightly long hair. He looked older than her, hard to tell by how much though, but there was something almost attractive about him. She wondered if he'd come about a job. He had a look of the scruffy tramp she'd thrust a flyer at yesterday, more as a joke than anything because the likes of him would never get a job with Romano's. But it couldn't be the tramp, because this guy was clean and reasonably well-dressed. She watched as he spoke to her stepfather and saw Luca gesturing to explain things. Then he pointed to Lenny over by the Ferris wheel and the man walked across. He shook Lenny's hand and Lenny hollered for Ronnie, who stopped what he was doing and ran over to them.

*

Jack couldn't believe his luck as the lad Ronnie took him to the hired hands' caravan. He stashed his bag away in an overhead cupboard and sat down on the bench seat that Ronnie told him would convert to his bed later. A sleeping bag, also in the cupboard, was for him to use. He couldn't wait to sleep on something comfy and clean after the flea-ridden straw-filled sacks.

'Follow me,' Ronnie said. 'Maria will be doing bacon butties and coffee in a minute for our break.'

'Maria?'

'Yeah. The boss's missus.'

'Right.' Jack nodded and followed him across the field to the largest caravan. It was a big fancy silver affair and a table was set up outside, laden with plates of food and pots of coffee.

Maria was officiating, pouring coffee into mugs and yelling for the girl with the long hair he'd seen earlier to get a move on with the milk. She came out of the caravan carrying a large jug and set it down on the table. Ronnie sat down on the ground and the girl flopped down beside him.

'Who's your friend?' She nodded towards Jack, lowering her lashes.

'Dougie,' Jack said before Ronnie could respond. He offered her his hand. 'Dougie Taylor, at your service.' He'd nicked the name of the pal from Garston bottle-washing plant as well as his accent. She took his hand and he held it for longer than necessary, giving a gentle squeeze. He smirked as she pulled it back and blushed slightly. 'And you are?'

'Eloisa.'

'She's Maria's daughter,' Ronnie said. 'The boss's stepdaughter.'

'Pleased to meet you, Eloisa,' Jack said. 'I think I'm going to like working here. Until the fair moves on, of course.'

'Are you just passing through?' Ronnie asked.

'Aye. Lost my job up in Edinburgh. Thought I'd take a bit of a trip, do some exploring. But a body needs to eat.' He smiled up at Maria as she held out a plate, and helped himself to a bacon butty. Yes, he was going to like working here, very much indeed.

*

At dinner break in the staff canteen, Cathy told Ellie the news about Jack. 'Please don't worry though. The police are certain he's not in Liverpool. I'm just letting you know so that you don't take any chances at night and walk alone in the grounds.'

'Flipping heck,' Karen said as Ellie's cheeks paled. 'We'll make sure none of us are alone. I guess he wouldn't chance coming round here again, but we'll make doubly sure we're extra careful, especially on nights.'

Ellie nodded. 'Thanks for the warning, Cathy. I hope he doesn't show up at your home.'

'If he does he'll have Johnny to contend with and we've to notify the police right away if we see or hear from him.'

Karen got to her feet. 'I suppose we'd better get back on the ward. I've never known it so quiet. You just wait though – calm before the storm. September and early October will be madly busy. All the Christmas and New Year celebration babies will be arriving.'

As they hurried back down the long main corridor, Cathy spotted a familiar figure dashing towards them. 'Davy,' she greeted him as he drew level. His blue eyes looked anxious and his hair stood on end as though he'd been running his fingers through it.

'Cathy, good to see you're on duty,' he gasped. 'I got a call from my mam at work. She'd gone to pick Jonathon up to take him to school and Debs was having pains. So when Mam got back to ours they waited a while until she was sure it wasn't wind or something and then Mam called an ambulance, and she is being brought in.' He took a deep breath. 'Excuse me gabbling. Don't know if she's here yet, but the baby's on the way. She'll be so glad to see you. Not sure what to do with myself. Pace the corridor like you see men do in films, smoke a fag, or what?'

Karen laughed. 'You dads! Come on, calm down and let's get up to the ward and see if Deb's has been admitted yet. We can make you a strong brew at least.'

'Thanks, Karen.' Davy looked relieved and followed them up the two flights of stairs.

'Just wait here,' Cathy instructed Davy as they reached the ward entrance hall, 'take a seat and I'll go and find out what's happening.'

'And I'll make you that promised brew,' Karen told him.

Cathy spotted Debbie right away near the bottom of the ward. Her auburn hair, piled up on top of her head, was so distinctive that she couldn't miss her. Her cheeks were flushed and she sighed with relief as Cathy stood beside her bed.

'Thank goodness you're here. I spoke to your mam earlier and she said you'd brought Granny Lomax in. I'm really sorry she's so poorly, Cathy.'

Cathy took Debbie's hand and squeezed it. 'Thanks, Debs. She was comfortable when I left her on the ward and there's been no further news. I'll pop in and see her again after my shift finishes. So, anyway, how are you doing? Has someone examined you?'

Debbie nodded. 'Yes and I'm six centimetres dilated. So I guess I'm over halfway there. Ouch—' She stopped and took a deep breath and then panted as another contraction washed over her. 'Oooh, funny how you remember what to do when it's not your first. I'm wondering if Davy's mam got in touch with him at work yet.'

Cathy laughed. 'She did. He's in the corridor at the top of the ward being looked after by Karen, he's having a cuppa.' She checked her fob watch. 'Fifteen minutes to visiting time. I'm going to pull your curtains round the bed and bring him down. The way you're doing, you might be in the delivery suite by the time visiting is halfway through and it would be a shame to miss out. Have you been shaved and given an enema?'

'I'm shaved but Sister said it was too late for an enema and I *have* been to the toilet already. I thought the pains were my tummy at first, giving me a bit of gyp, until they didn't go away and Davy's mam took charge and phoned for an ambulance.' Debbie's face screwed up and she took a deep breath before continuing. 'Oh good, I'm glad Davy's here. Thank you. I need to tell him that a letter arrived from the building society, after he went to work this morning. We've got our mortgage through. We can now buy Gianni's house. What a great day this will be for all of us. New baby and— Aghhhhh!' She reached for Cathy's hand and squeezed hard as another contraction racked her body. 'Will you be here to deliver it, Cath? It could be ages yet.'

'I hope so.' Cathy pulled the pink-and-blue striped curtains and wiped Debbie's face with a damp flannel from the top of her locker. 'It's great news about the house. Now let me go and get Davy.' She ran back to the top of the ward, where Davy was just finishing his cup of tea. The cup clattered back into the saucer and he jumped to his feet.

'Is everything okay?'

'Yes, she's doing fine. I'll just check with Sister that it's okay for you to go in and see her a bit earlier.' She retrieved the cup from his shaking hands and took it into the kitchen. Sister was finishing a phone call but looked up and beckoned her into the office.

'Yes, Nurse Romano?' she said, replacing the telephone receiver.

'Is it okay if Mrs Ayres' husband visits her now, Sister? She'll probably be in delivery before visiting ends and he's just dashed here from work.'

Sister nodded. 'Just this once won't hurt. We're very quiet today. I think you'll all be fighting over who delivers the Ayres' baby, although Mrs Ayres tells me you've been good friends since your infant school days so I guess you'll want to at least be in there with her.'

'I'd love that,' Cathy said. 'She's my best friend. It would be wonderful to deliver her baby today.'

'Then take Mr Ayres down the ward now and put his mind at rest.'

Cathy thanked her and beckoned for Davy to follow her. It was only ten minutes before official visiting time anyway and most curtains were pulled around beds as mothers fed their babies or freshened up in readiness for their visitors, so it was unlikely anyone would see him being sneaked in and complain about preferential treatment.

'Debs,' Davy said, slipping through the gap as Cathy held the curtain to one side. 'Are you okay, love?' He dropped a kiss on her forehead and Cathy went to get him a chair. Debbie grimaced as another contraction washed over her.

'Don't worry, Davy,' Cathy said reassuringly as she handed him a chair. 'We'll give her something for the pain in a few minutes.

It'll help relax her as well. Here, Debbie.' Cathy held out the mask from the gas and air tank that was standing by the bed. 'Take a few deep breaths on this and you'll be floating. It just feels like you've had one G&T too many.'

'Can I have a go as well,' Davy said, laughing. 'Floating sounds a nice place to be right now.'

Debbie shook her head and smiled. 'You'll be floating without any help in a minute when you hear the other good news.' She went on to tell him about the letter from the building society. 'New house, well new owners anyway, and a new baby on the same day. Cathy will let Gianni know if she speaks to him later. He'll need to make sure he's got things in place with a solicitor.'

'He's ringing me tonight,' Cathy said. 'Lots of good things to tell him now, well apart from Granny. Right, I'll leave you two alone for a while. Press that buzzer above the bed if you need anything. One of us will come and check you in fifteen minutes.'

By four o'clock Davy had left to pick Jonathon up from his mother's house, where he'd been taken after school, and Debbie was in the delivery suite, fully dilated and ready to give birth. Jean had come on her late shift and was the midwife in charge, with Cathy accompanying her. It was lovely to think her best friend's baby would be one of the total of forty that she needed to help deliver before she qualified. She was well on the way to completing that figure now.

'Okay, Debbie, now when I tell you to push I need you to put all your effort into it,' Jean instructed. 'As soon as that next contraction comes, give it your all, girl.'

Debbie grunted and signalled from behind the gas and air mask that she was ready to push. She let her chin fall to her chest, clutched the mask in her hand and, red in the face, pushed with all her might.

'That's it,' Cathy called from the end of the delivery trolley. 'I can see the head and it looks like it's got hair the same colour as yours. As soon as you get another contraction, push again. In the meantime, pant just like you've been taught to do.'

'Come on, Debs, we'll do it with you,' Jean encouraged as Debbie panted slowly and grabbed at the mask again to take a deep breath.

'Another,' she grunted and pushed hard again.

'That's it,' Cathy said. 'The head is born. Nearly there. Next contraction and it'll be all over. It's definitely got auburn hair and your little turned-up nose.'

As Debbie pushed one more time and Cathy eased out the shoulders and finally the slippery little body, she couldn't stop the tears rolling down her cheeks as she gazed at the perfect little daughter of her dearest friends. 'Debs, you've got a little girl. Oh my goodness, she's lovely.' She wiped her eyes, and then clamped and cut the umbilical cord. After wrapping the tiny baby in a white cotton sheet, she handed Debbie her daughter.

'Well done, Debs and Cathy,' Jean said, giving Cathy a hug. 'It's not easy seeing your friend in pain, but you both did great. She's a little beauty.'

'I'm amazed she's a girl,' Debbie said, choking on her tears. 'I never thought I'd get a daughter. Oh, Davy will be made up now we've got one of each. We'll definitely need an extension now so she can have her own bedroom. Thank you so much, you two.'

'All in a day's work,' Jean said. 'Isn't that right, Cathy?'

Cathy nodded and smiled through her tears. Debbie reached for her hand, sharing the special moment, but Cathy knew they were both also thinking of the baby Cathy had lost. She took a deep breath. 'I'll go and ring Davy at his mam's and let them all know. Any names yet?'

Debbie shook her head. 'I was so sure she'd be another boy that we've only picked boys' names. She was going to be Justin.

I quite like Alison though. I'll see what Davy says when he gets here tonight.'

'I'll get her weighed and properly cleaned up while Jean delivers the placenta and finishes sorting you out,' Cathy said, taking the baby from Debbie. She laid her on the table on a nappy and caught all the corners up together, slipping the hook of the scales through all four corners. 'Seven pound three ounces,' she announced. 'Smaller than Jonathon was, but a good weight for a dainty little girl.' She washed the baby's hair and gently wiped her body clean, pinned on a nappy and slipped a tiny cotton gown on her. Big blue eyes looked back at her and Cathy could see her friend in every inch of her face: her nose, lips, eyes and hair colour. She was the double of her mummy.

Chapter Eleven

Back on the ward Cathy finished her shift and said goodbye to Debbie until tomorrow. She spoke to Davy, who sounded delighted by the news and said he'd be there as soon as he was allowed back in. He reminded her to let Gianni know about the house. She set off to go back to Women's Medical. Granny was still sleeping and Sister told her she'd been like that all day. They'd set up a saline drip to stop her from becoming dehydrated. Sister asked her to come into the office and take a seat.

Cathy sat down and chewed her lip as Sister opened the sheaf of notes on her desk. 'I'm sorry, Nurse Romano but it really isn't good news I'm afraid. The X-rays showed your grandmother has a huge shadow on her lungs. We will conduct a further X-ray tomorrow depending on how she is, but blood test results also show her red blood cell count is low and the white count is very high. We also noticed that her gums bleed easily, and she had a nosebleed earlier. She has a number of bruises on her body, her arms and legs and her torso. This is common with a high white-cell count. But her lethargy and shortness of breath are also signs that Doctor Munro says point to a condition called AML, acute myeloid leukaemia.'

Cathy stared at Sister with her mouth open. 'She has had a few nosebleeds recently, but she put it down to blowing her nose too hard,' she said, her voice wobbling. She wiped her eyes. 'And those bruises Granny says are because she's always bumping into things now her eyesight's failing a bit. I should have guessed she had more than just a bad chesty cough, but she's so stubborn and refused to see a doctor for months. I feel terrible for not realising things were more serious.'

Cathy was silent for a moment as she choked on a sob, then went on: 'I know she has had angina for a few years now as well. I had to practically force her to go to the doctors' with me. I guess at Granny's age there's not a lot can be done now.' She sighed. 'I really do feel bad. So what will happen next?'

'Well, like I say, maybe another X-ray tomorrow and possibly further blood tests. But I'm afraid your grandmother is a very poorly lady and the best we can do for her now is make sure she's kept comfortable and hydrated. You'll find she will probably sleep most of the time. My nurses are preparing a small side room for her and we'll transfer her into it later. It'll be more private and you can pop in any time you like to see her. I know you are her only relative.'

Cathy swallowed hard and nodded. 'My mam works here a couple of days a week. Granny was her mother-in-law until my dad died. She's very fond of her. Can she come in too?'

'Of course. Tell her to make herself known to either me or any of my nurses.'

Cathy nodded. 'I will. She's Auxiliary Nurse Harrison. She works on the children's ward down the corridor from here.'

Sister smiled. 'Ah, I've met your mother. Alice, isn't it? I'll look out for her. Now you get yourself off home, you look worn out. If there are any changes at all we'll ring you at once.'

'Please do,' Cathy said, sniffing back her tears. 'No matter what time it is. My stepfather will bring me in.' She got to her feet and, thanking Sister, left the ward on legs that didn't feel like they'd hold her up for much longer. The bus was just pulling up as she got to the stop and she climbed on board and sank onto a seat at the back, dabbing at her eyes with a hanky.

'Bad day, queen?' the conductor asked as he gave her a ticket and took her fare.

'So-so,' Cathy answered with a half-smile. 'I'll be glad to get home and put my feet up for a while.' She closed her eyes for a few minutes. It had been the most emotionally draining day she'd had in a long time, and it wasn't over yet.

*

'Take my car and drive to Liverpool now. You should be with your wife,' Luca said and Maria nodded her agreement. Gianni had just come back from the phone box looking pale and anxious. Cathy's granny was very poorly in hospital, he'd told them, and Cathy had been really upset on the phone. 'Go on, boy. We can manage. Give you time to catch up with that little girl of yours as well.'

'What about the show? How will you do it with just the two of you?'

'Marco and I will improvise. Your place is with Cathy and Lucy. It sounds like it's the final days for her granny and she'll need you with her when the end comes.' He handed Gianni the keys to his two-tone, yellow-and-black Ford Consul, his pride and joy. Gianni had passed his test in the car at his dad's insistence and was familiar with it. Luca also handed him a five-pound note. 'Fill it up,' he instructed. 'There's a garage down the road. Drive safely and give our love to Cathy and our little Lucy. I'll call Cathy's mother's house tomorrow night before we start the show. Write down the phone number for me, son.'

While Gianni wrote down the number, Maria hurriedly packed him a bag of clothes and toiletries. She gave him a hug. 'Drive carefully and safely and stay with your family as long as you need to.'

'We're in Liverpool later this month so no need to rush back up here. Stay with them and look after them,' Luca said, patting him on the back. 'We've got that new labourer Dougie on board to help us for a while and he seems to be shaping up okay.' They waved him off and Luca shook his head. 'It's time Gianni settled down with Cathy; either her here with him, or him back home with her. One of them is going to have to compromise at some point. They can't go on forever living apart like this. It's not right for the child, as I well know.'

Maria rolled her eyes. 'That's wishful thinking on your part, my love. I feel they should be together, too. But they are as stubborn as each other.'

*

Alice opened the door, leaving the chain on. *Who on earth was knocking at this time of night?* Feeling jumpy, thinking of Jack, she peered cautiously through the gap and gasped. 'Gianni!'

'Hello, Alice, it's so good to see you,' Gianni said as she gave him a hug.

'Oh, come on in. Cathy will be so pleased to see you. She hasn't stopped crying since she came home from work. It's been quite a day for her.' Alice caught her breath and went on, 'She's in the front sitting room curled up on the big sofa bed. She may even have fallen asleep, but don't worry about waking her up, she'll be that thrilled to have you here.'

Alice pushed open the door and peeped in. The curtains were closed and the red-shaded lamp in the corner cast a warm glow around the room. The radio was playing softly in the background. Her daughter was half-dozing, but still sobbing softly into a cushion. She obviously hadn't heard Gianni's knock at the door. 'Cathy,' Alice whispered and shook her by the shoulder. 'You've got a visitor, love. I'll leave you to catch up with him. Call me when you want a drink or anything.' She nodded at Gianni to go in, closed the door behind him and rejoined Johnny in the back room. He was watching the news on the telly. Since her discovery in the paper about Jack they had watched every report they could but there was still no news of his capture. 'Gianni's just arrived,' Alice said, sitting down beside him.

'Oh that's good news, love,' he said, smiling. 'Just what Cathy needs right now.'

*

Cathy stared at Gianni as if she'd seen a ghost. She jumped up and he caught her in his arms and held her tight, raining kisses on her face as she sobbed in his arms. 'I can't believe you're here,' she said. 'I'm probably asleep and dreaming.'

'You're not,' he whispered into her hair. 'Dad told me to come home to Liverpool tonight. He's lent me his car. I came as soon as I could. I'm so sorry about your granny, Cath, I really am. But I'm here for you now and I'll stay with you until the fair comes to Liverpool at the end of the month.'

'Thank you. I don't think she's going to last that long if I'm honest, but I'm so glad you are here with me. Lucy will go mad when she sees you in the morning.'

'I can't wait to give her a cuddle.'

'Have you had anything to eat tonight?'

He shook his head. 'Maria was about to dish up supper when I got back from the phone box.'

Cathy nodded. 'Let's go in the back and I'll make you some cheese on toast and a brew. Johnny and Mam won't mind us invading.'

Gianni followed her into the back room, where Johnny greeted him and made room on the sofa. 'Good to see you, Gianni. Sit yourself down. Nice that you've come home to support our Cathy. We've just been watching the news. They've still not picked up that Dawson bastard. Well, there's nothing on the news again tonight to say different anyway. He'd better not show his face around here or he'll have me and Jimmy to answer to.'

'And me,' Gianni said. 'Couldn't believe it when Cathy told me he'd escaped. I hardly see the telly with working at night and I rarely catch sight of the paper after it's done the rounds. I suppose he'll be long gone now. Lost up in Scotland or lying low for a few months.'

Cathy shuddered. 'Don't let's talk about him. Makes me feel all weird, knowing he's out there somewhere. Anyway, Mam, Gianni's had nothing to eat tonight so I'm going to make him some cheese on toast and a cuppa. Do you two want anything?'

'No thanks, love. We've had some supper earlier while you were dozing. Go on back in the front room and I'll make Gianni something. You must have loads to talk about. You can grab some blankets and sheets and pillows from upstairs and pull out the sofa bed. You'll never both manage on that little bed upstairs in Lucy's room and besides, you'll want a bit of time to yourselves. Go on, get it sorted out and I'll bring your food through when it's ready.'

By the time Alice brought his supper in Gianni had pulled out the sofa bed mattress and he and Cathy had made it up with bedding, ready for the night.

'That looks nice and cosy. Gives you both a bit of space as well. Cathy's got a lot to tell you that she couldn't get out on the phone with her crying so much. I'll leave you both to it.' Alice left the room and closed the door as Gianni stretched out on the bed and held his arms out to Cathy, who joined him.

She reached for the little tray her mam had put his supper on and gave it to him. 'Eat first while I tell you all the news and then we can catch up properly.'

He smiled, a twinkle in his eyes. 'Good. I hate that your granny is so ill, but I'm really grateful that we have this time together. I'm looking forward to loving you all night long.'

Cathy stroked his cheek. 'So am I,' she whispered. 'It feels like it's been forever.'

'Right, well tell me what's been going on then, apart from Granny being so poorly.' He bit into his toast and rolled his eyes with pleasure. 'You can't beat nice strong Cheddar.'

'Well, for starters, I helped to deliver Debbie and Davy's baby daughter today,' she began. His eyes opened wide. 'She's beautiful. A tiny version of Debbie with the auburn hair.'

'Oh, sweetheart, I bet that was hard for you, seeing your best friend in agony as well as bringing back thoughts of the baby we should have had.'

'It was. But it was also a very special and precious moment in my life that I'll never forget. I felt so emotional as I held Debbie's daughter.'

Gianni nodded and held her tight. 'I'm sure you did,' he whispered into her hair. 'I can't wait to catch up with them. I suppose Debs will be in hospital for a while though.'

'About another week. She did very well, so apart from resting she won't need to stay in too long. I feel dead proud of her. And,' Cathy continued, 'they've got the mortgage through on the house. I was supposed to ask you tonight if you'd got things sorted with your solicitor but I couldn't speak, as you know.'

'Oh that's just brilliant!' Gianni exclaimed. 'I'll set the ball rolling tomorrow. I couldn't be home at a better time, well apart from the main reason behind it,' he added, shaking his head sadly. He finished his supper while Cathy snuggled up silently beside him.

'Right,' he said when he'd finished eating and drunk his tea. 'I need a pee and to brush my teeth. Can I have a quick look in at Lucy as well? I promise not to wake her.'

'Of course you can. Come on.' Cathy got to her feet and carried the tray back into the kitchen. She accompanied him upstairs and sat on the top stair while he used the bathroom. Together, they opened the door to where Lucy was curled up asleep on her bed in her little pink room, surrounded by teddies, her long dark hair fanned out all over the pillow and her long dark lashes flickering gently in sleep.

Gianni took a deep breath and blew a kiss into the room. 'She's growing up so quickly. She's just beautiful.' He took Cathy's hand and laced his fingers through hers. They stood silently for a few seconds, staring at their daughter.

'Come on,' Cathy said softly, closing the bedroom door. 'We need some time to ourselves now.'

*

Jack accepted the glass of vodka and coke from Eloisa, who invited him to sit on the grass and dropped down next to him. The mid-July night was warm and still fairly light from the half-moon shining in a clear starlit sky. Someone had lit a campfire away from the living wagons and a couple of the hands were strumming guitars and singing folk songs. The small crowd sitting around the fire seemed relaxed and called out greetings to him. Today had been good and he'd really enjoyed himself. Everyone was so friendly and helpful and had gone out of their way to make him feel at home. He'd been kept busy by Lenny, sorting out all sorts of problems: cleaning up after kids puking on the ghost train, selling tickets to Ferris wheel riders, and taking over on the rifle range when the lad in charge had been rushed to hospital with stomach pains. The stall was opposite Eloisa's hook-a-duck game and she'd been giving him come-on glances from under her dark fringe all night, making his pulse race and his balls tingle. Ronnie seemed oblivious to his girlfriend's flirty ways and Jack wondered what the score was between the pair.

Late afternoon the boss's son had turned up, looking anxious. It was the first Jack had seen of him and he was surprised to see it was Gianni, the biker Cathy had been seeing. He kept well back away from them and stayed hidden behind a tree while observing what was going on. That was all he bloody needed, Gianni spotting him and blowing his cover. It was a good few years since their paths had crossed and in his present guise Jack didn't think he would recognise him, but he was taking no chances. Eloisa was all over the lad, greeting him with a hug, but she'd been pushed to one side as he'd spoken agitatedly to Luca and Maria and had then been given a bag by Maria and had driven off in Luca's fancy car.

Jack had caught some of the conversation, that he needed to be home with his family, but who was his family and why did he need to be home with them when surely all fair people lived on site? He got the gist that Gianni was part of the bike show and was concerned about leaving his dad and uncle in the lurch. He'd need to make sure he kept out of Gianni's way when he came back until he got the measure of what was going on. There'd been no sign of Cathy. They must have split up and he'd got a wife and kids somewhere that he was going off to join. Cathy would still be nursing, he reckoned. Well, the hospital was where he was planning to start looking for her anyway, when he eventually made it home to Liverpool. That bitch had it coming to her.

He knocked the drink back and jumped to his feet. 'I'm off to bed, lads,' he announced to the other hands, who were sharing a joint now. He was surprised the boss allowed it, given that they were all pissed, too. Or more like, he didn't know what they got up to once the fair closed for the night.

Eloisa got to her feet. 'I'll walk you to your van, Dougie, in case you can't remember which one it is.' She giggled and hiccupped, flicking her long hair back and giving him that look again.

'I think I can manage,' he muttered, pushing her away as she grabbed his hand. He didn't want to offend Ronnie. After all, he had to share the van with him.

'The walk will do me good and clear my head.' She yanked on his arm and they set off towards the hired hands' caravan.

'Won't your bloke mind?' Jack said and lit a cigarette.

'He won't even notice I'm gone now they've started on the weed.' She pulled his fag from between his lips, took a drag and handed it back as they strolled around the perimeter of the recreation ground, Eloisa hanging on to his arm.

Jack could feel himself getting turned on and fought it. He needed sex like he'd never needed it before, but not with Ronnie's bird, no matter how easy a lay she might be. It wouldn't be right.

As they passed a gap in the trees Eloisa grabbed his hand and led him into a small glade. 'No one can see us in here,' she whispered seductively, batting her lashes.

Jack put his arms around her and looked into her eyes. She leaned back against a thick tree trunk and puckered up for a kiss. His lips met hers, his hands groping her breasts before he could even think about it. She ground against him and unbuckled his belt. Shit, his too-tight jeans were a struggle to get down but she persevered and pushed her hands inside, touching him. Not much he could do now, so he took a deep breath and let her get on with it. She dropped to her knees and gave him the best blowjob he'd had since Lorraine. He groaned as he exploded and his legs felt like they were about to buckle under him. She looked up with an expectant gleam in her eyes and he pulled her to her feet. He slid his hand up her skirt, not in the least bit surprised to find her naked underneath. She writhed on his busy fingers and before he even had time to get down beneath her she jerked and yelled, screaming his name and God's, and went limp in his arms.

'Well, that *was* a surprise!' Jack grinned as he leaned her back against the tree again while she caught her breath. He pulled up his jeans and fastened his belt.

'But was it good for you?' She seemed anxious now as she straightened her skirt and ran her fingers through her hair.

'Best I've had in a long time,' he said, truthfully. Beat his own handjobs any day.

She smiled. 'Really? We need more time and then I'll show you what's good.'

'I'll look forward to it.' He grabbed hold of her again, squeezing her breasts through her thin cotton top. Amazingly, considering how tired he felt, he could go another round. But they needed to get back. He wasn't risking losing his job on the first day. And sexy as the little bird was, that soft bed appealed to him too. 'Same time tomorrow,' he said. 'I'll make sure I'm prepared.' There was no way he was fathering more brats. He'd done his contribution for the world population.

She smiled and took his hand as they made their way to his caravan.

Chapter Twelve

Cathy awoke with a jump and rubbed her eyes. It took a moment for her to remember where she was and she lay still in Gianni's arms in the dark room, wondering where the noise was coming from. Then she realised it was the phone ringing in the hall and she shot out of bed, hastily wrapping a blanket around herself, and dashed to pick up the receiver. She knew it was the hospital before she even spoke. Granny Lomax had taken a turn for the worse and she needed to get there immediately.

Back in their room, Gianni, who'd heard Cathy's side of the conversation, was pulling on his clothes. Cathy dashed upstairs to get dressed and tapped on her mam's door. Alice called to come in.

'I heard the phone ringing, chuck. I presume it was the hospital. Is Gianni taking you?'

Cathy nodded, choking on her words as she spoke. 'I have to go and say goodbye, Mam.'

'I understand, love. Do you want me to come with you?'

'No, it's okay. Stay here with Johnny and the kids. We might be ages, I'll see you later.' She kissed her mam and dashed back downstairs to where Gianni was waiting in the hallway with the car keys in his hand. 'I am so glad you're here,' she said.

'So am I. Come on, darling.' He locked the front door behind them and handed Cathy the house keys to put in her pocket.

The roads were quiet at that time in the early morning and they were at the hospital in no time. Night Sister greeted them and accompanied them to the small side room that Granny had been transferred to earlier.

'She's peaceful, don't be alarmed by her laboured breathing. It's normal at this stage. Just talk to her and hold her hand. She'll be able to hear you; it's the last thing to go. It will be nice for her to hear your voice.'

Cathy smiled and thanked the sister. Gianni put a chair either side of the bed and they talked quietly to Granny, telling her how Gianni was here and about Lucy's antics. After a while Cathy glanced at the clock ticking slowly on the side wall. It was four thirty and Granny was struggling harder for breath. Gianni reached for Cathy's hand across the bed and squeezed it. She blinked back tears and came round to stand beside him. He slipped his arm around her waist and held her tightly as Granny Lomax shuddered and took her final breath.

Cathy sobbed. 'Oh, Granny, what will I do without you? We all loved you so much.' She pressed the buzzer by the bed and Night Sister came into the room. 'She's gone,' Cathy wailed and Sister patted her shoulder.

'I'm very sorry, Nurse Romano. I'm glad you managed to get in and be with her. It will have meant everything to her that you were here. I'll get one of my nurses to make you some tea in the family room.'

Gianni led her to the little room at the end of the corridor and she collapsed into his arms and sobbed against his shoulder while he held her tight. A nurse brought in a tray of tea things and then left them alone, closing the door quietly behind her.

When they arrived back home Cathy lay in bed sadly for a while before eventually falling into a fitful sleep for most of the morning. Alice had let the hospital know that neither of them would be in work that day. Johnny had walked the girls and Rodney to school and Lucy had been taken to Ben's mothers for a couple of hours while the family decided what to do next. Gianni went back to the hospital to collect Granny's death certificate and when Cathy woke he suggested that they go to the bungalow to see if she had left any instructions with regards to funeral arrangements.

'Older people are usually quite specific in where they would like their funerals to be held,' Alice said as she made Cathy some breakfast. 'I suspect that Granny would want hers at St Michael's Church and then to be buried with her husband and your dad in the graveyard attached.'

Cathy nodded wearily. 'I just remembered – as we waited for the ambulance the other day she told me she'd put a letter for me in her bureau and to read it if she doesn't come back.' Tears ran down her cheeks. 'I never dared to let myself think that she wouldn't.'

Alice rubbed her arm. 'When you've had your breakfast you and Gianni can go over there and look for the letter. Make sure everywhere is locked up and secure as well; check all the windows and doors. Do you think you could let her next-door neighbours know she's passed away as well while you're there? They've always been very good to her. I'll write to our Brian and tell him. She did a lot for Brian as a lad. He'll be really upset. I wonder if I should try and phone him. I'm not sure how easy it is to put a call through to America.'

'You could send him a telegram,' Gianni suggested.

'Oh, what a good idea.' Alice nodded. 'I'll go to the post office later and get it done. When you two come back from the bungalow we can sort out the funeral arrangements according to Granny's wishes.'

The lump in Cathy's throat threatened to choke her as she wandered from room to room in her second home on Linnet Lane. She'd spent half her life enjoying happy family times under this roof. Birthday parties, Christmases, picnics in the garden. Snuggling down in her little bed and living here with her mam and Uncle Brian, who'd had a bedroom in the loft space, many years ago. All the lovely meals Granny had cooked for them and the wonderful cakes she'd made. She turned to Gianni and gave him a watery smile. 'I'm trying to focus on all the happy times,' she said. 'There are no sad ones at all. I was so young when my dad died so I can't remember that, or how very sad *she* must have felt for years after. No matter what, she always made sure we had fun.'

'Then keep yourself focused on that. I did it when Mam died and it really helps.'

Cathy nodded. 'I'd better look at that letter she mentioned.' She opened the bureau in the hall. A large white envelope with Cathy's name written in Granny's neat, sloping handwriting stood propped in front of a large box. She carried it into the dining room, laid it on the table and stared at it for ages. Gianni reached for her hand and squeezed it.

'It won't open itself, Cathy. I'm here for you like you were there for me when we sorted through Mam's papers. Be brave, love.'

She picked up the envelope and undid the flap, sliding out a letter and several sheets of paper that she put to one side before starting to read. Granny had written the letter the same day Cathy had taken her for the X-ray. In the letter she told Cathy she wanted to be prepared for the worst, as she felt it was soon to come. 'She knew she hadn't got long,' Cathy said tearfully. 'That's why she wrote this letter with her instructions. They are on the sheets of paper.' Cathy read the letter out to Gianni, her voice faltering from time to time.

My Darling Cathy,

I know I don't have long left on this earth. I don't want to go, but I fear it's God's will and he won't listen to any arguments from stubborn old me, so I will go along with whatever he has planned. I just want you to know that you and Lucy have always meant the world to me and have brought such joy into my life.

After losing my dear boy Terry I didn't think I could go on, but one look at your smiling face made me feel so grateful for what I had left to live for. I never want you to struggle like your mother had to do at times, and everything I have in the world is yours now I'm gone, including the bungalow. I know you will look after it and make it as nice a home as you can for you and Lucy and Gianni, when he can join you. In the box in the bureau are the details for my solicitor, who will instruct you how to go about things. The pages in with this letter are my funeral details. I know I can trust you to carry out my last wishes. Goodbye, my darling girl, and be happy. Thank you for making me the proudest grandma that ever walked the streets of Liverpool.

All my love, Granny Lomax. Xxx

Cathy looked across at Gianni, who also had tears running down his face. 'I don't know what to say,' she said. 'I'm stunned.' She looked around and shook her head. 'She's left me her home. I can't believe it.'

Gianni wiped his eyes with the back of his hand. 'Cathy, you are her only relative, well you and Lucy. It's no surprise really, love. I can see from your face that you're shocked. But it's always been your home too.'

She shook her head. 'I'm beyond shocked. It's going to take me a while for it to sink in.'

'Let's go back to your mam's then and she can help us sort out the funeral details. It's best to keep busy for the next few days, love, and I'll be here for you too.'

*

Jack hovered at the rear of the caravan and listened in to the conversation between Maria and Luca, who had just come back from the telephone box. The window above his head was open and they must have been sitting just underneath it because he could hear every word. He caught the name Cathy and his eyes widened. He got the gist of the tale Luca was telling Maria. Gianni's wife was called Cathy. So they had got married – but why didn't she live here with him? Gianni was staying in Liverpool until the fair pitched up there towards the end of the month. Cathy's grandmother had passed away and left her a bungalow. That would be the one on Linnet Lane, then, where the old witch had lived.

Then he heard Alice's name mentioned, along with Johnny, who appeared to be her husband the way Luca was talking about him. He felt a rush of anger surge through him. Johnny was the name of Jimmy, the neighbour's, brother. He'd always had a thing about Alice. So the bastard had married her then? Not that he was bothered, but the thoughts of Alice getting on with her life while he'd been banged up filled him with fury. One day they'd all pay for it, he was determined. Especially that little cow Cathy. Just wait until he got his hands on her.

He jumped out of his skin as a voice said 'Boo!' down his ear. 'What the fuck,' he said, spinning round to find Eloisa standing grinning behind him.

'What are you doing round here?' she said.

'I er, I think I dropped my packet of fags earlier. Been covering everywhere I've walked to try and find them,' he fibbed.

'Have you checked your caravan?'

'Not yet, because I was sure I had them in my pocket, but maybe I left them in there after all.'

'Shall we go and look?' Eloisa shot him that teasing look and his balls tingled. She knew the caravan was currently empty as everyone was working on site.

'Why not,' he replied, grabbing her hand and dragging her towards it. He opened the door, shoved her up the steps and, looking around to make sure no one was watching them, followed her in and locked the door.

Eloisa pulled the curtains across and sat down on the bed that Jack hadn't folded away from this morning.

He looked at her with narrowed eyes, imagining that she was Cathy. He lunged for Eloisa before she had a chance to say anything. The look of shock on her face as he handled her roughly spurred him on and he was inside her quicker than a rat up a drainpipe. She lay beneath him while he banged away, looking too shocked to say anything. He swore at her and bit on her lip to silence her when she finally gave a squeal. 'You like it rough, don't you?' he growled, almost forgetting to do his Scottish accent. 'All you girls like it rough.' He looked down at her terrified face and grinned as he came. He rolled off her and lay on his back as she lay silently beside him.

'Dougie, why did you do that?' she asked eventually. 'There was no need to force yourself on me. I was willing to make love with you.'

'Love, ha, what's love got to do with anything? You bloody women think that's all there is to life.'

She started to cry and he sat up, suddenly filled with remorse. She wasn't Cathy. She was the boss's stepdaughter and if she told her ma what he'd just done to her he'd lose his new job and the roof over his head. They'd probably get the cops involved as well. *You stupid sod, Jack*, he thought. He put his head in his hands. 'I'm sorry, Eloisa. I don't know what came over me. I've been so screwed over by women that I don't recognise a good one when she's right under my nose.'

He reached for her and pulled her close. He could be tender when he tried; he just needed to make the effort. 'Let me make it up to you.' He kissed her gently and laid her back on the pillows, stroking her face. 'Just give me a bit of time to get my breath back and I'll show you how nice I can be. Please don't tell anyone what happened then. I care about you, you know I do,' he fibbed as he felt her beginning to relax in his arms.

Eloisa sighed and snuggled into him. 'I care about you too, Dougie. You're different from anyone else I've ever been with. But please don't do that to me again. There's no need. I will never refuse you.'

'I promise.' He needed to keep on her good side so he could drop random questions into their conversations about Gianni and Cathy. Not only that, she had said she was always willing and he'd been sex-starved for years.

Chapter Thirteen

Two days before Granny Lomax's funeral, Alice answered a knock at the door. She opened it just in time to see a taxi pulling away and a tall man with his back to her waving at someone passing by on the opposite side of the street. Her hand flew to her mouth as he turned and smiled. 'Brian! Oh my God, Cathy, look who's here.'

'Looks like I've beaten the letter I sent you after reading your telegram,' Brian said. 'I should have listened to Lori and sent a telegram back. Well, surprise!'

'Well come on in then, don't stand on the step.' Alice threw her arms around her younger brother and he gave her a bear hug in return and then pulled Cathy into his arms as she appeared behind his sister.

'I am so, so sorry to hear about Granny's death,' he said as she clung to him. 'I hope I haven't missed her funeral.'

'No you haven't,' Cathy said, smiling for the first time in days. 'It's on Friday. You've got time to recover from your flight. Oh it's so good to see you, it really is. Granny will be thrilled if she's looking down on us.'

'That's good,' Brian said. 'It's good to see you two as well. Such a shame it has to be in sad circumstances. But never mind. We'll make sure she has the best send-off.'

'We certainly will,' Alice said. 'Come on through to the back. Leave your case in the hall for now and it can go upstairs later.

We're bursting at the seams with Gianni here as well, but we'll manage to fit you in somewhere.'

'I can pop Lucy in with Rosie, she won't mind,' Cathy said. 'Then you can have her little room for a few nights, Brian. I'm afraid it's a bit on the pink side though.'

'I can live with pink for a while,' Brian said with a grin.

Alice dashed into the kitchen and made them all a cuppa. They sat down at the table and Brian smiled and picked up his mug; he took a sip, savouring the first mouthful.

'Best brew I've had for years,' he declared. 'I'm looking forward to seeing the kids again. I bet they've grown a lot.'

'They have. Sandra's all legs and long hair now *and* lad-mad,' Alice said. 'Rosie hasn't changed much and neither has Roddy. The girls will be in from school shortly. Gianni has taken Lucy to meet Roddy but you can bet your life he'll have been dragged into the café on Lark Lane for jam tarts and orange juice.'

'And how is little Lucy?'

'Not so little any more,' Cathy replied. 'She starts school in September. I can't believe how quickly the time has flown. She hadn't seen Gianni for a while until he came home and she's already got him wrapped around her little finger. He falls hook, line and sinker for her demands though.'

'What about your two boys?' Alice asked. 'Have you brought photos with you? And congratulations on the new one.'

Brian beamed and reached into his pocket for his wallet. He pulled out two coloured studio photographs of his sons. 'Samuel's on the right and little James is of course the baby.'

'Oh, you've called him after our dad. That's lovely, Brian. Do you remember? That's what I was going to call Cathy if she'd been a boy?' Alice said, her eyes filling. 'How thoughtful of you.'

'Sammy is Lori's dad's name, so we thought James would be nice for the little one. In a year or two, when they're a bit older, we'll bring them on a visit to Liverpool. Lori can't wait to meet my family and I'm dying for you all to meet her too.'

'I'll get that,' Cathy said as someone else knocked on the door. She hurried down the hall and smiled as Davy greeted her with a wide grin.

'Just to let you know I've brought Debs and the baby home. Pop across later if you've got a minute.'

'Oh I will. I'm so sorry I haven't been back to the ward to see them.'

'Hey, don't you worry about that. You've had quite enough on your plate. We're both very sorry to hear about your granny. Catch you later.'

'See you in a bit then,' Cathy said and waved goodbye as he hurried away.

'Debs and the baby are home,' Cathy announced, going back into the sitting room. 'I'll nip over later.'

'Have they chosen a name yet?' Alice asked. 'I saw Davy the other day and they were still dithering.'

'Oh, damn. I forgot to ask. No doubt I'll find out tonight. Right, I'll refill our mugs seeing as Brian really enjoyed his first brew.'

'I did,' Brian said and laughed. 'It might sound a bit daft but a proper cuppa is one of the things I've missed most. Americans either make it like gnat's pee or so you can almost stand a spoon up in it.'

Cathy laughed. 'But *you've* got Elvis Presley, Bobby Vee and the Ronettes.'

'Well *you've* got the Beatles, so don't you be complaining,' Brian teased.

'We have and loads of others too. I'm not complaining really. We're very lucky music-wise in Liverpool.'

*

Cathy gazed down proudly at the beautiful baby in her arms. 'She's really filling out, Debs, and she's gorgeous. How are you feeling?'

'Absolutely fine,' Debbie said. 'I'm raring to go now. Can't wait to push her out in the pram.'

'Don't be in too much of a rush or you'll tire yourself out. Night feeds can take it out of you. Make sure you get a nap in the day when she's asleep.' She looked up as Davy and Gianni came into the room carrying glasses and a bottle of sherry.

'A little toast to our new arrival,' Davy announced, pouring tots of sherry into the glasses and handing them round. He raised an eyebrow in Debbie's direction and she nodded. 'It's taken us a while to choose a name that we feel suits our little girl, but here's to our Catherine Alison Ayres. May she have a truly wonderful life.' He raised his glass and smiled at Cathy as her hand flew to her mouth and tears spilled down her cheeks.

'Oh my goodness. Thank you. I wasn't expecting that.'

Debbie smiled. 'Well, you brought her into this world, Cathy. We'd also like you and Gianni to be her godparents, and I want to ask your mam to be the other godmother. She's always looked out for us since we moved in here.'

'Oh, Debs, she'll be thrilled to bits. She really will. So much is happening at the moment. I don't know if I'm on my head or my heels right now. But this has just made my day and I know Gianni will be absolutely chuffed too.' She beamed at them both as Gianni nodded his agreement.

'Oh that's wonderful Cathy, we really hoped you'd say yes. We know you've had so much going on. How are you feeling about Granny?' said Davy.

'I really wish she was still with us, but we've got everything planned for the funeral on Friday, so that's a relief. And she left me her bungalow, which has really knocked me for six.'

'She's left you the bungalow?' Debbie gasped. 'How wonderful. It's lovely and the garden is gorgeous too. When will you move in?'

'Not for a while. I love it, as you know, but I'll feel strange living there alone with just Lucy and no Granny.'

'But surely now you'll have a roof over your head you can be a real family and all live there?' Debbie looked pointedly at Gianni. 'And you might want to try for another baby again soon too. Lucy starts school this year. The age gap will be too big if you leave it much longer like we nearly did.'

Gianni smiled and sat down on the sofa next to Cathy. 'It's a nice thought and when Cathy feels ready we will try again. We have a lot to talk about, but we need to get Granny's funeral out of the way first. I think Cathy will find things easier when we've said our proper goodbyes.'

Cathy took a deep breath and nodded. 'I will. I feel a bit in limbo at the moment.'

After saying goodnight to Davy and Debbie, Cathy and Gianni joined her mam and Johnny and Brian for another drink before going to bed. Johnny was showing Brian his ideas for the Woodlands Road house and telling him all about the girls' plans for a private maternity home.

'We're almost at the finishing post with the purchase, just need a completion date now,' Johnny said. 'We need to invite your friends round soon for another meeting, Cathy. When you get back to work you can maybe organise something.'

Cathy nodded. 'Yes sure, I can call Jean and she'll arrange for the girls to come over one night next week if that's okay.'

'That's fine, love. Just let me know what night and I'll ask Jimmy over as well.'

'Sounds like a really sound plan to me,' Brian said. 'I know the house, it's really nice.'

'Have you been in there?' Alice asked.

'Well it looks like the one where Jack had a room when he worked at the Legion, before you and he married—' He stopped quickly. 'Ah, I'm sorry, Alice, I shouldn't have brought that up.'

'It's okay,' Alice said. 'It was a long time ago and we've all moved on.'

Cathy turned to Gianni. 'Shall we go to our room? I'm really tired and we've loads to do tomorrow. Granny's solicitor wants to see me at eleven and I'd like Gianni to come with me.'

Gianni nodded and got to his feet. 'See you all in the morning,' he said.

Cathy said goodnight to them all and Gianni followed her out of the room.

As they lay in bed Gianni turned to her and said, 'I've been thinking things over, Cath. If you want us to be together as a family now, I'm willing to leave the fair and make a home with you and Lucy. I've loved us being together here, and I've really enjoyed my time with Lucy as well, little madam that she is.'

'You give in to her too much. You need to learn to say no more often and mean it,' Cathy said, an amused smile on her face. She thought about the last few days, and how wonderful it was to be a proper family at last. She tried to keep her voice level. 'You love the fair, Gianni, and I would never ask you to give it up. That decision must be yours alone. But if it's what you really want, I've got another five months before I qualify and then I will be on a much higher salary scale, so I could work to keep us both. And we'd have no mortgage to pay.'

'We're very lucky. I've got the money from Mam's house to come when the sale to Davy and Debbie is completed. Erm, by the way, I want to offer half to you to put into the maternity home project. I think it will be a good business for us to invest into. That's if you want it, of course.'

Cathy sat up and stared at him. 'Are you sure? I mean, I thought you'd want to put it away or buy a bit more of the fair from your dad.'

He shook his head. 'I think Dad is itching to go back to Italy at some point. Maria too. Marco will buy him out eventually.

Nothing has been said yet, but it's just a feeling I get. The quarter I own, I will willingly let go. I've got it out of my system. The bikes I mean. I saw you growing up without a real father figure and so did I. I don't want that for our Lucy. She needs a proper home with both her parents always around. I'll see this season through with them, but by November I'll be finishing for the winter anyway, and I'll tell Dad I won't be going back. I can get a job here, I'm sure. I've got my draughtsman qualifications and there'll be the money we'll have left from my house sale to live off that will tide us over for ages.'

'There's nothing I'd like more than for us to be a family again,' Cathy said, moving into his arms. 'But like I say, the decision to give up the fair and the opportunity to work with your dad has to be yours and yours alone.'

Cathy sat open-mouthed in front of Joseph Trent, her granny's solicitor. He'd just told her that as well as the bungalow, Granny Lomax had money invested in various accounts that would now be transferred to Cathy. There had been two life insurance policies in the box at the bungalow that would more than pay for the funeral. Cathy had already made calls to both companies and cheques had been issued within days. They were awaiting clearance in Cathy's bank account. Mr Trent said once he'd finalised all the details and transferred the money and the deeds of the bungalow into her name, he would send her a bill for his services. He handed her a sheet of paper listing the names of the banks and building society that held Granny's money, plus a written statement for each account. He assured her that all would be dealt with as soon as possible, commiserated over her loss and shook her and Gianni's hands. They left the Bold Street office in the city in a bit of a daze and wandered hand-in-hand for a while as the news sank in.

'Let's go and get a coffee in the Kardomah,' Gianni suggested. 'I need to see if I can find a cheap black suit for the funeral tomorrow as well. I guess I'll need one anyway, for job interviews later in the year.'

'Then get a decent one,' Cathy suggested. 'It'll serve both purposes. You'll need a white shirt and black tie as well. Good job I've just been paid. We'll go in Lewis's and see if Millie can get us a bit of a staff discount.'

Gianni smiled. 'It's mad isn't it? Between us we've got more money than anyone we know and no access to any of it yet.'

'Mam and Johnny will sub us if we need it. But Granny's policy cheques will clear by tomorrow. Then I can pay the funeral and the buffet bills and there'll be a fair bit left over.' Cathy led the way into the café and Gianni ordered two coffees and cakes.

'Oh, this is lovely,' Cathy said, taking a bite of the rich chocolate sponge cake. 'I'll be glad when tomorrow is over. I hate the thought of saying a final goodbye, but Granny will be reunited with my dad and granddad and I have to keep that thought in my mind.'

Gianni smiled and reached for her hand across the table. 'She will.'

In Lewis's Millie greeted them both with hugs and was more than happy to oblige with her staff discount. She took a break from her cosmetics supervisor duties and accompanied them to the men's clothing department. She and Cathy hung around while Gianni tried a couple of suits on and when he called them over from the changing rooms, Cathy's hand flew to her mouth.

'Oh my God, I'd forgotten how smart you can look in a suit.' Gianni was so handsome with his thick dark hair and brown eyes, and now, as he stood in front of her in that suit with an amused smile on his face, she was glad he was so willing to give up the fairground for her and Lucy. At least he'd be away from that slutty Eloisa, his stepsister.

It was funny how she never gave the girl a thought any more, and she trusted Gianni always to be faithful to her – after his one night of indiscretion when they were split up – but she was glad he'd be away from her soon. She would never trust the girl as far as she could throw her. She shook her head to clear her mind while Gianni went back into the cubicle to take the suit off. Millie accompanied them to the till and the salesman sorted out her discount. They walked back to the ground floor, said goodbye to Millie and made their way to Lime Street station.

'Feels weird being here,' Gianni said, looking round. 'Back home I mean. I didn't realise how much I missed Liverpool. It'll be great to be back for good.'

Cathy nodded. 'I would hate to be away from the city.'

'That's because you're just a sweet little Liver Bird at heart,' he teased.

Chapter Fourteen

Granny Lomax's funeral was the perfect send-off for a lady who had been so well loved and respected in her community. The church was packed with friends, neighbours and people Granny knew from church, as well as Cathy's family. Rosie and Sandra had been allowed the day off school as Granny had been the only grandparent they'd ever known. They sobbed quietly while the vicar of St Michael's read the eulogy he'd prepared a few days ago with Cathy and Alice's help and they sang Granny's favourite hymns. Saying Psalm 23 almost finished Cathy off, but with Gianni by her side she held it together.

Brian had written a eulogy too and got up to read it. He said how grateful he was to Granny Lomax for all the help she'd given him with his education, teaching him at home during the war and helping him to achieve his school certificates, which had led to him gaining his university degree. He made everyone laugh when he said she was a terrible cheat at board games though and had always beaten him at ludo and snakes and ladders.

The vicar thanked him and led the final prayers and hymn before the congregation filed out of church. They gathered by the prepared graveside and Alice wept as she saw Terry's name etched in gold on the marble headstone. Johnny slipped his arm around her waist and Gianni held on to Cathy as Granny's coffin was lowered into the grave and she gave way to her tears. Both Cathy and Alice picked up a handful of soil and scattered it on top of the coffin, followed by the other mourners, and then they led the way into the church hall where the buffet was being held.

Cathy, Alice and Brian stood by the doors to welcome everyone inside. As the last mourners passed them, Cathy blew out her cheeks and turned to her mam and Brian. 'Thank you. I couldn't have got through this without you both by my side.'

Brian gathered the pair into a group hug. 'That's what families are for,' he whispered. 'I remember the times when it was just us three after Mam died and Granny was always there to help and look after us.'

'She was,' Alice said. 'And I go and repay her by marrying that swine whose name I'm not even going to mention.'

'Mam, you need to forgive yourself,' Cathy said. 'Come on, let's go and do our hostessing bit. The Lark Lane café have really done Granny proud with the lovely buffet.'

*

Jack ran a comb through his beard. It was growing really long now and he had a moustache that beat Jimmy Edwards' into a cocked hat. He twirled the ends out and smiled. Eloisa didn't like it. She complained it tickled and made her want to sneeze. Well tough, the facial hair was part of his disguise and no way was it getting shaved off to suit her. By the time he got to Liverpool, Jack hoped, he'd be unrecognisable.

It had been difficult to hide his wooden foot from her, and she ribbed him about leaving his socks on in bed, but it was a dead giveaway as it had been reported in the papers. He'd told her he had an ugly scar on his foot from a serious war injury that he didn't like people to see and preferred to keep it covered. So far she'd bought his story, and had told him the reason she also had a slight limp was because she'd had a broken leg a few years ago due to an accident at the fairground.

He'd panicked last night when he'd seen two police officers patrolling the fairground and showing people his and Andy's mugshots. But from the shaking of heads it was clear that not one of the hands recognised him, which was great to know. When he'd asked Eloisa what the cops had been saying to Luca before they started patrolling around, she'd replied that Luca's daughter-in-law's stepfather, a man named Jack Dawson from Liverpool, along with another man from Glasgow, whose name she couldn't remember, were on the run for the murder of a prison officer.

'Wonder why they came here to look for him?' Jack mused with what he hoped was a scornful tone. 'What a waste of time.' So Cathy was definitely married to Gianni then. 'Somebody on the run is hardly likely to take shelter with people he knows, is he? Family contacts and friends would be the first places they'd check.'

Eloisa laughed. 'No idea what he'd do, but we've been told to report any sightings if he does turn up.'

'Fair enough.' Jack laughed it off, but he would keep a firm eye on anyone he felt was looking at him too closely. 'Is the boss's son still away?' he asked.

'Yep. We won't be seeing him again now until we pitch up in Liverpool. And *she'll* be around, making sure to keep a watchful eye on him, when we do get there.'

'She?'

'Cathy, the moaning wife. She doesn't trust him around me. We have a bit of history, me and Gianni. We were going to get married at one time. But he's tied to her and the kid now, so that's that. She's well and truly got her claws in him.' She strolled away and Jack watched her go, wondering what the history she'd referred to was all about. She's jealous of Cathy, no doubt about that, he thought. And she said the couple had a kid. Well, that was news, but then it would be.

No one had told him, not even Lorraine in her letter when she'd written to let him know Alice had got married again. But, maybe *she* didn't know either, because she hadn't even told him Alice's new husband was that bloody Johnny that used to make eyes at Alice when they ran the Aigburth Legion. Ah well, just another week or two and he'd be seeing them all for himself – only they would have no idea it was him.

*

'Thank you for putting me up,' Brian said as he stood in the hall very early on Sunday morning waiting for a taxi.

'It was our pleasure,' Alice told him. 'It was such a long way for you to come for so short a time, but we truly appreciate that you made the effort.'

'We certainly do,' Cathy said, coming into the hall. 'We miss you so much.'

'You and Gianni must come out for a visit soon. You'd both love it.'

'Love it, she might,' Alice said. 'But don't you dare get any ideas about persuading them to move to the USA. I couldn't bear it.'

'We're going nowhere for now,' Cathy said. 'We've got a business to get up and running and I've got my training to finish this year. But you never know, some day we may well take a trip.' She stopped as a horn tooted outside. They walked with Brian to the taxi and waved him off. 'We really will miss you,' Cathy said quietly as the taxi turned the corner on to Lark Lane.

Gianni gave her a hug as she walked back into their room and started to cry. 'I stayed in here so you and Alice could have him all to yourselves for the last few minutes. We said goodbye in the kitchen.'

'He said we should visit one day,' Cathy said.

'Well maybe we will once everything is sorted out. I'd love that. America always fascinates me. The music, the clothes, the cars.' Gianni took her hand and twirled her around and Cathy smiled. 'One day,' he said. 'We never really had a proper honeymoon, so maybe we could aim for that in time.'

Cathy nodded. 'I'd really like that.'

'What shall we do today? We could take Lucy to the park and have a picnic maybe.'

'Shall I ask Davy and Debs if they fancy coming with us?' Cathy said. 'She might feel like a walk to give the baby an outing.'

'Good idea. Lucy and Jonathon can play on the swings together.' Gianni glanced at the bedside clock. 'Let's try and grab another hour's kip before everyone gets up. It's only half seven.'

*

'So have you thought any more about what you will do?' Debbie said as she and Cathy lay on a picnic blanket in Sefton Park while Gianni and Davy were out on the boating lake with Lucy and Jonathon. It was a beautiful day but not too hot and the park was crowded with families, dressed in their summer outfits, all taking advantage of the good weather. Baby Catherine was asleep in her pram, parked under the nearby tree with a sun canopy shading her.

Cathy hitched the skirt of her pink-and-white striped summer dress up her legs to try to get a bit of colour to them. 'I think so. After this season has finished with the fair, Gianni is going to leave it and live with me and Lucy at the bungalow. He said he'd look for a job in Liverpool. He can take his time as we've a bit of spare money to live off and we've no rent or mortgage to pay.'

'You're in a very good position,' Debbie said. 'I envy you.'

'We are.' Cathy told her about the plans to create a new maternity home at the Woodlands Road house. 'I haven't been able to say anything before now, so keep it to yourself until it's all sorted. I'll be able to tell you more when we get the plans passed and the money side of things in place. Johnny and Jimmy are dealing with all that and Jean has written to the National Childbirth Trust to see if they can help with funding. Hopefully they will agree.'

'Sounds like a fabulous idea to me. Some of those poor unmarried girls have an awful time. I mean, look how my mam turned on me when I was expecting Jonathon. If Davy hadn't wanted to marry me, I'd have had to give my baby up for adoption. It would have broken my heart. You lot are so kind and understanding, not like the nuns in the Catholic homes. And the women who can afford to pay privately will have the best midwives in the area. I'll definitely have my next one in there. Except' – she stopped and sighed – 'there probably won't be any more. Davy says two is quite enough and we're lucky to have one of each.'

Cathy laughed. 'I'm inclined to agree with him on that score. Two is definitely enough.' She shaded her eyes and looked across to the boating lake, just making out her daughter and Gianni in a pea-green boat heading to the shore. Good. She could murder an ice-cream cornet and no doubt Lucy would be mithering for a lolly as soon as she got out of the boat. Davy's red boat was still in the middle of the lake, so they'd be a while coming in to shore. She watched Gianni clamber out and lift Lucy up onto his shoulders. He waved in Cathy's direction and pointed to the ice-cream van.

'Two cornets with raspberry please,' she called out to him. He stuck a thumb up to show he'd understood and went to wait in the queue.

'This area will soon be full of fairground rides,' Debbie said. 'You'll get to spend a bit of time with your in-laws.'

'I will. But most of the time I'll be back at work. Gianni can look after Lucy when he's not riding the bikes and Maria absolutely loves her to bits so she'll see to her when he's working.'

'Is Eloisa still around?'

'As far as I know. I haven't asked and Gianni hasn't mentioned her. No doubt she will be.'

'Does Maria still do the crystal ball thing? I might have my fortune told when she gets here. See what the future holds for us.'

'I think she does, but you'll have to ask Gianni.'

'Ask me what?' Gianni said, appearing at their side with two dripping cornets. Lucy had red ice lolly juice running down her chin and he wiped it away with his hanky. 'Sit down next to your mammy now, there's a good girl.'

'Does Maria still tell fortunes? Debs wants to know,' Cathy said.

'Yeah, she does. Always seeing danger in everything,' Gianni said with a laugh.

'Well I still might give it a go,' Debbie said, licking the ice-cream that had run down her fingers. She waved at Davy, who was signalling from the shore towards the ice-cream van. 'We've got ours, thanks.'

'Hmm, I'd rather not know, if I'm honest,' Cathy said. 'About the future I mean. I prefer to wait and see what happens.'

Chapter Fifteen

Gianni was sitting on the old bench in Alice's back garden, under the shade of an apple tree, sketching his daughter as she played on the small lawn with her dollies. He was looking after Lucy while Cathy went into work to get her rota and catch up with the other midwives. She'd been off nearly three weeks and said she felt ready to go back. He and Lucy had taken a stroll along to school with Roddy and then called into the post office on Lark Lane for a pad and pencils. He'd left all his art things back in the caravan in York and he was missing sketching.

He loved spending time with his daughter. She was cute, intelligent and funny as well as a right little bossyboots. There'd be few who would get the better of Lucy when she started school. Heaven help her teachers. The fair would be arriving in Liverpool very soon now and he couldn't wait to show her off to his dad and Maria. It was almost a year since they'd seen her as they'd spent last winter in Italy with Maria's elderly parents while Gianni spent it with Cathy and Lucy at Granny Lomax's bungalow.

He hoped his dad would understand when he told him of his decision to leave the fair. He'd really enjoyed himself and he would miss everyone, with the exception of Eloisa. But it was time to put his family first. He hoped they would have more children, eventually. They hadn't really discussed the subject since Cathy's miscarriage as she was still so career-driven. She'd started to take the new contraceptive pill, so the decision had to be hers when she was ready. It wasn't really the time yet either, with the new business under way, but Debbie was right, the age gap would be too wide if they left it much longer. Ah well, time would tell. 'Lucy, would you like a drink of orange juice?'

'Yes please, Daddy. Granny Alice always gives me a biscuit with my juice.'

'Does she now? Well let's see what I can do. Will you show me where she keeps them please?'

'There,' Lucy said, running indoors ahead of him. 'In the lellow barrel.' She pointed to a pottery biscuit barrel on the sideboard in the shape of a beehive with a chrome lid.

He smiled, loving the way she said lellow. He'd done the same as a little lad. 'I'll have one as well with a coffee. You choose it for me.' He put the barrel on the table and removed the lid and Lucy climbed on to a chair to make her choices.

Gianni put the kettle on and made himself a mug of coffee. He smiled when he went back into the sitting room and found she'd chosen a custard cream for him. His favourite. 'Now how did you know that Daddy loves those?' He handed her a red beaker of orange juice.

She shrugged. 'I don't know, I just did.'

'Clever girl.'

She beamed at the praise and bit into her pink wafer.

*

'So everything is coming together,' Jean announced as the midwives and Cathy met in the canteen. She placed a letter on the table. 'We've had a reply from the NCT and it seems like they're all for independent units. We'll be expected to supply antenatal and post-natal services as well as delivery and care. We need to be linked up with the hospital and the nearest doctors' surgery, but I can't see that being a problem. We will still be NHS paid nurses. It just means we'll be working in a smaller and more pleasant environment for us and our patients. We can also, if we've got the space, run a little clinic as well, for baby weighing and feeding advice, that sort of thing, for after the post-natal stage. It's often a time when a new mum struggles and baby blues set in.'

'Sounds great,' Cathy said. 'Gianni is giving me some money from the sale of his mam's house to put in the kitty. And actually, if we need it there's some of my granny's money in accounts that I will have access to eventually.'

'I heard she's left you the bungalow,' Karen said. 'Are you and Lucy going to live there now?'

Cathy nodded. 'In time. Gianni is leaving the fair after this season. We'll be together as a family and will all live there.'

'Oh, that's really good news, Cathy,' Jean said. 'It's not before time. You'll have completed your course by then as well. Once we're up and running you can pick your days and hours to suit your family needs.'

'And of course it means I don't need a bedroom at the house,' Cathy said. 'So it leaves plenty of room for you three to make it your home as well as the business premises.'

'All our dads have agreed to put something towards the renovation work and I'm hoping we can get some funding from the council towards it as well,' Jean said. 'I've written to just about everyone I know and one of the young doctors told me his dad's quite high up in the council and he's going to push for it at their next planning meeting.'

'Brilliant,' Ellie said. 'It seems everyone is onside with us.'

'Johnny wants a meeting as soon as we can all get an evening off together,' Cathy said. 'He'd like to go through some figures with you all, so that everyone is in the picture with what they're doing.'

'Well we're all off on Thursday evening if that's any help,' Karen said. 'Me and Ellie are on earlies, and Jean has the full day off.'

'That's great. I'll let him and Jimmy know. Cheers to our future.' She lifted her mug and the others clinked theirs against it, laughing.

*

'What you got there?' Jack asked as Eloisa shoved something behind her back as he approached her while she was sitting on his caravan steps.

'Nothing,' she muttered, her cheeks going red as he stared at her. She made to push whatever it was she had hidden into the canvas bag that lay by her side. 'I've brought you a sandwich.'

'Oh, good, I'm starving. Shall we go inside then?' He led the way and she followed him.

'Right, hand it over then,' he demanded once they were inside.

She pulled a greaseproof-wrapped package from her bag and held it out to him. 'It's cheese and tomato.'

He snatched it from her and said, 'Not that, whatever it is you are hiding from me. We can't have secrets if we're supposed to be serious about seeing one another. Otherwise, we might as well as not bother and you can bugger right off back to lover boy.' He knew that threat would get to her as she constantly told him he was a much better lover than Ronnie and was glad she was no longer his girlfriend. He wondered if Ronnie knew that he'd been dumped, as he still hung around her with his puppy-dog expression. It was as though Ronnie wasn't that bothered; he certainly hadn't said anything to Jack. Eloisa needed Jack more than he needed her and he knew she had fallen for him big time, or so she kept telling him.

'I don't want to go back to Ronnie,' she said, her expression sulky.

'Then hand it over. What have you got that you don't want me to see?' He wagged a finger at her and she backed away looking worried. 'You'll have me thinking it's something to do with another bloke in a minute and I'll warn you now, I don't like being cheated on and messed about, lady.'

'I'm not cheating on you. I never would.' She dug a sketchbook out of her bag and handed it to him. 'Here.'

He opened the first page and tried not to let any expression of recognition cross his face when he saw a likeness of Cathy dressed in skimpy underwear. Well, the little tart! Mind you, it didn't surprise him. 'Whose sketchbook is this?' he demanded. 'Who's the girl and why have you got this?'

'It's Gianni's and that's his wife, Cathy. She poses for him.' Her voice held a tone of scorn and he glanced at her as he flicked to the next sketch. It nearly took his breath away. There was no doubt that Cathy had become a very beautiful woman.

'I know I could pose better than her,' Eloisa muttered.

'Maybe you could. But this isn't yours. It's private and not for yours or anyone else's eyes. You need to put it back where you found it.'

She shook her head. 'No. I want him to think he's lost it when he comes back. I was going to hide it somewhere. He'll go nuts if he can't find it when he checks in the cupboard where he keeps his art stuff. He looks at those sketches every night.'

Jack shook his head. 'It's going right back to that cupboard now, or I'll look after it and return it to Maria later. I'll tell her I found it behind their caravan, to save face for you.'

He held the sketchbook above his head when Eloisa reached for it. She stared at him.

'You're not having it,' he said and shoved her roughly out of the way. 'I don't trust you to return it. Now go on, get out of my sight while I have my dinner.' He practically pushed her out of the caravan and locked the door behind her.

She hammered on the door but he ignored her and switched on his transistor radio to drown out her noise while he made a mug of coffee. He sat down at the little table and wolfed the sandwich Eloisa had brought him, washed it down with his coffee and lay on his bunk with Gianni's sketchbook. He looked through it from cover to cover. There was no doubt about it; Gianni was good at his art. But Cathy was beautiful. He felt the heat rising and his balls tingling as he stared at her almost naked body. There was no way this sketchbook was going anywhere but in his own cupboard, to look at when the fancy took him. One way or another he had to have her. Roll on Liverpool.

*

The meeting at Alice's house turned into a bit of a party as they all toasted the plans with sherry and pale ale. Millie came in halfway through the night to take a look at the various ideas Jimmy and Johnny had put to the girls for the kitchen and bathroom fittings. The owner had accepted their offer of six and a half thousand pounds and the money had been raised for the mortgage. It was less than the asking price because of all the works that needed doing. The roof needed new tiles in various places and there were a couple of large areas where damp had appeared where rain had leaked in. Two of the big back windows needed to be replaced.

'That's a really good price,' Gianni said, 'Considering I got two and a half grand for my mam's two-bedroomed terraced house. Woodlands Road is three times the size and loads of garden and parking as well.'

'We thought so,' Johnny said. 'But it's not the sort of place that gets snapped up by families so it could have been on the market for a long time. I think the owners just want it off their hands as soon as possible before winter comes round and more damage is caused by the bad weather.'

'How will we heat it?' Jean asked. 'It needs more than a couple of fires downstairs. We need a certain temperature for newborns, especially if we have cold winters. I don't fancy lighting fires in the little fireplaces upstairs. It won't be very hygienic.'

'We'll put a heating system in for you,' Johnny said. 'There'll be radiators in all the rooms. They'll run off a boiler from that utility room at the back of the kitchen. We'll look into what will be best, solid fuel or gas. It'll heat your water as well, so there'll be constant hot water from the taps. Just the job for baths and all the washing you'll have to do.'

'We'll need some help with all that, the cleaning and washing side of things,' Jean said. 'Maybe a housekeeper.'

Alice smiled. 'I know a lady I used to work with at Rootes munitions factory during the war. In fact Millie knows her too. Bet she'd love to work with us. She does a bit of cleaning for local people in the area and she used to mind my kids when they were little. She also delivered Cathy in an air raid shelter, believe it or not.'

'You mean my other godmother, Marlene,' Cathy said with a grin. 'She's a lovely person.'

'I'm sure she'll jump at the chance,' Millie said. 'She's used to cleaning and cooking for quite a few. She had a large brood before they all fled the nest, and she also looked after her mam and dad until they died.'

'She sounds like the perfect housekeeper,' Karen said.

Jean nodded. 'She does indeed. Will you line her up, Alice? Let her know what we're doing, and see if she's interested.'

'I will,' Alice replied. 'And I've just had another thought. We had a foreman called Freddie who was a great gardener and he's also Cathy's godfather. He's semi-retired now and always looking for odd jobs in the area. He has a card in the post office window. Do we need a part-time gardener?

'We will do, definitely. We won't have time to do it ourselves so we'd need to get a man in. He sounds perfect. Put him on the list, Alice.'

'This is great,' Millie said. 'It'll be like old times back at the factory, but instead of planes and bombs, it'll be prams for transport, and babies on the production line. I feel quite left out of things now, but I'm no nurse or midwife, so I'd be no use to you as staff.'

Jean raised an eyebrow. 'How are you at office work and answering the phone, Millie? We'll need a receptionist and someone to man the office. There'll be a lot of filing of notes and records to keep. It needs to be done properly as the powers-that-be from the NCT, and no doubt the NHS and social services, will do checks on us from time to time. It'll be a case of keeping the books balanced and all that.'

'Millie does all my books and paperwork,' Jimmy spoke up. 'And she's never off our bloody phone! She can talk for England. I reckon she'd make a cracking secretary and receptionist. Might as well as keep it in the family and if Cathy's going to be surrounded by her godparents she might as well as have her other godmother on board as well,' he teased.

'I'll put you on the list then,' Alice said, grinning. 'This is all so exciting. I can't wait.'

'Just the permissions to be granted now and we'll crack on,' Johnny said.

'I told Cathy I'm giving half of the money from my mam's place to her to put into the business,' Gianni said. 'I think it's a good investment.'

'Thank you, Gianni,' Johnny said. 'That's more than generous of you. Property is always a good investment if you pick the right place and I feel we're onto a winner here. We can pay some of the mortgage off with your contribution.'

Gianni smiled and looked at Cathy. 'You're okay with that, aren't you?'

'I am, if you are. Feels like we're doing something really good together and that makes me very happy.'

'All our dads are willing to chip in as well,' Jean said. 'Every penny helps.'

'Well I think this has been a very productive meeting. Let's all drink a toast to Woodlands Maternity Home then,' Jimmy said, raising his glass. 'Here's to Woodlands, and all who give birth in her.'

Chapter Sixteen

Jack packed his belongings away and stowed the bag in his allocated cupboard in the shared caravan, placing Gianni's sketchbook underneath and making sure it was well hidden from view just in case the door flew open when the caravan was on the move. He swigged down the mug of coffee he'd made and limped back outside to join the other hands on what was proving to be a very busy afternoon.

The fair was in the process of packing up for the long-awaited move to Liverpool, where they'd be staying until the end of August. He couldn't wait. He'd been told by Lenny that they'd be hitching up in Sefton Park for two full weeks. He missed his home city but he wouldn't be reacquainting himself with any old friends when they got there. He'd check out a few places, see what was happening, but his visit was mainly to see what Cathy was up to.

He wondered if his eldest daughter Sandra was still at school; at fifteen she was due to leave, surely. In his opinion kids should be getting jobs, not idling around taking exams until they were old enough to vote. His own teens and early twenties had been ruined by the war and then he'd lumbered himself with Alice and her brat. His life had not been his own from that day on, until his recent escape from that prison van. It felt good to be free of all responsibilities and to only have himself to think about.

He'd become closer to Eloisa in the last few days, but not so close that he wanted to get too involved. A man in his position couldn't afford to get too close to anyone. When she questioned him about his past he'd had to think on the spot and make stuff up. Keeping track of what he'd told her wasn't easy. Still, not long now; he'd take his revenge on the woman who'd ruined his life and then he'd be off. He might take the steamer to the Isle of Man when he left Liverpool. He quite fancied living by the sea and he'd need another place to hide out as by the time he'd finished in Liverpool, there'd be more than a search warrant out for his arrest.

*

Alice laughed as Marlene flung her plump arms around her. 'So you fancy the job then?' she asked her old workmate, whose face was wreathed in smiles.

'I'll say I do,' Marlene replied. 'It sounds right up my street. What a lovely idea to open a nice home like that.'

'I'm so glad you want to join us. I'm not sure what hours you'll be working until we get going properly. But I'm sure it'll all work out to suit you.'

'We can play it by ear,' Marlene said. 'When do you think it'll be ready to open?'

'Johnny reckons by the new year. They've got the keys now and are clearing stuff out and doing repairs to the roof. The plans for the home go before the committee this week and we're just hoping it gets past. It's all hands on deck once that happens. They've got most of the finance in place.'

'I can't see they'll turn it down,' Marlene mused. 'There are plenty of young girls in need of a bit of help when they get themselves into trouble.'

Alice nodded. 'Many have no one to turn to. Our midwives are kindness itself. They'll help them get back on their feet, no matter which path they choose to take after giving birth.'

'I'm sure they will. And them that can pay a fee will get the best care there is. Better than a hospital bed any day.'

Alice got to her feet. 'Right, well I'll pass on the good news to the others and as soon as I can let you know about when you can start I will. It'll be before we open so that you can get the kitchen organised and let the girls know exactly what you'll need. I'm off to see Freddie now to offer him a gardening and odd-job man position. Keep your fingers crossed that he'll join us.'

'He'll jump at it,' Marlene said. 'You mark my words. Be like old times. I'm looking forward to it already.'

'And me.'

Freddie was just going out as Alice called on him, but he welcomed her indoors.

'I won't keep you a minute,' she said. 'I should have phoned you but I was round the corner at Marlene's and thought I'd take a chance that you were in.'

'I'm only off to the allotment for an hour to get from under my missus's feet,' he said. 'It's good to see you, Alice. Come through to the back room.'

Alice followed him into the tidy room and took a seat of the sofa he pointed at. She could see his wife through the window, pegging out washing.

'Now what can I do for you?'

Alice told him why she was there and he beamed and nodded.

'That would be smashing, queen. I'd love to be involved. And you say Marlene and Millie will be working there as well? It'll be Rootes part two.'

'Freddie, I'm so happy you'll be joining us,' Alice said. 'And the others will all be thrilled to bits. It'll be a great team and I'm sure the whole thing will be a success. I'll get in touch again as soon as I have more news. I need to get off now so I can pick Roddy up from school.'

Freddie showed Alice to the door, his wide smile splitting his face. 'Catch up with you soon, gel.'

Alice waved and dashed away, feeling accomplished. She couldn't wait for everything to fall neatly into place. She thought back to how far she'd come since she had first worked with Millie, Marlene and Freddie at Rootes during the war, and the twists and turns her life had taken since then and now how all the threads were pulling them together again. She was a great believer in fate and the saying, 'what will be, will be'. Hopefully the next few months would fly by with no major problems and they could start 1964 with everything to look forward to.

*

Gianni stood by Sefton Park gates with Lucy on his shoulders as the trucks and caravans drove past him and found places to park. They waved to everyone as each truck arrived and Lucy laughed as the passengers waved and made silly faces at her. Once Luca had parked, he came dashing across the grass to greet them. 'Good to see you again, Dad.' Gianni lifted Lucy down and bent to whisper to her, 'This is your grandpa, Lucy, remember, I told you he was coming today.'

Lucy nodded and smiled shyly. Luca got down to her level on one knee and spoke gently.

'Hello, Lucy. It's so nice to see you again.' He held out his hand and she took it, looking up at Gianni for permission to go with Luca. 'You have to pull me up. My knee hurts a bit today. Can you do that for me?'

'Which knee?' Lucy asked, frowning.

'This one.' Luca pointed to his left knee, the one he wasn't kneeling on.

Lucy let go of his hand, leaned over and dropped a kiss on his knee and then patted it. 'That's better now. Come on, I help you up, Grandpa.'

Gianni smiled. 'She's taking after her mammy. Another nurse in the making.'

'No bad thing there,' Luca said, giving Lucy a hug. 'And she'll be a good one. My knee feels so much better already. Let's go and see Maria. She has something special for you to do.'

Gianni followed them to his dad's caravan, where Maria flung open the door, her arms open wide. 'Welcome, come on in. Oh it is so good to see you both!' She gave Gianni a hug and a peck on his cheek and enveloped Lucy, who happily hugged her back and gave Maria a kiss.

'Oh, she's not at all shy,' Maria said with delight. 'I was so worried she wouldn't remember us at all,' she said to Gianni. 'Lucy, come and see what I've made for you.' Maria led the way to the dining area and opened a tin that was sitting in the middle of the table. She lifted out several gingerbread men and put them on a plate. 'Would you like to give them all eyes and a mouth? I'll show you how while your daddy and grandpa take a look around the fairground.'

Lucy nodded and climbed up onto the bench seat, smiling broadly.

Maria covered her clothes with a dainty pink-and-white gingham apron. 'I made this for you. We don't want to get your dress messy, now, do we?'

'Thanks, Maria,' Gianni said.

'I thought doing this would keep her occupied. It's too busy out there right now, and far too dangerous for a little child to be wandering around. I know you two will want to get ready for working together again.'

Luca nodded. 'It's been a long time. We need to get the wall of death barrel erected and do a rehearsal as soon as possible.'

'Well off you go then. Come back in an hour and I will have some tea and cake ready for you both.'

*

Jack slunk down behind the trailer housing the waltzer ride as he watched Luca and Gianni make their way across to the wall of death trailer. He frowned, wondering what the score would be now they'd all arrived in Liverpool and whether Gianni would be back working with the bike show. He'd need to keep as low a profile as he could until he knew what was happening. He didn't for one minute think Gianni would recognise him, but even so, he was taking no chances. Eloisa would no doubt fill him in with updates when she found out if Gianni was back for good. He could also do with finding out where Cathy was living now and, if she was still nursing, at which hospital she was based. 'All in good time, Jack,' he muttered as Lenny called out for him to come and help unload the waltzer cars. 'All in good time.'

As the fairground hands and Jack lifted the cars from the trailer, and Lenny and two others fixed the sides and the floor of the waltzer together, Jack spotted Eloisa making her way to her mother's caravan. He whistled through his fingers to gain her attention and she spun around and waved at him. He beckoned her over but she shook her head and mouthed 'later' as she ran up the caravan steps. He frowned and carried on with his chores. Not like her to practically ignore him. Maybe she thought Gianni was in the van. He felt a twinge of jealousy. Well she'd soon find out he wasn't because Jack could hear the roar of motorbike engines and guessed Gianni and Luca were preparing to ride around the park. He turned his attention to what Lenny was saying about making sure each car was firmly bolted to the floor.

*

Eloisa hurried up the steps of the caravan, a smile fixed firmly in place. She'd just heard from her hook-a-duck assistant that Gianni had been seen earlier. She hoped he'd be inside talking to his dad. But the smile quickly left her face when she spotted Lucy with Maria at the table. 'What's *she* doing here? Where's Luca and Gianni?'

'Eloisa,' Maria chastised. 'That's no way to speak to the child. She's here helping me to decorate the biscuits while her daddy and grandpa are erecting their ride. And she's doing a very good job too.'

Lucy smiled with importance and stared at Eloisa with her solemn dark eyes.

Eloisa looked away. The brat was so like her mother, apart from her eyes that were Gianni's eyes, deep, dark and huge. 'So they're out unpacking everything? I'll go and see if I can help.'

'Don't you be getting under their feet, now. You should be setting up your own stall.'

'It's ready. There's nothing else much to do. It only took us half an hour.'

'Then make yourself useful and see if anyone else needs a hand. There's a lot to do before tomorrow's opening night, as I'm sure you are well aware.'

Eloisa rolled her eyes. 'See you later,' she said and stomped off outside, slamming the door behind her.

Maria shook her head. 'That girl,' she muttered.

'Is she naughty?' Lucy asked, peering up at Maria from under her fringe.

'Sometimes, yes, she's very naughty,' Maria said, smoothing Lucy's hair from out of her worried eyes. 'But don't you worry about her. Let's finish these gingerbread men and then we can have them with our tea when your daddy and grandpa come back. And you can pick one to take home for your mammy later.'

Eloisa hurried over to the wall of death ride and looked around for Gianni. Marco popped his head over the parapet and asked her what she wanted.

'Just came to say hi to Gianni,' she said, flicking her long hair back over her shoulders. She didn't really like Marco and he made it quite clear he didn't really approve of her. Since she'd lost the baby that his son had fathered, he'd always treated her coldly, only speaking to her when he had to. He'd been angry with Alessandro and sent him back to Italy to his grandparents' home, but he was always saying how much he missed him, probably just to make her feel bad, Eloisa thought.

'He's out across the park with Luca, giving the bikes a run.'

Eloisa nodded and walked away. She looked up at the cloudless blue sky and smiled. Looked like they were in for a hot weekend, which meant the punters would be here in droves tomorrow. She loved it when the fair was busy and the weather was warm and sunny. It made all the difference to her working day. She wandered over to the waltzer, where Dougie had his back to her, stretched out on the floor of the ride fiddling around with a bag of tools. She tapped him on the leg and he looked up.

'That was a short visit to your ma's,' he said, raising an eyebrow and shuffling forward to the rail to pull himself upright.

'I just needed to use the bathroom quickly,' she fibbed. 'Portables are not up and running yet.'

'Oh, aye, thought you might have been to see if she'd got any visitors.'

Eloisa snorted. 'She has. Gianni's little brat is with her.'

'And where are they? He and that wife you're always telling me you can't abide.'

'He's out on the bikes with Luca and *she*, I presume, is at work. Looks like she's lumbered him with the kid and he's dumped her on my mother.'

He shrugged. 'Maybe your mother likes having her there.'

Eloisa stared scornfully at him. 'Are you mad? Why would she? It's not as if it's her own flesh and blood.'

'What's her name, the wee one?'

'Lucy. Why?'

'I just wondered. That's all. Wouldn't do you any harm to be nice to the girl. Not her fault she's got parents who leave her with anybody.'

'Yeah, right. See you later.' He was obviously not going to sympathise with her, so she might as well make herself useful elsewhere. 'Oh, by the way, Dougie,' she said, turning back. 'No one has mentioned it being handed over yet, but did you sort out giving that sketchbook back? Because likely as not Gianni will want to take the rest of his stuff later if he's staying elsewhere with Cathy and not at the van. There won't be enough room for all of them with the brat as well. And I just know that sketchbook will be one of the first things he'll look for.'

'Err, no I forgot,' he muttered. 'We've been so busy with packing up in York and then setting up here. Leave it with me.'

'Oh my God, you are joking? How the hell are you going to give it to Mum without him finding out it's been missing? You can't say it was dropped down behind the caravan today because we've only been here a few hours, and if you told Mum you picked it up in York she'd have expected you to hand something so private back immediately. You are such a stupid idiot, Dougie. You promised me—'

He grabbed her arm and pushed his face close to hers. 'Don't you ever, and I mean *ever*, call me an idiot again. If you hadn't taken it in the first place we wouldn't have this problem. Now piss off out of my sight. I don't want to see you again today.'

'But the sketchbook…' She faltered as he stared at her with such an evil look in his eyes it made her stomach flip. 'I'll tell Gianni you stole it and then you'll be for it. You'll get fired. I'll make sure Luca gets rid of you. I'll tell them what you did to me that time.'

Dougie grabbed her arm again and lowered his mouth to her ear. 'And I'm telling you that if you don't keep your mouth shut you'll rue the day you were born,' he growled. 'Do I make myself clear? Now get out of my way, or you'll be very sorry.'

Eloisa stifled a sob and hurried away without a backward glance. Dougie seemed to hate her today and she had no idea why. All she'd ever done was be nice to him and give him more affection and love than she'd ever given to Ronnie.

There was something about him though and she wondered what he was hiding. He'd just appeared from nowhere in York, had told her so little about his background, and he sometimes told her one thing and then contradicted it with another. She had only questioned him once about that and he'd been angry with her and told her he got confused at times. The painkillers he had to take for his scar on his foot addled his mind a bit, he'd said. She wondered if he'd kept the sketchbook on purpose so that he could look at the sketches of Cathy. Maybe he thought she was better-looking and had a nicer body than hers.

Well he could just sleep on his own tonight. She certainly wasn't sharing a bed with him and that was certain. He wasn't always as clean as he could be lately either, didn't shower very often, never trimmed his beard, and she hated the way he left his big thick socks on when they made love, using his scarred foot as an excuse. It wasn't very romantic but he just wouldn't budge on the matter. She did like him though and he was the best lover she'd ever had, even if he was a bit heavy-handed with her at times. Anyway, he could just get lost until he apologised now. See how *he* liked being ignored.

Chapter Seventeen

'Wow, this is lovely, Lucy,' Cathy enthused as her daughter proudly handed her a gingerbread man, complete with coloured Smarties buttons down the front of his body. 'Aren't you a clever girl? Maria is very kind to let you make them.'

'She's been working hard all afternoon,' Gianni said, ruffling her hair. 'Maria is great with her. I've been helping Dad get the ride up and ready for tomorrow. We had a spin around the car park on the bikes just to get the feel again. I'll go back over later to finish helping before it gets dark. The more we can complete tonight the less there will be to do tomorrow. But I thought it best to bring her home for her tea, knowing you'd be back from work by now. She's really tired as well so I think you'll get her into bed early.'

Cathy nodded. 'Good. I'm shattered. We've had a really busy day on delivery. I'm planning a long soak in the bath and an early night. Is the fair still closed on Sunday, by the way?'

'Yep, so I'm all yours for the day.'

'That's great. I'm off all weekend too. I'll bring Lucy to see everyone and to have a go on the kiddies' rides tomorrow afternoon. Karen and Ellie are off too, so we'll all come down.'

She smiled up at Gianni. 'Thinking about Sunday, I feel I'm ready now to start having a bit of a clear-out at Granny's place. Thought we could make a start this weekend? When we've cleared out what we don't want to keep, Johnny said he'd go and have a good look over to make sure it's all sound and no repairs need doing and then maybe we can have a think about some decorating. If we do a room at a time it will be ready to move into for when you leave the fair. I don't suppose you've said anything to your dad yet?'

He shook his head. 'It didn't feel like the right time this afternoon. But I will do soon.'

'You haven't changed your mind then?'

'Not at all. I told you what I want to do. I'm ready for us to settle down.'

'And be that boring couple we always said we didn't want to be?' she teased.

'Cathy, life with you will never be boring. Look at all that's happening right now. The new business, a new home for us, and Lucy will be starting school in just a short time as well. Big life changes for us all. We should make the most of these next few weeks with her while we can.'

'Are you two ready to eat?' Alice called from the kitchen. 'I'm just about to dish up.'

'We are,' Cathy called back. 'And yes, you're right,' she said to Gianni. 'We should.'

*

'Right, I'll see you later,' Gianni said after tea, kissing Cathy goodbye. 'I won't wake you, don't worry.'

'I bet you do,' Cathy said, grinning. 'Get some more of your clothes from the caravan tonight, then you've got a few extra things to wear. It's hard keeping on top of the washing when you've only got a few bits here.'

'I will. I've a few other things I need to bring over as well. I'll take your holdall bag with me. It's bigger than the one Maria lent me.'

'It's in the cupboard in Lucy's room. I'll go and get it for you.'

'I'll say goodnight to her while you do that.'

Cathy headed upstairs and he went into the back room, where Lucy was ready for bed and sitting on the sofa with Rodney and

Rosie, who was reading them both a bedtime story. He dropped a kiss on Lucy's head and waved goodbye to the others. Sandra looked up from reading her magazine at the table and smiled.

'We're coming to the fair on Saturday afternoon,' she announced. 'Well, I'm coming early with Ben. Mam and the others will come along later after Johnny finishes work. Can't wait for a go on the waltzer, and to see you riding your bike.'

'I'll watch out for you and give you a special wave. See you all tomorrow. You'll be in bed by the time I get home.' He turned as Cathy came into the room with the holdall and she accompanied him to the front door. 'See you later.' He dropped a kiss on her lips and strolled off up the street.

When they moved on from Liverpool the fair would head for Chester and he could still come home some nights if his dad lent him the car. Mind you, he could now actually afford to buy one of his own. It was something to look into when he had a bit of spare time. He quite fancied a Volkswagen Beetle. A nice shiny black one. He patted his jacket pocket to make sure his dad's keys were still in there. Pointless driving to the park tonight as it was only a short stroll away and saved him time looking for a parking space. He'd left the car outside Alice's where he knew it would be quite safe.

When he got to his dad's caravan he decided to pack his things before going over to help them finish erecting the ride. The door was unlocked, as he'd expected it would be; fairground folk were trusting and never stole from their own kind. The place was empty. His storage cupboard was at the bottom of the van over the bunk that he'd slept in. He opened the doors and lifted down a pile of T-shirts, socks, underwear and jeans. He left his show clothes neatly folded where Maria had placed them on the shelf after washing and ironing them for him. She was good to him, just like his mam had been.

He swallowed the lump that had risen in his throat as he thought of his mam and how proud she would be of Lucy. But he knew too how disappointed she would have been at him joining the fair. Well, this lifestyle would soon be over and he would be the hard-working draughtsman that she'd wanted him to be, as well as the good stable husband and father that Cathy and Lucy deserved. He opened the next cupboard along, where he stored his art stuff. He lifted down packs of pencils and pens, sticks of charcoal and two small drawing pads. Where the heck was his large sketchbook containing his sketches of Cathy? He climbed up on to the bunk and peered inside. It was empty. He took a deep breath and jumped down, scratching his head. *Where the hell was it?*

Cathy would go absolutely mental if anyone saw it. He'd promised her faithfully that he would never show a soul those drawings. They were for his eyes only. She had no idea that Eloisa had once looked at it. The sketchbook had been well hidden, placed flat to the shelf in the cupboard. Whoever had taken it knew what they were looking for.

He knew it was unlikely that either his dad or Maria would do something like that. The only cupboard Maria went in was the one with his clothes. So the obvious culprit was Eloisa. She knew about the sketchbook; but he'd kept it hidden from her eyes for ages now. She must have had a good root around to find it. But why would she want to look at pictures of his almost naked wife? That was a bit weird to say the least. He finished packing everything away and zipped up the holdall, leaving it on his bunk to collect later.

Gianni felt his pulse quicken with a mixture of anger and fear, wondering who else had seen the drawings of Cathy. The only way to find out was to go and ask Eloisa, if he could find her. Outside the caravan area the park was teeming with people going about the business of setting their stalls up and getting the rides in place for tomorrow. He waved and smiled as people called his name in greeting. Eloisa's stall was being looked after by a young lad. He was busy filling the shelves with china rabbits and stuffed toys, prizes for those lucky enough to hook a duck with a matching number. For the others there were smaller consolation prizes too. 'Hi, Tony, any idea where Eloisa is?' Gianni asked, glancing round in the hope she'd magically materialise.

'Nope, sorry, Gianni. I haven't seen her since this afternoon and she was having a right old row with that Scottish bloke near the waltzer.'

'Scottish bloke? Oh, you mean that new hand we hired over in York?'

'Yeah, him. Dougie Taylor he's called. She's been seeing him but don't let on I told you. It's a touchy subject because Ronnie's my mate and she wasn't very nice to him when she dumped him for that bloke.'

'Fair enough. I'll see if she's hanging around with my dad at the ride. See you later.'

Gianni walked across the grass and passed Maria's gypsy fortune-telling tent. He popped his head inside to see Maria looking perplexed as she polished her crystal ball with a large white handkerchief. 'Do you have any idea where Eloisa is?' he asked as she looked up and half-smiled at him.

She shook her head. 'Not right now. She had her supper and then went straight back out again, not long after you left with Lucy.'

'Can't you ask your crystal ball?' he joked and then as her face clouded he wished he hadn't said anything. 'What's wrong?'

She sighed and shook her head. 'I see danger again. It is everywhere around us and this fairground. It worries me; it's a feeling that I get in here.' She patted her chest. 'In my heart. Protect your family, Gianni. They need it. I was right before when I warned you and you took no heed of me that time. Well, I am warning you once again. Look after them.'

Gianni shrugged and thanked her before going on towards his dad and the bikes. She had been right a few years ago when he and Cathy had split up for a while. But now, surely everyone would be okay. Cathy wasn't pregnant and roaming the country on her own looking for him; she was here safe and sound with her family, and so was Lucy.

And Jack, one of the dangers back then – well, he was in Scotland, about as far away as he could be. He wouldn't dare to show his face in Liverpool. Too many people knew him and would be on the lookout for him. He had no place to hide round here. Gianni waved at his dad and Uncle Marco and pushed any thoughts of danger from his mind. He'd have to find Eloisa later and have it out with her about his sketchbook.

'We've finished putting everything up,' Luca said, breaking his train of thought. 'Let's have a go at our routine now, see if we can all remember it.'

Gianni climbed onto his Indian Scout bike, the buzz of adrenaline flowing through his veins. The thrill never left him. It would be so difficult to live without it, but a nice car would be so much better for family trips out. He'd get used to it, given time.

When Gianni left the fairground that night he still hadn't managed to find Eloisa, nor that Dougie bloke she was supposed to be involved with. Well, he was blowed if he was going knocking on the door of his caravan, in case they were in there together. Ronnie and the other lad who shared with him were both sat on the grass in the middle of the caravans having a drink and a sing-song. He picked up his holdall and set off for home, shouting goodbye to his dad, Maria and Uncle Marco. He'd have to wait until tomorrow now to try to corner Eloisa.

Chapter Eighteen

Cathy cleared a space in the wardrobe in Lucy's room and hung Gianni's clothes up. She put his sketchbooks and pens and the rest of his art stuff in the sideboard cupboard downstairs. She frowned as she reached into the bottom of the holdall and realised that the big sketchbook he'd used in the past to draw pictures of her wasn't in there. She hoped he hadn't left it lying around in the caravan to be found by his dad or Maria. She'd be mortified to think anyone else had laid eyes on it. He was in the bath and when she took the empty holdall upstairs to put back in the bottom of the wardrobe, she tapped on the bathroom door. 'Only me,' she called out.

'Come in, only you, it's unlocked.'

She slipped inside and closed the door. He was relaxing in the steaming pine-scented water and smiled up at her. 'Nice stuff this Radox.'

'It is,' she said. 'Um, I've just unpacked your bag and put everything away, including your pens and stuff. But there were only two small sketchbooks in there. Where's the big one, with, well, you know?' She chewed her lip as he rolled his eyes.

'I'm not sure, Cath. It wasn't in my cupboard when I took everything out.'

'Oh no. Where the hell is it then? You must remember what you did with it.'

'Yes, I do remember perfectly well. I had it the night before I left the fair in a hurry. I put it back exactly where I always put it. But it wasn't there when I looked today. Someone has taken it out and I doubt very much that it was Dad or Maria, which only leaves one other person.'

Cathy stared at him, feeling her eyes widening in horror. 'Eloisa? But why would she take it?'

'No idea. I've looked for her everywhere today to tackle her about it, but couldn't find her. I'll have it out with her tomorrow.'

'Well if you don't, I will,' she said. 'Why would she want to look at pictures of me?'

Gianni shook his head. 'No idea, love and I'm so sorry. She's obviously done it to be spiteful, or to get at me, or something, but God knows why. I always avoid her like the plague.'

'She a bitch,' Cathy spat. 'I hate her. She's jealous of what we have.'

He nodded. 'Yes, I think you're probably right. Don't worry, Cath. I'll get it back one way or another.'

*

Eloisa snuck out of Dougie's caravan at two in the morning just before the other hands arrived back. In spite of him telling her where to go earlier, he'd searched her out later in the day and dragged her back. He'd said very little about the sketchbook other than that he would make sure it was returned tomorrow and not to mention it again. He'd hardly spoken to her while they'd been together tonight. No apologies or any tender words.

They'd shared a couple of bottles of ale and a small bottle of whisky until she was too drunk to care what he did. He'd been rough and growling out commands in a voice that didn't sound like his, but she hadn't dared to say anything to stop him in case he hurt her. Afterwards he'd fallen asleep with his back to her and she'd taken her leave and crept home to the safety of her own bed. Earlier she'd seen Gianni going home to his family and had been told by a few people that he'd been looking everywhere for her.

She knew why and just hoped it would all be sorted by the time the fair kicked off tomorrow afternoon. She could live in hope. No doubt Cathy would be around at some point tomorrow, so she'd have to face her if she was.

*

Cathy smiled as Lucy hung onto Karen and Ellie's hands, lifting her feet off the ground as she swung between them squealing with joy. Cathy had invited them to have a look around the bungalow first and then they'd all taken their time strolling along to the fairground.

'It's perfect. You are lucky, Cathy,' Ellie had said as they stood out in the back garden that was starting to look a bit like a jungle now. She would need to get in touch with the gardeners Granny had used next week before it got completely out of hand.

'I know,' Cathy said. 'We're very lucky. I can't wait now for us to move in and make it our own. We always had really nice times here, Uncle Brian and I, as children. I want to replicate some of that for my own family. Well for Lucy anyway, and our little Roddy as I know he'll love to come and play with her. I'm hoping we can be in for Christmas.'

'You might have another little one of your own when you feel ready,' Karen said. 'And you'll know where to come and give birth and get first-class care.'

Cathy sighed. 'To be honest, I'm a bit scared of getting pregnant again after my miscarriage. Maybe, in time. But for now I'm looking forward to being part of our new venture.'

'There's Daddy,' Lucy shouted excitedly as they walked onto the fair site. 'Daddeeee.' She let go of Karen and Ellie's hands and shot across to Gianni, who swung her up into his arms and then transferred her onto his shoulders.

'Afternoon, girls,' he greeted them, dropping a kiss onto Cathy's lips. 'Lovely day again. It's getting a bit crowded already. I've just been back to the caravan to get changed ready for the first show.

We've been rehearsing most of the morning. Come and say hi to Maria. She'll be really pleased to see you.'

'You go and see your family and we'll have a wander around,' Karen said. 'Catch up with you later. What time does your bike show start, Gianni?'

'The first performance is at two thirty,' he replied.

'We'll meet you by the wall of death then, Cathy,' Karen said. 'I fancy some candyfloss. Where's the stall?'

'Over in that direction.' Gianni pointed ahead. 'Doreen makes the best candyfloss and toffee apples in the world. Just follow the smell.' He waved them off as they linked arms and hurried away.

'Did you speak to Eloisa?' Cathy asked, following him over to the caravan, where Maria was sitting on the steps with a delicate china cup in her hands. She was turning it this way and that and frowning, tutting every few seconds.

'Reading the tea leaves?' Gianni said, making her jump.

'Oh, Gianni, I had no idea you were there. I'm just seeing if there's anything good about to happen today but all I can see is—'

'Danger,' Luca said for her as he appeared at the top of the steps, and rolled his eyes.

'You should not mock me,' Maria scolded.

'But you see danger in everything you look at, love,' Luca said as Gianni and Cathy hid their smiles. 'You always have done.'

'And I am always right. Is that not so?'

'Well it depends on who you're doing readings for. I mean, you told Lenny's wife he was seriously ill the other week when he said he'd got a pain in his foot. She'd all but got him dead and buried and was dusting off the policies. Turns out he had an ingrown toenail.'

'Yes and it was turning septic. If he hadn't come to me, he might have died before he'd got help. You mock me but we'll see. There is something not good in the air right now. Mark my words.'

'Yes, dear,' Luca said. 'I'm listening. Anyway, here's my little nurse, Lucy. Come to Grandpa, my darling.'

He held out his arms and Gianni lifted Lucy down and passed her to his dad.

'Is Eloisa around?' Gianni asked. 'I need a quick word with her.'

Maria looked at her watch. 'She should be on her stall now getting ready for opening.'

'Thanks. Can we just leave Lucy with you for a few minutes?'

'Of course. I'll take her on one of the little rides. I'll call out for one of you if I'm needed in my tent for fortune-telling.'

'We won't be long, and then Cathy will take her from you.' Gianni grasped Cathy's hand as they walked across to Eloisa's stall.

She was busy with a customer, so Gianni and Cathy stood close by watching. Her assistant Tony nudged her as she finished and she looked across, her cheeks pinking slightly. She swept her long hair back over her shoulders and came out from behind the stall with a swish of floaty skirts, her low-cut top revealing her deep cleavage. Eloisa looked at Gianni, her heavy-lidded eyes roving up and down his body. Cathy held his hand tightly, aware of how sexy her handsome husband looked in his show outfit of tight black leather trousers and red satin shirt. His dad and Marco wore the same, but Gianni looked the best, she thought.

'What can I do for you, Gianni?' Eloisa said with a smirk. She deliberately ignored Cathy and licked her glossy red lips as she continued to stare at him.

'You can tell me what you did with my sketchbook,' he began. 'It's missing from my cupboard.'

She shrugged. 'Sketchbook? No idea what you mean. I've not clapped eyes on any sketchbook.' She turned to walk away but he grabbed her arm and pulled her back.

She looked at his hand holding on to her and smirked. 'See, he just can't keep his hands off me, Cathy.'

Cathy gritted her teeth and took a step forward but Gianni held up his hand to stop her coming any closer. 'You do know what I mean,' he said, raising his voice. 'You're the only one who knows where I keep my art stuff in the caravan. Now tell me what you've done with that sketchbook, or I'll…'

Eloisa raised an eyebrow. 'Or you'll what? I haven't got it and I don't bloody well know where it is. Now if you'll kindly let go of me, I have customers to see to.'

He let her go and stepped back, a look of fury on his face.

'I'll see to the customers,' Tony called. 'Sounds like you need to sort things out with Gianni.'

'There's nothing to sort out.' Eloisa turned to Cathy. 'I don't know what *you're* looking so smug about. Think you can trust him, don't you? Well I know better. He's always making passes at me.' She flounced away, leaving Cathy staring after her.

'Take absolutely no notice of her,' Gianni said, holding Cathy's hand tight and leading the way back to the caravan. 'She's totally insane. I wouldn't go near her for all the money in the world.'

'She's horrible,' Cathy said. 'I can't believe she's Maria's daughter.' She glanced back over her shoulder to see Eloisa standing with a tall, bearded man who had his arm around her waist and was leering down her top. 'Who's that she's with? Looks old enough to be her father.'

Gianni glanced back. 'Some fella called Dougie that joined us in York. She dumped Ronnie for him.'

'She's actually seeing him? Bloody hell. Is she desperate? I'm so glad you're leaving this fair. I want you all to myself.'

'Can't be done,' he said, a teasing look in his eyes. 'What will the other lady in my life say to that?'

'Other lady? Oh, you mean little madam,' she said as Lucy came hurtling towards them and flung herself at Gianni's legs.

'I rode a motorbike like your one, Daddy,' she announced as Maria came into view, panting behind her.

'I couldn't get her off the little ride,' Maria said. 'She wouldn't come off the bike. She had three goes on it. It was the only bike on there as well; the other vehicles were cars and a bus. She made a beeline for the bike.'

'A boy was crying. He wanted a go,' Lucy said. 'But I told him, "no you can't, it's my bike" and he went back to his mammy and cried. What a big baby.'

Cathy hid her smile. 'Now that's not very nice, Lucy. Poor little boy. You have to be kind to people and learn to share.'

'It's okay, he's having a go now,' Maria said. 'It's nearly showtime for you,' she directed at Gianni. 'Did you find Eloisa?'

'We did, for what it was worth. Right, I'll get off and join my dad and Marco. Catch up with you later.' He kissed Cathy lips, ruffled Lucy's hair and strode away.

'Be careful,' Cathy called after him.

He turned, waved and mouthed, 'I will.'

*

Eloisa's stomach twisted in a knot of jealousy as she watched Gianni and Cathy walk away hand-in-hand. She jumped as a hand fell on her shoulder.

'Hope that's not a wistful look you're giving him,' Jack whispered in her ear.

'Oh, Dougie, you scared the life out of me. You daft thing, of course it's not a wistful look. But you can guess what he's been asking me about, can't you?'

He nodded. 'I've been thinking about that and how best to go about it. To be honest, I reckon it's best if we burn it, don't you?'

'No, we can't do that. It needs to go back and I'll have to do it when no one is around. You'll have to give it to me later and I'll put it in the cupboard when Mum and Luca are sleeping. When Gianni comes back to the fair for good after this stint in Liverpool he's got to put his stuff away in those cupboards anyway and he'll find it then. With a bit of luck he won't ask any questions.'

Jack raised an eyebrow. 'Hmm, let me have a think about it. Right, I'd better get to work. I'm on ghost train duties. See you later.' He gave her a squeeze around the waist and dropped a kiss on her lips – after taking an eyeful of her cleavage.

*

Sandra and Ben walked hand-in-hand up Lark Lane and made their way to Sefton Park. Her mam and Johnny and the kids were just in front. Sandra felt so excited. She was dying to watch Cathy's husband ride the bikes. Cathy hated him doing it but it sounded so exciting to Sandra. She wished she and Ben could swap places with her sister and Gianni and do all that travelling in a caravan. So much more exciting than being stuck in Liverpool all week. At the park, they wandered around. Ben bought her some fluffy pink candyfloss and she shared it with him.

She loved this, the smell of frying onions, the noise and fumes from the generators and the music blasting over the tannoy system. She did a little wiggle to the Everly Brothers' song 'Cathy's Clown' and then Ben led her over to the waltzer. The operator spun them round and round, Sandra clinging onto the bar across their laps and then screaming as she was thrown across Ben. She felt dizzy when they got off. At the hook-a-duck stall Ben won her a white pottery duck. She glanced sideways at the girl who took Ben's money and handed him his prize, and pulled on his arm.

'Think that's the girl that fancies our Gianni,' she whispered. 'Cathy was always moaning about her.'

Ben laughed and led her away from the stall. 'What do you want to do now?'

'Let's just stroll around a bit more. Then we'll have a ride on the ghost train. Also, I want to find a fortune-teller but I don't know if I'm brave enough to get my palm read or see the future in a crystal ball.'

Ben laughed. 'I don't believe in all that sort of stuff, but my mam does.'

Sandra smiled. 'Well I know what my future will be anyway. I'm gonna be a nurse like our Cathy. Just gotta pass my exams and I'm off.'

'I want to join the police force,' Ben said. 'Me and you would be set up for life with good jobs.'

Sandra smiled at him and they stopped at the fortune-telling tent and read the posters pinned up outside.

Maybe she'd have a go later. But for now Ben was calling her name and heading for the ghost train.

*

Jack walked away from Eloisa, his mind in a whirl. He'd spotted Cathy with Gianni earlier and she was as beautiful in the flesh as Gianni had made her look in his drawings. She was as slim as she used to be, but curvy in the right places. Glossy dark hair that swung freely down her back and moved around her face as the gentle wind lifted it. He couldn't part with that sketchbook, but had no idea how to stop Eloisa having a hysterical fit on him and snatching it from his hands. He took his seat in the ghost train kiosk and prepared himself for the onslaught. There was already a queue of kids and teenagers beginning to form.

'Hey, Sandra, over here, gel. Let's go on the ghost train,' a young lad was yelling at his girlfriend, who was busy eyeing up the fortune-telling tent. The girl turned and ran towards him, her neat white skirt showing off her shapely legs and her long dark hair streaming out behind her.

Jack frowned. The girl looked vaguely familiar. And then as the couple drew nearer he realised with shock that it was Sandra, his eldest daughter. Fuck, *she'd* grown up. He hoped she wouldn't recognise him. 'Yes, son,' he mumbled in as strong an accent as he could manage. After giving him the once-over, but showing no signs of recognition, Sandra was now looking over towards the fortune-teller's tent again. Good.

'Two please.' The lad handed over a two-shilling piece and Jack gave him his change. Keeping his head as low as he could, Jack pointed them in the direction of the platform, where the operator showed them which car to get into. He was just getting over the shock of that when he spotted the rest of his estranged family in the distance. Alice, his other two kids, Rosie and young Rodney, along with Millie from next door and her little lad, and with them were Johnny and Jimmy, the brothers. Jack felt genuinely sick and thought he might throw up any minute. He had to get out of there before anyone recognised him.

What on earth had he been thinking, staying with the fair once it arrived here? His whole past was standing around in this park. All he needed now was for bloody Sheila or Lorraine to come strolling in and that would be that. No matter how much he'd disguised himself, they weren't *all* daft. So far he'd been with folk who wouldn't know him from Adam, but this was dangerous. He called to the bloke doing the operating. 'Frankie, mate, I can't do this. My stomach's playing me up something shocking. Must have eaten something dodgy. I'm gonna have to go back to the van for a while before I throw up.'

'Okay, Dougie. I'll ask Lenny to pull someone off another ride. Hope you feel better later.'

'Ta.' Jack hurried back to his caravan. He needed to get away from here. Though God only knew where. He packed his belongings in his rucksack and then decided it wasn't big enough for all the stuff he'd accumulated over the past few weeks, so had a root through Ronnie's cupboards and found a small suitcase. Just the job. And that bloody sketchbook would fit at the bottom.

Or should he leave it behind and let one of the lads find it and give it to Luca? It had Gianni's name on the cover, so whoever found it would surely hand it over right away. Even if they had a bit of an ogle at Cathy first, he was pretty sure it would end up back with its rightful owner. He lay down on his bed, trying to think what to do next. He'd best leave it here. It was one less thing to identify him by if the police picked him up. He decided to stay put for a few hours, and pretend to be really ill if anyone came to look for him. If Eloisa came knocking, he wouldn't answer the door. Once the crowds started to thin out and darkness fell, he'd make his escape, but to God only knew where. He had a few quid saved, but it wouldn't last him long.

Running away was not going to help him get his hands on Cathy. He'd need to think this out carefully while he had a bit of time. He'd have a rifle round the clothes lying around in a minute or two. See if anyone had left any cash in their pockets.

Chapter Nineteen

By the time it was starting to get really dark and the remaining punters were leaving, Jack had managed to accumulate a fair few quid. He'd snuck into nearly all the unlocked caravans close by and rooted through pockets, bags and jam jars left on shelves with handfuls of loose change in them. He'd also got his hands on a set of car keys.

Gianni had left a jacket hanging over the back of a chair in Luca and Maria's caravan. He knew Luca had lent him his Ford Consul and that it would likely be parked outside Alice's place on Lucerne Street or even Ma Lomax's bungalow. Absolutely perfect; neither place was far. He'd wait until the family was all in bed and head over to Alice's first. He couldn't see them being up much beyond midnight with the kids. Tomorrow was Sunday and they would no doubt have a lie-in, so he could be well away by the time anyone realised the car had gone. He hadn't driven for a long time and he hoped he could still manage it with his bloody wooden foot.

He wondered how long it would take for anyone to realise they'd been robbed. Probably ages because they were a very trusting community who never locked their doors. He looked through the window as he heard voices outside getting closer. The stall and ride owners were slowly making their way back to their caravans. It would be a while before Ronnie and the other lad showed up here as they usually sat around outside, sharing a few bottles of ale. That was good because they would be three sheets to the wind, fall asleep as soon as their heads hit the pillow, and he'd be able to slip away unnoticed.

He made a mug of coffee and a sandwich; it might be a while before he ate again. Although if he headed for the Dock Road in the morning, there used to be a café down there that did a good breakfast for next to nothing. He'd have the car by then, so getting to it wouldn't be a problem. He couldn't chance getting on a bus for fear of being recognised. Then he'd head to North Wales or the Isle of Man on a ferry; but for now he needed to focus on getting out of Liverpool until he had a proper plan. Stupid of him to come here in the first place. Getting revenge on Cathy was hardly worth going back to prison for. But then again, it was very tempting to hang around and take his chances – but it seemed like she was never alone. There was always someone with her.

*

Eloisa took a lengthy drag on her cigarette and frowned as she watched a shadowy figure moving stealthily between the copse of trees at the side of the caravans. The person had their back to her, so she couldn't tell in the half-moonlight if it was male or female, but from the height and build she'd guess at male. She'd been unable to sleep, tossing and turning long after everyone else had gone to bed, and had decided to sit on the steps of the caravan. The night was stifling but it had clouded over and there'd been rumblings of thunder. She was feeling a bit fed up because Dougie hadn't let her in when she'd gone to see if he was okay. She'd been told he was unwell and had gone to his caravan to rest. It had been all in darkness when she'd last knocked on the door, giving up after calling his name twice and getting no response. If he'd been poorly, he was probably sleeping it off.

She stared at the person for a few seconds longer and then as they turned sideways on she thought she saw a beard. Dougie? Hard to tell really. At least four other hands had beards of varying lengths. He had a large rucksack on his back that made him look like a hunchback in this half-light and she was sure now that she saw him limping. If it *was* Dougie, where the heck was he going? She dashed back inside and quickly pulled on a pair of jeans and a lightweight sweater, thrust her feet into shoes and left the caravan, keeping her distance, creeping stealthily behind him.

The trees thickened after a few more yards and Eloisa shivered as the branches took on sinister shapes. The moon was behind the clouds now and every shadow spooked her. She almost jumped out of her skin as she trod on a twig and it cracked loudly. She was aware of whoever it was stopping ahead of her. They stayed quiet but she thought she could hear them breathing.

An owl hooted above her head, and she jumped and gave a stifled squeal. She lost sight of the figure and didn't know which way to go. Straight ahead probably led towards the park entrance. Taking a deep breath as thunder rumbled in the distance, she crept forward, glancing from left to right as she walked. She felt really scared now. Maybe she should turn back. As she concentrated on finding her way back, keeping her head down to make sure she didn't trip, a hand shot out from behind a tree and grabbed her. The owner of the hand spun her around so that she couldn't see him and, before she could scream, had clamped a hand across her mouth.

'What the fuck do you think you're doing?' a rough Scouse voice growled in her ear. 'Why are you following me?'

Eloisa couldn't see the man but from his familiar smell, sweaty body mingled with Old Spice and nicotine, she knew it was Dougie. But that wasn't his voice. She wriggled and tried to kick out at him – if she could get him on the knee he wouldn't be able to hold on to her with his bad foot as he would wobble and lose his footing. But he spun her around and held on to her. He slapped her across the face and split her lip, swearing at her in that strange guttural accent. He knocked her to the floor and sat astride her.

'Dougie, stop it, it's me, Eloisa. Why are you doing this?' Maybe he hadn't recognised her. She felt her nose crunch as he punched her in the face, all the while telling her to shut her bloody mouth.

'You're all the same, bloody women. Alice, Sheila, and that brat Cathy. All needy and bloody useless. And you, you're no different. None of you are worth doing time for.'

Eloisa gritted her teeth and with all her strength pushed him as hard as she could. He fell backwards and she struggled to her feet, holding on to a nearby tree trunk to steady herself. She was seeing stars and felt very wobbly from the punch to her face. Why had he mentioned Cathy, and wasn't her mother called Alice? And that accent – where was the gentle Scottish accent Dougie usually spoke with? A sudden streak of lightning flashed overhead, highlighting the man struggling now to get to his feet. As she stood close to him she saw him raise an arm and push her to the floor. She fell backwards and the last thing she was conscious of before oblivion took over was him fiddling with the foot she lay near and covering it with his long thick sock that had rolled down in the scuffle.

*

Jack caught his breath and looked at the crumpled form of Eloisa lying near his feet. There was a pool of blood forming at the back of her head where she'd hit a rock as she'd dropped backwards. Shit, her eyes were closed and she wasn't moving. *Was she dead?* Her face was covered in blood from her broken nose and her lips were badly swollen. She was hardly recognisable. He felt a sudden rush of guilt for the mess she looked, but it was her own fault for following him. There was no way she was going to stop him making his escape. With a bit of luck he'd be well away before anyone found her. There'd been loads of punters at the fair today, and any one of them could have been responsible for attacking her. He took a deep breath and limped away as fast as he possibly could. He just hoped Luca's car was on Lucerne Street and easily accessible.

He peered down Linnet Lane first but could see no sign of the distinctive black-and-yellow Consul. Good. That must mean the car was at Alice's. He shuffled along to Lark Lane and, taking a few furtive glances over his shoulder, turned onto Lucerne Street. The houses were all in darkness, just the streetlights casting a glow. The moon was hidden behind clouds again. Lightning flashed, followed quickly by rolling thunder.

He could see the car parked a few houses down and unlocked the door, sliding onto the driver's seat. He looked across at Alice's house but all was dark and silent, as were the next-door neighbours and the houses directly across the street. Hopefully he wouldn't be seen.

Jack took a deep breath and started up the engine. It purred to life immediately and he slipped it into first gear and pulled gingerly away from the kerb. He held his breath as he changed gear, pushing down the clutch with his good left foot. Even on the side with the wooden foot he still had feelings in his leg, and he put gentle pressure on the accelerator pedal. The car moved along almost effortlessly. It was almost new and smooth to drive. Once he was out on Aigburth Road he carefully headed for Liverpool city centre and the docks. He checked the petrol gauge and smiled with relief when he saw the tank was half full. He had enough money to put a bit more petrol in if he needed to, but then he'd have to abandon the car and make his way on foot to heaven knew where. Fortunately he'd got a rolled-up sleeping bag tied to his rucksack so at least he wouldn't be cold at night if he had to sleep rough.

*

Maria banged and clattered around the caravan kitchen, muttering loudly to herself, until Luca could stand it no longer. What the hell was wrong with her now? She'd been edgy all day yesterday, muttering on about danger until it had nearly driven him mad. He slid out of bed and joined her.

'Maria, it's Sunday morning. I was hoping for a lie-in after the busy day we had yesterday. What on earth is wrong with you?'

'Eloisa. She stayed out all night.' Maria banged a frying pan onto the stove. 'No doubt with that man, that Dougie. I don't like him. He's too old for my daughter. You need to tell him.'

Luca shook his head. 'Eloisa is a grown woman. She's old enough to know what she wants. I've no idea how old Dougie really is, he just said in his thirties, but that could mean one end of the scale or the other. He works hard and keeps his head down and doesn't get under my feet.'

'Well I still don't like him. I will tell her so when she rolls home later.'

But by three o'clock Eloisa still wasn't home and Gianni had arrived with Lucy.

'You were up early this morning, Dad,' Gianni said. 'I was quite shocked when I pulled back the curtains and saw the car had gone. Cathy said maybe you'd taken Maria out for the day. We've been at Cathy's gran's place doing some sorting out and this one has been playing with Rodney—' He stopped as a puzzled expression crossed Luca's face.

'Son, I haven't got the car. You say it's gone from outside Alice's?'

Gianni nodded. 'Well you're the only other one with keys, so I assumed you'd taken it.'

Luca rummaged in his pockets and pulled out a set of keys. The car key was on the ring. 'Where are yours?' he asked Gianni.

'Right here.' Gianni felt in his jacket pockets, then frowned. 'Well they were there yesterday, definitely. I left my jacket in here while we worked.' He paused as someone hammered on the door.

Maria opened it and let in an agitated Lenny and his wife.

'Lenny,' Luca said. 'What's wrong?'

'We've been robbed,' Lenny's wife Irene said. 'My Lenny's wallet has been emptied and the few bob I had in me purse has gone. And them next door said they've had stuff nicked from their caravan as well.'

'My car keys were taken from Gianni's pocket here yesterday,' Luca told them. 'And my car has been stolen overnight from outside his mother-in-law's house on Lucerne Street.'

'Where's that then?' Lenny asked.

'Over that way' – Luca pointed over his shoulder – 'Just off Lark Lane.'

Lenny rubbed his chin with his fingers as though deep in thought. 'So who would have known that car keys taken from inside this caravan would belong to a car parked a few streets away?'

'Only someone who knew that it was,' Maria said. 'It has to be family. But there's only Eloisa, apart from us.'

Luca grunted. 'Unless she told someone. I think we'd better go and get her over here.' He stormed off out of the caravan, leaving the others with puzzled expressions.

'Where is she?' Gianni asked.

'With that Dougie man. She hasn't been home all night as far as we know. Please, sit down all of you and I will make us strong coffee.'

'Well that may sort out who took the car, but what about the money?' Lenny said, handing round cigarettes. Maria and Gianni declined but Irene took one and Lenny held out his lighter. She puffed frantically.

'We ain't got no money for food now,' Irene said. 'It's downright disgusting. We've never had no trouble like this before. We're all as honest as the day is long on this fairground. Like one big happy family.'

'Luca will see you're all right for money, Irene. Please don't worry,' Maria assured her as Luca came back, shaking his head.

'She's not there and neither is that Dougie fella,' he told them. 'All his belongings are gone and so is Ronnie's backpack and sleeping bag. Seems they've all had money and stuff stolen as well. In fact as I'm walking around people are telling me they've all been robbed. Even loose-change jars are empty.'

Maria's hands fluttered and she cried out, 'I told you there was danger in the air.'

'Yes, you did,' Luca said. 'Right, we need to call the police, tell them we've had several thefts and see what they make of it.'

'But where is my daughter?' Maria said. 'She's a good girl; she wouldn't steal from her own. Maybe that man made her do it and he's kidnapped her.'

Gianni rolled his eyes. 'Maria, I doubt anyone would kidnap Eloisa. She'd kick up too much of a fuss. More like she's gone off with him of her own accord. I saw the pair of them from a distance yesterday and they seemed very close.'

Luca nodded his head. 'I think Gianni is right. I'll go and use the phone box by the park gates. Tell anyone else that comes knocking on the door about the theft that we have it all in hand.'

*

Tony, the Ferris wheel operator's son, shouted his dogs to heel but they ignored him, gambolling on ahead and barking relentlessly in the little copse near to where the caravans were parked. He rattled their leads and called their names again. The barking continued. 'I suppose I'd better come and see what you're barking about. I hope you haven't found another hedgehog or you'll be covered in fleas again and Ma won't like that,' he called after them.

He ploughed through the fallen branches and brittle pinecones – and stopped dead. One of the dogs was nosing at something on the ground and whimpering. 'Jesus, Mary and Joseph,' Tony gasped and made the sign of the cross in the air. 'Come away, boys.' He grabbed the dogs' collars, fastened their leads back on and ran as fast as he could back to the caravans, screaming, 'Help, help! There's a body in the copse.'

Chapter Twenty

Leaving Lucy in the care of Irene and Lenny, Gianni hurried back to Lucerne Street to get Cathy and Alice. His garbled story of needing help at the fairground had them throwing all the equipment they could find into Cathy's nurse's bag and dashing back with him. He'd told them police and an ambulance had been called but not that the injured person was Eloisa.

When they arrived Maria was crying, 'Is she dead? Is my daughter dead?' and Cathy realised who the young woman on the ground was. Luca held Maria in his arms as Cathy knelt beside Eloisa's still form.

'There's a faint pulse,' Cathy said quietly to Alice. 'She's alive, but only just. I'll clean her face up as best I can, but I'm not moving her as she seems to have a serious head wound.' The blood was congealing on the ground and matting Eloisa's thick hair. 'She's going to need X-rays to determine the damage, as well as stitches. Looks like she fell backwards and hit her head on that big rock. But her facial injuries tell me she was assaulted first. Whoever did this really went for her.'

She set to work with Alice's help and by the time the ambulance and police car arrived, Eloisa looked a bit less bloody. Her eyes were starting to bruise and her nose was crushed. She was still only semi-conscious but had moaned softly as she was lifted on to a stretcher and whisked away in the waiting ambulance with the bells clanging. Maria had gone with her, but Luca was asked by the police to stay behind while they talked to him and took some statements.

Gianni stayed with his dad while Cathy and Alice took Lucy back home. She was upset; she had clearly realised something was wrong when all the adults had been so worried. 'I'll see you later,' Gianni said. 'Perhaps Johnny will take my dad to join Maria when we've finished here with the police. I'll bring him home with me.'

As the two police officers sat in the caravan with them after taking short statements from all the other members of the fair, Gianni and his dad tried to piece together the happenings of the last twenty-four hours. While they were talking, Gianni got up to answer a knock at the door. An agitated Ronnie stood there, clutching the missing sketchbook.

'Gianni, I found this under Dougie's pillow when we were folding his bed away. It has your name on it. It fell on the floor and I saw a drawing of a lady that looks like your wife.' Ronnie's words were garbled as though he was embarrassed. 'Not that I've ever seen your wife without clothes on,' he added quickly. 'And I didn't look no further, honest, mate. I closed it up right away and brought it straight over here. Don't know how he ended up with it, but that doesn't sit right with me.'

'Thank you for returning it, Ronnie,' Gianni said. 'Please don't worry. Odd though, like you say, that it should end up on Dougie Taylor's bed. You don't have any idea where he is, I suppose?'

'Not a clue. Is it true that they found a woman's body in the copse?'

Gianni nodded. 'It's Eloisa. She was in a bad way, but still alive, when they took her in the ambulance. I'll let you know more when we know ourselves.'

'Thanks, Gianni. Me and her were good friends until that Scottish bastard showed his face. He'd better not be the one responsible for doing that to her.' He turned and walked away but not before Gianni saw his shoulders shaking and him wiping tears away.

He rejoined the officers and his dad and told them it was the young lad Ronnie who had shared a caravan with the missing hired hand. 'He just brought back a sketchbook of mine that had somehow fallen into the hands of Dougie Taylor.'

One of the officers looked up from the notes he was making. 'So, none of you really knew this man that you say joined the fair in York a few weeks ago. You took him on as a casual hired hand? Yet you tell me he was in some sort of relationship with your stepdaughter, the young lady found injured in the copse, Mr Romano?'

Luca nodded. 'That is correct. He was a hard worker and got on well with all the other hired hands that I've had for years.'

'Do you know anything of his background?'

'Very little, I have to admit. Said he was from Edinburgh, had lost his job and fancied doing a bit of travelling around the country. He just wanted a bit of casual work to be going on with. He had a bit of a scruffy appearance, longish hair and a beard that could do with a good trim. He'd got a tooth missing from the bottom, one of the middle two.' Luca tapped his own tooth with his finger. 'This one. You only noticed the gap when he laughed, which wasn't that often, actually. He was a bit moody at times. Oh, and he walked with a bit of a limp, said he had a bad foot.'

The police officers looked at each other.

Gianni frowned. 'Did he, Dad? Can't say I noticed that. Mind you, I've had so little to do with him. I've been so busy with coming home to help Cathy, and Granny's funeral and what have you. Our paths rarely crossed. He seemed to keep out of my way.'

'One young man said he heard you arguing with Eloisa yesterday, sir,' one of the officers said, addressing Gianni. 'Is that correct?'

Gianni nodded. 'It is. We were arguing because I accused her of taking my sketchbook. In fact, the one Ronnie just returned to me that was found in Dougie's bed.'

The officer nodded. 'Someone also said they saw her arguing with Dougie but then she was seen going into the caravan with him all smiles a while later.'

Gianni shrugged. 'No idea about that – oh, though Tony, her assistant, did say she was arguing with him. Might be the same argument.'

Luca shook his head. 'I don't wish to speak ill of my step-daughter while she is so badly injured, but that girl could cause an argument in an empty room, Officer.'

Both officers hid a smile and continued to question Luca. 'Now you say many of the fairground people have been robbed of money from their caravans and that also you have had your car stolen? The keys were taken from a jacket here yesterday afternoon, and the car from Lucerne Street. That's outside your mother-in-law's house, sir?' He directed that at Gianni, who nodded.

'Yes, my dad lent me the car a few weeks ago to come home for family reasons, and because it saved messing about finding a parking space here and we're in easy walking distance of the park, I left it on the street.'

The elder of the officers scratched his chin thoughtfully. 'Your wife's mother, is that the lady that helped with the first aid earlier?'

'Yes, Alice Harrison,' Gianni replied.

'I visited Mrs Harrison a few weeks ago but she wasn't home. I had some news for her. Mrs Harrison was the former Mrs Jack Dawson, wasn't she?'

Gianni felt his jaw dropping. 'She was.'

'Sir, would you mind if we got that sketchbook checked for fingerprints right away?' the older officer asked. 'If it's been kept by this Dougie Taylor fellow then it may have his prints on it. In view of the seriousness of the attack on the young lady it's very important that we do this. It will be looked after and returned to you at a later date. We just need the cover, if you'd like to detach it from the contents for me, please.'

Gianni nodded and removed the staples holding the sketchbook together. He slid out his drawings, handing the cover to the officers.

The older officer's radio crackled and he answered it as a disembodied voice spoke. 'I'll take this outside,' he told Gianni and Luca. When he came back he was smiling. 'Eloisa has come round. She has a fractured skull and a broken nose but she's going to be all right. This might be a good time to get someone to take Mr Romano to the hospital. We will be making our way in to see her tomorrow. We'll need to take a statement and with a bit of luck she may recall who her attacker was and then we can put out a search and bring him in. He's a very dangerous man to do that to a young girl and leave her for dead.'

'That's really good news,' Gianni said, breathing a sigh of relief. Although his stepsister drove him mad at times, he would hate anything bad to happen to her. He loved her mother, who had been nothing but kind and loving towards him, and knew she would be heartbroken if she lost Eloisa. 'And I'm sure my stepfather-in-law will oblige with a lift. You've got my dad's car's description, haven't you? It's a very distinctive Consul in black and yellow.'

'We have. We'll get this sketchbook cover to the station now and if there are any matching prints on our files we'll have a name to work with at least. Hopefully it will be the same name Eloisa gives us. We'll be in touch as soon as we have any further information. It'll probably be tomorrow before we get any results as our forensics chap doesn't work on Sundays.'

Gianni thanked them and gave them Alice's phone number so that they could let him know as soon as possible. They said their goodbyes as he showed them out of the caravan.

*

Tears ran down Eloisa's face as a kind police officer drew up a chair and sat down by the side of her bed. A nurse had told him that he couldn't be too long; her head injury was severe and she needed to rest. Eloisa was in a small side room and he closed the door to give them privacy.

'Now, in your own time, Eloisa, just tell me what you can remember,' the officer said quietly, taking out a notebook and pen.

'Not a lot,' Eloisa said, sniffing. 'I know who it was though, and I don't understand why he would do this to me when all I've ever done is be nice and loving towards him.'

'I spoke to your mother earlier and she said you're convinced it was a man called Dougie Taylor that attacked you?'

'Yes. He was sort of my boyfriend. We'd been seeing each other since he joined the fair in York. But on Sunday morning I saw what I thought was a prowler or something near the caravans. Then I realised it might be Dougie and that he was leaving without saying goodbye to me. I was upset so I followed him. Then he turned on me for no reason and hit me several times. He was saying things in a funny accent, like a Scouser, but very deep and nasty. It was almost like he was a madman and wanted to kill me.'

'Did this man tell you anything about himself while you were, err, seeing him?'

'Very little. He told me one thing and then changed it to another. He said he got confused because he'd been on medication for his injured foot and he did like to drink a bit too much.'

She frowned and gasped as something came back to her from that night. 'I've just remembered something a bit odd that I saw before I passed out. His right sock had rolled down. I was lying on the ground by his feet and he lifted his trouser leg and pulled the sock up over his ankle and up his calf. Where his leg joined his foot it didn't look right. Sort of brown and shiny not like real skin – which is why his sock slipped down maybe. Does that make any sense to you? It sounds weird, I know, but I did see it, I'm sure.'

The officer nodded. 'It does make sense, thank you. I'm going to leave you now to rest. But can you just take a quick look at this picture and tell me if you think this is Dougie Taylor?' He held a mugshot of Jack Dawson in front of her.

She frowned. 'I've seen that before. Officers came to the fair to ask if we'd seen him. He's Jack Dawson.'

The officer nodded. 'That's right. He's a wanted man. Does he resemble Dougie Taylor in any way?'

Eloisa studied the picture again. 'I'm not sure. Maybe. But Dougie had long hair and a beard and a missing front tooth at the bottom. His face is a bit thinner too.'

The officer took a deep breath. 'This man also has a missing front tooth.' He tapped a bottom tooth with his pen. 'This one.'

Eloisa frowned. 'Same as Dougie's.'

'This man could have grown his hair and a beard and he may also have lost weight. He also has a right foot missing, which has been replaced by a wooden one.'

'But what about his accent? Jack's from Liverpool. Dougie's from Edinburgh and has a Scottish accent; well, he did have until the other night. He and that Jack fella can't be the same man, surely?' She yawned loudly and the officer got to his feet.

'I'll leave you for now. Get some sleep and if we need to speak to you again we'll come back. Rest assured we're doing our best to catch the man responsible for attacking you, Miss.'

*

Gianni took a call from the police station just after twelve noon on Monday. Officers would be calling at the house within the hour.

'I'm glad I'm on a late one today,' Cathy said. 'I don't start until three, so I can hear what they have to say first-hand before I head for the bus.'

'The chap I just spoke to said there will be a heavy police presence in the area around the park for the next few days. It's a shame – it'll put punters off coming to the fair.'

'Only if they've got something to hide,' Cathy said. 'I wonder how Eloisa is doing. I don't like her that much, as you know, but what's happened to her is just awful. Did they say if they've got any news on your dad's car yet? That was really odd how it vanished from here but the keys were taken from your pocket in the caravan. How would a random thief know that?'

Gianni nodded. 'I don't know, but it is indeed very odd.' He had his own theory on who was responsible for attacking Eloisa and stealing his dad's car, but until he knew for certain, or the police confirmed it, he didn't want to scare Cathy half to death with his thoughts.

*

'Are you sure?' Cathy felt her face draining as she stared at the two officers seated opposite her on the sofa in the front sitting room.

'We're certain, Mrs Romano,' one of them said. 'Fingerprints on the cover of your husband's sketchbook match up to prints held in our system of the escaped prisoner Jack Dawson.'

'But this man from the fair, Dougie Taylor, how is he involved?'

'He and Dawson are one and the same. After escaping from a prison van in Leeds, he grew his hair and a beard and adopted a Scottish persona, including the accent.'

'So he's been living that close to us since the fair arrived in Liverpool.' Cathy shuddered and felt sick. 'Why on earth would he come back here when he knows he's wanted and people are on the lookout for him?'

'That's what we'd like to know, Mrs Romano. The reasons for his return are a mystery. However, he's taken Mr Luca Romano's car so will no doubt be out of the area by now. It's a distinctive car, so we're hoping the TV bulletin on tonight's news and a report in all tomorrow's papers will bring us some results. That car is easy to spot anywhere. Our main worry is that he'll abandon it.'

Gianni shook his head. 'I'll come and meet you from work tonight,' he told Cathy. 'It'll have to be on my motorbike though now we've no car. But I'm not having you trying to get home on your own on late-night buses.'

Cathy blew out her cheeks. 'I don't care what you meet me on, just as long as you do. Mam is going to be so worried when she hears he's been near the house, but I've got to warn her. I'll get off now to the hospital and tell her.'

'Can we offer you a lift?' one of the officers said. 'We're just going to speak with Eloisa again. You might as well as come with us.' He scribbled something on a piece of paper and handed it to Gianni. 'Any sightings or anything at all that you think will help us, please ring that number right away.'

'Thank you for the lift offer.' Cathy got to her feet. 'Just let me finish getting ready and I'll be with you in five minutes.'

Chapter Twenty-One

Cathy hurried down the main corridor of the Royal and headed towards the staff canteen. She hoped her mam was still on her dinner break as it would be easier to speak to her here than on the children's ward. She pushed open the canteen door, scanned the tables and spotted her sitting with another of the auxiliary nurses.

'Hiya, love,' her mam greeted Cathy. 'What up? You look mithered to death. Sit down and I'll go and get you a cuppa.'

'I've no time, Mam. I'll have one on the ward later.'

The other nurse got to her feet. 'I'll leave you two to talk. See you later, Alice. Nice to see you, Cathy.'

'You too,' Cathy said.

'Right, tell me what's wrong,' Mam said as the nurse walked away.

Cathy told her that two police officers had called on them earlier and why.

Alice's eyes opened wide and her hand flew to her mouth. 'It was Jack? Oh my God, what the heck did he think he was he doing, holing up with the fair like that?'

Cathy shook her head. 'No idea. Probably just luck on his side that it was in York when he escaped in Leeds and made his way there. He's been in disguise with long hair and a beard and he's been having a relationship with Eloisa. It makes me sick to think he nearly killed her, perhaps because she tried to stop him from leaving. He's a really dangerous man. It terrifies me to think he's on the run out there again. It's definitely him though, because they've matched his fingerprints, and Eloisa saw his wooden foot.'

'She's lucky to still be alive,' Alice said, shaking her head. 'We all need to be on our guard now. I can't see him getting far with Luca's car. He's going to struggle to drive it. I would have thought it was almost impossible that he could, so he may just dump it.'

Cathy nodded and got to her feet. 'I'll see you later tonight. Gianni's going to meet me. His dad brought his bike down here in one of the trailers, so he'll pick me up on that.'

'You just be careful on the back of that bike.'

'I will. Better the bike than walking home after dark though.'

Alice nodded her agreement. 'I'll ring Johnny to come and collect me later.'

*

'Bloody hell,' Karen said as Cathy told her the events of the last few hours. 'I can't believe it. We saw that girl on Saturday when we had a go on the hook-a-duck stall. Hope she'll be all right. Ellie's on nights tonight so we'll warn her as soon as she comes on duty. We should let Sister know as well and she can get the news over to other ward sisters so their staff can be warned. No one should take any chances. Unlikely he'll put in an appearance here, but best to be on the safe side in view of what happened to Ellie.'

'Better go and find out what's been happening on here today,' Cathy said. 'Get some work done to take our minds off things.'

Karen nodded. 'Hopefully there'll be something in my pigeon-hole when I go off duty from the powers-that-be about our venture. I didn't have time to check before I came up here.'

*

Jack sat in the car near the Dock Road and pondered on what to do next. He would need to abandon the car soon as after the first few miles he had been finding it too much of a struggle to drive.

He knew he'd be at risk of an accident and that would attract unwanted attention, which was all he needed. Plus the car stuck out like a sore thumb.

He debated using his stolen money to take a steamer from the docks across to Douglas on the Isle of Man, until things calmed down a bit here, but then how would he get back? It looked like he had no choice but to go back to living in allotment sheds again and stealing food as and when he could find it. His plans had all gone to pot. It had been a big mistake coming back to Liverpool and now he would be in even deeper shit when they found Eloisa's body. His picture would be everywhere once they realised he was missing, and who he was.

That coupled with the shooting of the prison officer might warrant a death sentence. Taking Luca's car had been a final moment of madness. Who else would have known which house it would be parked outside? He wasn't cut out to think like a criminal. He knew he liked to have his way with women, and he was an accomplished petty thief, but anything else he was rubbish at. He should have gone up to Scotland with Andy and the lads. They'd have taught him a thing or two. He'd been so obsessed about finding Cathy that nothing else had mattered.

He needed a plan of action and had no idea now whether he should speak with a Scottish accent still or his normal Liverpool one, or try something else altogether. Who would the police be looking for? Dougie Taylor? Or had they worked it out by now and were looking for Jack Dawson? Life was shit at the moment and he couldn't see how it would ever get better, but he really needed to get pissed tonight. He started up the engine and drove further up the road until he spotted an open off-licence, where he nipped in and stocked up on booze and fags. There was a small chippy next door and he bought a fish supper, then walked back to the car and drove to a nearby fire-damaged factory and pulled into the deserted car park. He switched off the engine and lights, ate his supper, and washed it down with a few good slugs of whisky. He had a quick pee up the side of the car, got back in and, unzipping the sleeping bag, curled up on the back seat, his mind working overtime. There was one place he could go where he might be able to hide for a while.

The old house he'd stayed in as an injured soldier had an outbuilding that was never used. It had an upstairs room accessed by a wooden staircase that he might be able to manage, and was situated at the bottom of the garden. Maybe the people who had owned it back in the forties were still there, or more likely it had been sold on – they'd probably be dead by now. It was worth a try as he was unsure if there were any allotments nearby where he could take shelter.

Tomorrow he'd dump the car near the docks and take a very early bus back to Aigburth. He could be hidden away before people started to get up for work. He could do with a haircut and a trim to his beard. But then if he did that he'd be more recognisable as Jack. The one good thing if he hid up that way was that Cathy was almost around the corner. He smiled and closed his eyes, remembering her curves and her beautiful full breasts in Gianni's sketches of her. What he'd give to get his hands on them, and show her who was boss.

*

Gianni met Cathy after work and the pair walked Karen across to the nurses' home.

'Any more news?' Cathy asked as they headed back to where he'd parked his motorbike. This was the second night running that he'd come to pick her up, and she was so grateful that he was here.

'Nope, not a sighting of him anywhere yet. But Dad's car was found abandoned on the Dock Road today. It's been taken to the station and is being checked for fingerprints right now.'

'So he didn't get very far then?'

'Unfortunately he's probably still in Liverpool, so we need to make sure we are extra careful. Dad has closed the fair for the time being. No one has got the heart to work. Everyone is in a state of shock. He said they'll all stay on Seffy Park for now in case the police need them for further questioning. Maria needs to be close to Eloisa so she can visit as often as she likes.'

He sighed. 'Cathy, even if Jack has been caught, when it's time to move on I'm not going with them. I've made up my mind.' He grasped her hands and looked straight into her blue eyes. 'I love you. You and Lucy need me more than the fair does. I'll do a bit of work helping Johnny and Jimmy to get Woodlands ready. And we can get the bungalow sorted and move in sooner now. Give your mam a bit more space in her own home.'

Cathy flung her arms around him. 'Thank you. I would never have asked you to do that, but I am so glad you've decided to stay with us.'

When Cathy and Gianni arrived back at Lucerne Street the TV news was on.

'You're just in time,' Johnny announced from the sofa, where he and Alice were seated, as they walked into the back room. He pointed at the screen. 'They're just coming up to the bit we've been waiting for.'

Cathy and Gianni sat down on dining chairs as the newsreader began his report.

Liverpool Police have issued another warrant for the arrest of an absconded prisoner. Jack Dawson, who also goes by the name of Dougie Taylor, is wanted in connection with a serious assault on a young woman near a Liverpool fairground, the newsreader said, adding that he was also wanted for questioning in relation to the murder of a prison officer. An enlarged copy of Jack's mugshot and an artist's impression of how he looked now filled the screen. 'A team of police are searching the area near the Dock Road where a vehicle, believed to have been stolen by Dawson, has been found abandoned.'

Cathy remained silent and chewed her lip anxiously as Gianni shook his head and picked up the *Echo* newspaper from the dining table. The headlines were accompanied by Jack's old mugshot side by side with the same artist's impression that had just been shown on the TV.

'Hopefully by tomorrow someone may realise they've seen him,' Gianni said as he read the report. 'That artist's impression is a really good likeness.'

'Let's hope so,' Alice said with a shudder. 'The thought of him out there makes me feel ill. Seeing his picture on TV has given me the creeps.'

*

Olive Gould put down her empty cup and pushed her glasses further up her nose as she watched the news on the TV. She picked up a pen and the *Radio Times* from the coffee table and scribbled down the phone number the newsreader was giving out. She squinted again at the picture of a man on the screen. Yesterday, just before locking up for the night, she'd served a man a bottle of whisky and twenty Woodbines. He'd been a scruffy-looking type but his money was as good as anyone else's. Times were hard, so beggars couldn't be choosers.

'Gerald,' she called to her husband, who was making a cuppa in the kitchen.

Gerald appeared in the adjoining doorway, wiping his hands on a tea towel. 'Yes, my love?'

Olive pointed at the television screen. 'There's a report of a man wanted by the police and I'm sure he came in the shop last night. They've just given out a number. Shall I ring it and let them know?'

Gerald frowned. 'Are you sure it's the same man?'

'No, not really. But the artist's impression they showed looks a lot like him. He's wanted in connection with the shooting of the officer in Yorkshire a few months ago and an attack on a young girl recently left for dead in Sefton Park.'

'Then yes, you'd better let them know he might have been around these parts. No doubt he'll have left the area by now though.'

Olive jumped to her feet and turned up the sound on the TV as the newscaster with the stern face repeated the number. A stolen car had been found abandoned on the Dock Road and police believed there was a possibility that the man may have taken a ferry either to Ireland or the Isle of Man. The broadcaster stated that the man should not be approached as he was deemed dangerous, but any sightings should be reported immediately.

Her heart almost pounding out of her chest, Olive stared again at the artist's impression on the screen and knew for sure it was the same man she'd served yesterday. She picked up the phone and, her fingers shaking, dialled the number she'd written down. An officer told her they would send someone to see her right away to take a statement. She didn't know what use that would be as she had no idea where the man had gone when he left her shop, but at least they'd have it on record that he'd been seen in the area.

*

Jack knocked on the door of Lorraine's flat and stood back, waiting for a response. The door opened a fraction and he heard the safety chain being removed, then Lorraine was standing in front of him, her hair in rollers and her dressing gown pulled tightly around her waist. She stared at him, her mouth open. 'What the hell do you want? It's nearly midnight.'

Jack was surprised that she'd recognised him. 'That's a nice welcome, I must say.'

'Well what do you expect, Jack after what you've done? You'd better come in before my neighbours see you. But you're not staying so don't get any ideas.'

He followed her into the narrow hallway and through to the small sitting room.

'Sit down.' Lorraine ordered. 'The police are everywhere looking for you.' She picked up a newspaper from the table and threw it at him. He was plastered all over the bloody headlines. The old mugshot alongside an artist's impression of what he looked like now, which was why Lorraine had recognised him, no doubt. 'And why have you come here? I don't want to get involved.'

Jack shrugged. 'I thought with you writing to me, like, you might help me.'

'Writing to you?'

'Yeah, when you told me Alice had got remarried.'

'Jack, that was over three years ago and you never wrote back. What gives you the right to think you can land on my doorstep now?'

'I've nowhere else to go, gel. I'm wanted for murder.'

'Murder? Oh you mean the prison officer? You're wanted in connection with that and running off, but you didn't pull the trigger. You should have given yourself up there and then.'

Jack fiddled with his beard and scratched his chin. 'Not the officer. A young girl at the fairground.'

Lorraine nodded. 'She isn't dead, Jack. No thanks to you.'

He stared at her. 'Isn't she?'

Lorraine shook her head. 'You left her for dead, which in my book is as bad as actually murdering her.'

'I had no choice, she'd recognised me.'

'Well *I* bloody recognised you too.' She jumped to her feet and grabbed a poker from a stand beside the tiled fireplace. 'So what you gonna do? Try and kill *me*?' She advanced towards him, swinging the poker.

He got to his feet. 'There's no need for that. What should I do? I thought you'd help me.'

'No chance, Jack. I want you out of here and go and give yourself up. You won't last five minutes out there. There's scuffers all over the place. If I had a phone I'd be on to them right now.'

Jack took that as meaning he should go and she wouldn't phone the police. He hurried out of her flat and Lorraine slammed the door behind him.

He walked out of the communal hallway and onto the dark street. He had nowhere to go and not a soul to turn to. All he could do was try to find an allotment, bed down in a shed again and take it from there. He'd no doubt that Lorraine would phone the police as soon as she could.

*

Jack settled down in his sleeping bag on a pile of old sacks in the outbuilding of the old house on Woodlands Road. He'd decided to head over here after spending the night after his visit to Lorraine's in an alleyway. He couldn't think of anywhere else to go. He was starving, but couldn't chance going out to get anything to eat.

When he'd arrived at the house early this morning, he'd been surprised to find it in the middle of a lot of changes. There was no one on-site when he'd arrived and he'd kept out of the way all day, listening to the men doing the work and carrying on conversations. He had been shocked when he'd peered through the dirty old window to see that it was Millie's husband Jimmy, and that bastard Johnny who had married Alice. Well, there was little he could do about it now as he'd struggled up the stairs – which were steeper than he remembered – and there was no way he'd get down there again in a hurry without breaking his neck. He wondered what the hell they were doing working here.

Had Johnny bought the house for Alice and the kids? Typical of her to fall on her bloody feet while he was facing life in prison. He reached for his rucksack and pulled out the bottle of whisky he'd bought last night. There was just over half of it left and he slugged it down to try to shut out the pain in his leg.

He threw the empty bottle across the room and lit a cigarette, hoping he'd sleep okay tonight. He'd need to be up and off again first thing before he was found. God knows where to though. He certainly couldn't stay here with Johnny around. Before he gave up all hope, though, he would have one final shot at seeing if he could get Cathy on her own. She'd either be at Ma Lomax's bungalow or Alice's place. He'd be lucky, but he could dream, he thought, and lit another cigarette, a smile playing on his face. He'd show her what she was missing, married to that bloody biker. She needed a good seeing-to by a real man and Jack felt he was the one to show her. She wouldn't forget him in a hurry.

*

When the news was conveyed back to Lucerne Street that Jack had been seen in the area buying drink and cigarettes, Alice felt sick. An officer had been dispatched to tell them they were combing every inch of Aigburth in their search for him. Alice cried in Johnny's arms after the officer had left, and Gianni comforted Cathy. A report had also come in from someone Jack had been acquainted with who'd seen him in the area.

'He could be anywhere,' Alice sobbed. 'It terrifies me to think of him out there, just waiting to get vengeance. That's why he came back here with the fair, to get his own back for being sent to prison. Knowing how his warped mind works, he'll think it's all our fault. Anybody else would be miles away by now.'

Maria and Luca stopped by after visiting Eloisa, who was making a good recovery.

'I can't believe they haven't caught him yet,' Maria said. 'I hope they hang him when they do.'

'Not sure if they will do that, love,' Luca said. 'He hasn't actually committed a murder as such. But he was an accessory to the prison officer's death in that he ran away and didn't report it, according to the officers that were also involved. He left Eloisa for dead, he's no idea if she's still alive, and he raped Ellie. He's a very dangerous man, especially to women, and needs to be kept in a secure prison when they catch him. One from where he can never escape again.'

'Well I for one hope they chuck away the key,' Alice said. 'I hate him for everything he's done, except my children. But the poor kids don't deserve a father like him. Thank God they have you, Johnny. Hopefully Rodney won't remember him, and Sandra and Rosie never mention his name. I just hope this doesn't stir up bad memories.'

'We'll give them all the support they need,' Johnny assured her. 'Eloisa is getting better and that's what matters right now.'

Luca looked at Gianni. 'Son, it's time you re-evaluated what's important to you. I've seen how much you enjoy being with Cathy and Lucy. Maybe it's time to put your family first now. The fairground isn't where you should be.'

'Dad, I'm really glad you've brought the subject up,' Gianni said. 'I've decided I want to leave. To stop riding the bikes and settle down here with my girls. I was going to finish the season with you and Marco, but to be honest I'd like out right away, if that's okay with you.'

'It's more than okay. You've got a lovely home waiting for you here. Ideal for bringing up Lucy and any more bambinos you may have. Maria and I have been talking this over for a while. I'm going to retire early. Marco wants to buy me out and bring in some younger riders. We will go back to Italy at the end of the season and take Eloisa with us so she can make a full recovery and think about what she wants to do for the rest of her life. I will pay you your quarter-share when Marco pays me. That way you can take your time finding work. Get your home sorted out and enjoy all the new adventures coming your way.'

Chapter Twenty-Two

Woodlands Maternity Home January 1964

Alice and Sandra took off their coats and hung them on the hall stand. The first week of the New Year and it was all hands on deck at Woodlands in a final mad rush to get ready for their open day at the weekend. Sandra had been helping as much as she could and had been offered a place to start as a cadet nurse at the Royal at Easter. Alice was thrilled that her second daughter was following in her older sister's footsteps, and that she'd had the opportunities to do so. For the next three months Sandra was going to get a bit of hands-on practice in and assist where she could at Woodlands. Things really had improved for the Lark Lane girls, even if Jack was still at large…

All planning applications for the business had been passed with no problems and the necessary permissions had all been granted. The financial matters were in place, the building works almost completed, deliveries of furniture and equipment were all under way and the NCT, social services and NHS were supporting the project. The midwives were helping to clean the downstairs rooms of their new home and business premises. Marlene had put herself in charge of all cleaning operations and as well as issuing orders she provided pots of tea and sandwiches to keep her small army of helpers fed and watered.

The bedrooms and bathrooms were ready to use. New beds and bedside tables were being delivered later today and then the patients' rooms could be organised. Carpets had been fitted this week and curtains hung. Johnny and Jimmy, with Gianni's help, had built wardrobes and cupboards in all the alcoves for storing towels, linen and clothes. Jimmy had made the suggestion to do that and had told the girls it would save on floor space and the need for free-standing wardrobes. They were all pleased with the neat and tidy streamlined look.

The washing machines and dryers had been going all morning and the freshly laundered sheets were folded on the table ready to take upstairs. 'That's much better,' Marlene said, smoothing out the creases in a cotton sheet she'd just fished out of the dryer. 'They were a bit too starchy and rough to the touch to put straight on the beds. Nice and soft and they smell fresher too. I'm going to set to and iron the bedspreads now, ready for later. They need to look nice and crease-free.'

Karen smiled and gave Marlene's arm a squeeze. 'You're a good one. We'd have probably just put them straight onto the beds without thinking. We'll definitely be ready for our open day on Saturday. We're bang on time with everything.'

'I can't wait,' Cathy said. 'I can't believe it's happening at last.'

'I know. And we've already had enquiries for our services after our leaflet drop-off sessions,' Karen said. 'I think we'll have the first bookings this weekend. It's all come nicely together. And to think we've got council approval too.'

'Doctor Kelso from the surgery on Aigburth Road is being really supportive as well,' Ellie said, her eyes shining. 'He's told a few of his patients to get in touch if they want to have their babies here. He said any time we need him for a delivery, just to pick up the phone.'

'Is that for the patients or you, Ellie?' Karen teased as her friend blushed prettily. Ellie and the young doctor had grown close during meetings over the last few weeks. It was the first time she'd shown interest in a member of the opposite sex since Jack's assault on her a few years ago. The other girls were waiting with bated breath for him to ask her out. He was also shy, but they looked good together, so fingers were being crossed all round.

'This place will be like a home from home,' Marlene said. 'It's more like a posh hotel than a hospital environment. Right, you girls get stuck into that pile of sarnies before those beds arrive. Then we'll get the rooms ready upstairs. We could do with a few vases of flowers as well. I know it's not spring, and choices will be limited, but I'm sure the florist on Lark Lane would do us proud if we asked her nicely. A colourful display on the table in the hall so visitors can see it as they walk in, now that would look lovely. It's the little touches that make a difference. Oh, and by the way, has anybody had that big cheese and onion pie that was in the fridge?'

They all shook their heads.

'Well that's a mystery. I'm sure it was in there, I wrapped it in greaseproof to cut up for later. Must have a pie-loving ghost on the premises.'

Alice smiled. Bringing Marlene in on this enterprise had been a good idea. 'Perhaps you dreamed it. I'll get the flowers sorted,' she said. 'The lady who runs the florist is an old friend of mine. She'll maybe give us a discount. Johnny said he and Jimmy will be over mid-afternoon to put the beds together.' She strolled into the large, light and airy sitting room that Jean insisted on calling the lounge as it sounded so much posher, and looked around with pride. Three large sofas and a coffee table were arranged in front of the fireplace and a unit with a decent-sized television stood in one alcove, with a record player on a built-in cupboard on the other side. It was a lovely room for expectant mothers to gather and to get to know each other.

The rooms were tastefully decorated in pastel shades, with contrasting colours in the floral curtains and cushions, and the carpets were neutral, mainly light beiges with small unobtrusive patterns. Millie's Lewis's staff discount had come in very handy in the last few weeks, and Alice had picked up some china figurines and brass ornaments at Paddy's Market, which gave the place a homely feel. The girls all had stylish taste and together they'd worked their magic. Cathy and Gianni had brought boxes of books over from Granny Lomax's bungalow and Johnny had built shelves in one of the dining room alcoves, where the books had found a new home. Granny's old grandfather clock now stood in the hallway, where it had chimed away the hours while they'd all scrubbed and polished over the last few days.

Freddie had come to look at the grounds but due to the cold weather and the ground still being frozen he'd been unable to do much in the garden, so had helped with the painting and decorating. He said he loved being with the lads and feeling like part of a team again and they'd welcomed him with open arms.

Cathy had finished her course and passed her final exams, both practical and theoretical, and she and Gianni had toasted the fact that she was now a fully qualified midwife at the same time as they celebrated moving into the bungalow just before Christmas.

The month before the Christmas celebrations, the country had been plunged into a period of mourning following the assassination of the American president John F. Kennedy in Dallas, Texas. Alice couldn't believe that anyone could do something so wicked and cold-blooded. That wonderful man, the head of the nation and the great source of hope, was gone. Everyone in Liverpool had been deeply affected and it was all anyone talked about for weeks after.

Cathy and Gianni had waved his dad, Maria and a fully recovered Eloisa off to Italy at the end of November. They kept in touch frequently and Luca said he was missing the bikes, although he was delighted to be back in Italy. Eloisa had met Dino, a boy she'd known years ago, and had been dating him for a few weeks. Luca said Dino seemed to be the making of her and they were keeping their fingers crossed that she would settle down at last. Maria was hoping for a grandchild in the not-too-distant future. She was missing Lucy and kept seeing baby images in her crystal ball, Luca had told them.

'Probably the maternity home keeps popping up,' Gianni joked, adding, 'just as long as danger keeps a low profile from now on, once they finally catch Jack.'

*

The ringing alarm woke Cathy with a start. She sat up, rubbing her eyes. Gianni was sprawled out beside her, dead to the world. He'd sleep through a bomb dropping on the roof, she thought, climbing out of bed and sliding her feet into warm slippers. Today was the day. She'd worked her final shift at the Royal yesterday and was raring to get going at Woodlands. Today was going to be a busy day.

There were no sounds coming from Lucy's bedroom, so she shut herself in the kitchen and made a mug of strong coffee to help wake herself up properly, and pushed two slices of bread under the grill. She looked around the shiny new kitchen that Johnny and Gianni had fitted in place of Granny's old one, which had been there since the bungalow was first built. Even though it now looked different, Cathy was often struck by memories of Granny cooking her wonderful dinners here and the smell of freshly baked bread that she remembered so fondly. She missed Granny, but was so pleased to be living in her home, the place where she had always been happiest.

Gianni had done the planning and designing for the new kitchen and had really enjoyed it. There were more cupboards than you could shake a stick at, but Cathy had nearly filled them with new stuff as well as keeping some of Granny's favourite china and glassware for best. Gianni had bought her a new cooker and fridge and a smart twin-tub washing machine. She loved the way everything just fitted in the spaces he'd made for them and how the new worktops in black-and-yellow-speckled Formica set off the yellow cupboard doors that were all fitted with shiny chrome handles. It was very modern, like a smart magazine kitchen.

Some of Granny's pieces had gone across to Woodlands and she'd kept some here. The old and new complemented each other and Cathy felt happy that there were still many of Granny's things around. They'd kept the dining room furniture, reupholstered the chairs and added a nice cloth on the table to protect it from Lucy's paints and crayons. Gianni had taken up the old carpets that had been down for over forty years. He'd painted everywhere in a fresh cream emulsion and he and Cathy had chosen a mid-green carpet with a small leaf design, which had been fitted throughout, apart from Lucy's bedroom, which was carpeted in her favourite pink.

Cathy buttered her toast, carried her mug and plate through to the lounge and put them on the coffee table. She pulled back the curtains on the wide bay window and the bright winter sunshine lit up the room. Their new three-piece suite in a light beige fabric had been a bargain in the January sales and had only been delivered last week. George next door had taken Granny's old one off their hands for his eldest grandson, who was just setting up home with his new wife. Cathy sat down and took a sip of coffee, looking round her lovely room with pride. She still felt the need to pinch herself from time to time to remind herself that this was where she now lived with Gianni and Lucy. It hardly seemed real some days when she thought back to all they'd been through since they first got together. And now, today, beyond her wildest dreams, she and her good midwife friends were about to throw open the doors on their new maternity home.

*

'When you've shown them round, tell them tea and cake is available in the dining room and Marlene will serve it,' Alice instructed as the four midwives stood on ceremony in the lounge, all smartly attired in their new uniforms. They'd chosen pink dresses to go under their white aprons. Jean felt it set them apart from the customary blue at the Royal. 'That way they'll stay longer and will ask questions they may not have thought of when they were looking round,' Alice continued. 'There are leaflets about what we offer on the sideboard in there too with all our contact details. Make sure you don't let anyone go out empty-handed.'

'Do we all look okay?' Karen asked, pushing an unruly strand of hair back under her starched white cap.

'Very smart,' Alice said reassuringly. 'You all look most professional. I'd let you deliver my baby – not that I'm planning on having any more,' she finished with a grin.

Millie appeared in the doorway. Her navy-blue suit evoked an air of confidence that she wasn't feeling. 'God I'm a nervous wreck,' she said. 'My heart's pounding. You girls look lovely.'

'There was a loud knocking at the front door and Alice rushed to open it. A man stood in front of her with the largest bouquet of flowers she'd ever seen. He handed them over with a smile and a nod and hurried back to a white van that stood on the drive. She carried them through to the lounge and put them down on the coffee table. The flowers were in a container and arranged beautifully. A small white envelope was pinned to the cellophane wrapper that surrounded the assorted blooms. On the envelope were written the words, 'For the staff at Woodlands.'

'Oh my goodness, where did those come from?' Jean asked, her mouth agape. 'Alice, take a look inside the envelope.'

Alice removed the envelope from the bouquet and slid out a pretty card. She smiled. 'Well, fancy that. It's from our Brian and family in America, wishing us all the very best for our open day today.'

'How wonderful,' Jean said. 'Those are beautiful. He must have done it by some sort of international flower-sending service.'

Alice nodded, feeling close to tears. Bless her thoughtful brother. 'This card has a Liverpool city florist address on the back, and it says Interflora. It's very kind of him. I'll take the cellophane off and put them in pride of place on the sideboard. Marlene did say that flowers are a nice touch and these knock spots off all the others.'

Marlene looked up from her cake-slicing duties as Alice carried the display into the kitchen. She wiped her hands down her flowery pinny and smiled. 'They look lovely, Alice. Proper colourful.'

'From our Brian. I'm putting them in the lounge.'

Marlene nodded. 'They've done well coming all that way in the post and not getting battered around.'

Alice smiled. 'A chap brought them in a van from a florist in the city. Interflora is a special way of sending flowers when you live abroad.'

Marlene stared at Alice. 'Get away. Didn't know they could do things like that. It's a blooming clever idea. Whatever will they think of next?'

'Think it's been around quite a few years now. Not that we ever usually get flowers in this way.'

'Aye, I'm lucky to ever get any.' Marlene laughed and carried on with her cake-slicing. 'I've just pulled some scones out of the oven. Nice change from cake for anyone that wants them. There's enough stuff here to feed an army but I've a fruit cake missing. I put it on the table to cool and it's gone walkies. What with that pie going missing as well, it's a bit odd. Anyway, we've enough.'

'I'm sure our midwives will see that nothing goes to waste after the visitors have all gone home,' said Alice, smiling at the gorgeous smell in the kitchen. 'Right, get ready; we've ten minutes to go.'

*

The doorbell rang at exactly two o'clock and Millie let in a tall, middle-aged woman with a green silk hat, decorated with feathers, perched on top of her head; she wore a dark-brown fur coat that almost swamped her bird-like frame. She introduced herself as Mrs Swain-Foxton from Woolton Village. Millie wrote down her name on the visitors' list and showed her into the lounge, where Jean took over and shook the lady's hand. Millie rushed back to answer the door and let in two young couples who'd arrived on the doorstep at the same time, the ladies both heavily pregnant. She took their names and ushered them through into the lounge. By three o'clock the house was packed, and the midwives were answering question after question. Marlene was rushed off her feet in the kitchen and Alice took up position behind the teapot to give her a hand. Marlene's fruit cake was praised enthusiastically and one young man said he almost wished he was having the baby if the food was going to be this good.

At six o'clock, the last of the visitors shown out, the girls gathered around the dining table to polish off what was left of Marlene's scones and cake.

'So, girls,' Jean began. 'That went very well. Two young unmarried mums joining us on Monday for long-term care and four ladies booked in who are all due next week. But please God, don't let them all go into labour on the same day,' she pleaded, looking up at the ceiling. 'Anyhow, they've all paid a reservation fee, so the beds are theirs. We've still got room for two more unmarried mums in the four-bedder. We may get referrals from the local doctors' practice now as they know we are up and running from Monday. I'll let Doctor Kelso know what availability we'll have by then. All our single rooms are booked up. I think that's a really great start. What do you lot think?'

'That's wonderful,' Karen said. 'They were all raving about how lovely everywhere is and how homely-looking. And one lady who is expecting her second said the delivery suite looks friendly and not like a butchers' shop. Wonder where the poor girl had her first?'

'What's the history behind our unmarried mums, Jean?' Ellie asked.

'Well, the lady with the green feathered hat wants us to take her sixteen-year-old granddaughter off her hands as soon as possible.

The girl is called Penelope Swain-Foxton. Her parents have washed their hands of her and sent her to her grandmother's, who in turn is packing her off here to us on Monday. She's five months pregnant and we're to keep her here until after the baby is adopted. She's paid us up front for Penelope's care and just said if we need more because she goes over her time, then we only need to make a discreet phone call. She was difficult to engage in conversation and just wanted to be off as soon as I said we could take her granddaughter and look after her and the baby. Poor kid. No doubt we'll hear her side of the story when she arrives. The Swain-Foxton chauffeur will bring her at ten o'clock on the dot. They sound like quite a posh family.

'The other girl is nearly seventeen and is called Sarah Young. Boyfriend has let her down and her mother says she can't bring a baby home as they already have six kids in a small house in the city centre and are waiting to be rehoused. The girl's father says she's not to bring it back to the house under any circumstances. They don't want any contact with her or us until she's ready to go home. She's a supported patient so her forms will need to go to the address we have for council and NHS assistance.

'Both of the girls will need to feel we are here to help them and not to judge their situation. I know I can rely on everybody here to give them the help they need. The married patients will just be here for their confinements and will go home as soon as they and their babies are ready to be discharged.

'And the phone's been ringing off the hook; we have a waiting list stretching to May so far. We'll have our hands very full, but it should be fun. I feel we'll enjoy our midwifery life here much more than at the hospital. We'll be more hands-on with our patients and have far fewer restrictions than with strict ward routines. We all work in a similar manner with the same ideas and as long as we follow a simple basic routine it should all work well for us.'

'I think a small sherry by way of a celebration toast will go down well right now,' said Marlene, getting to her feet. She reached up and lifted down a bottle of cooking sherry from her ingredients cupboard. 'It's for Sunday-tea trifles, but I can get more in.'

'I think a toast might be right,' Alice said as the doorbell rang. 'Who the heck's this? Don't they know the open house was only until six?'

But when Millie went to answer the door, she found Jimmy, Johnny, Gianni and even a smiling Doctor Kelso, who'd turned up to see how they'd got on.

'We thought there might be a need for this,' Johnny said, and pulled a bottle of champagne from a brown paper carrier bag. 'But for those who don't like it, there's also this.' He produced a large bottle of cream sherry. Spotting Marlene's cooking sherry, he said, 'Get the glasses out, Marlene, you can save that sherry for your trifles. We'll have a toast, and then our girls can tell us how today went.'

'Let's take the drinks into the lounge and make ourselves comfy,' Jean suggested. 'And we'll also drink a toast to mine, Karen and Ellie's lovely new home as well.'

Chapter Twenty-Three

Alice and Johnny had only been in bed an hour when they were awakened by loud hammering on the front door. Johnny rushed to answer it followed by Alice, an anxious expression on her face. It was Jimmy, looking worried to death. He was fully clothed and had his car keys in his hand.

'Quick, get dressed,' he directed at Johnny as Millie appeared behind him. 'The police just called us. There's a fire at Woodlands. The fire brigade is already on its way there.'

'Oh my God,' Alice gasped as Johnny ran back up the stairs to put some clothes on. 'Is it in the house? Hurry up. Karen, Jean and Ellie are asleep in there. Come in, Millie. Do we need to come with you?' she asked Jimmy.

'No, you girls stay here while we see what the hell is going on. We've only just had new wiring put in so I hope it's not something to do with that. We'll be back as soon as we can,' he finished as Johnny appeared by his side. 'Phone Gianni at the bungalow and tell him to meet us there.'

Alice made a pot of tea and Millie joined her at the table in the back sitting room. 'I hope it's not too bad,' Alice said, shaking her head. 'All that money we've got tied up in the place as well.'

'Oh God, yes,' Millie said, stirring sugar into the mug Alice handed her. 'Our homes, we could lose our homes.'

'Oh, Millie, don't say that.' Alice's lips trembled and her eyes filled. 'I couldn't bear it.' The phone rang and Alice dashed to answer it. 'It's Cathy,' she mouthed at Millie. 'I've no idea, love,' she replied to Cathy's question. 'Has Gianni gone to join them? I just hope the girls are okay, never mind the house.'

'Yes he has, Mam,' Cathy said. 'Who called the fire brigade? That must have been one of the girls. Hopefully they're out of the house safely. We can't lose it now; we've got so many plans.'

'I'm just wondering if I should throw on some clothes and run round to see what's happening?' Alice said. 'If I do I'll come and see you.'

'Okay, Mam.'

*

'Good job it was the outbuilding, Mr Harrison.' The chief fire officer was speaking to Johnny. 'I think we can get these young ladies back inside the house now.' He looked at Jean, Karen and Ellie, who had been shivering in slippers and dressing gowns by the back door while a couple of the firemen had done a safety check all around the house.

Another fireman came out of the now-damaged outbuilding carrying something in his hands. 'Looks like someone was sleeping rough in there,' he said and handed a rucksack to the chief.

Johnny scratched his head. 'I haven't seen anything untoward, but it was unlocked. Our gardener just kept a few tools in there.'

'This was upstairs along with the remains of a sleeping bag,' the fireman said.

Gianni looked closely at the scorched rucksack and his hand shot to his mouth. 'This might be a really long shot, but that bag looks like one that was stolen from a caravan on my father's fairground. The man who stole it is on the run from the police. His name is Jack Dawson. We need to let them know. Oh God, Johnny, we also need to warn Alice and Cathy. I'll go and phone them both now.' He headed for the kitchen. 'Tell them to keep all the doors locked,' Johnny called after him. 'And we'll be home soon.'

Both numbers were engaged. Gianni growled with frustration. 'No doubt yapping to one another,' he muttered. He left it a few seconds and then tried again: still engaged. He dashed back outside. 'Can't get through to either of them.'

Johnny nodded. 'Alice usually has the place locked up like Fort Knox, so she should be okay.'

'So does Cathy as a rule. Hope she remembered to lock up after seeing me out.'

The chief fire officer was on his radio when Gianni came back outside. He said, 'Over and out' and turned to Johnny. 'I've informed the police and they're on their way here to collect the evidence.'

Johnny nodded. 'Okay, we'll hang around until they get here. Gianni, you get back to Cathy. I'll try them one more time.'

Gianni said goodbye and set off back to the Linnet Lane bungalow.

*

Jack limped away from the house as the fire brigade arrived. He'd been hiding in the bushes by the front gate as the engine had sped past him down the drive. As he neared the end of the road he saw two men running towards him and dodged behind a tree. He recognised them as Alice and Millie's husbands and wondered where Cathy's was.

He stayed put for a couple of minutes until he saw Gianni puffing up the road. He smiled. Good. All the menfolk were now here and the women were at home on their own. His tactics in starting the fire to cause a distraction were paying off. He was sick and tired of hiding and stealing what food he could to stay alive. That woman who did the cooking at the big house had started locking the door now, so he'd had hardly anything this week. He knew his days of being on the run were numbered.

He slunk along the road, keeping as close to the hedges and bushes as he could, and made his way to Linnet Lane. The double-fronted bungalow stood out from the others in the row with its freshly whitened exterior. There was a light on in the front window, which he took to be a bedroom. The other side was a bay and was the lounge. That much he remembered from his visits here when his mate Terry was alive.

He slid down the side passageway to the back door and tried the handle. The door was locked, but he recalled from times past that Ma Lomax had always left a spare key on the shelf in the garden shed. If Cathy hadn't remembered or even known about it, then maybe it was still there. Heart thumping, he opened the shed door carefully and felt along the shelf. Among the dust and cobwebs his hand closed around something small and cold. Unless the locks had been changed when Cathy and Gianni had done the place up, he was in with a chance.

His pressed his ear up close to the back door and could hear Cathy's muffled voice. Sounded like she was talking on the phone. She'd be in the hallway then. He tried to recall the layout of the house. The window to the right of the small bathroom would probably be where the kid was sleeping. Then he remembered; the back door opened straight into the kitchen. He pushed the key into the lock and it turned easily.

He let out the breath he hadn't realised he was holding. The door swung open quietly as though the hinges had been oiled. He closed it behind him. He heard Cathy say goodbye and smiled. Praying she'd go straight to her bedroom, he held his breath. He heard a door closing in the hallway.

On the back of the kitchen door was a lightweight scarf. He pulled it off the hook and crept out of the kitchen. The hall leading to the front door was directly in front of him, with doors off to the lounge and front bedroom. To his right was an inner hallway that had three doors, the end one being a cupboard, he knew, as he'd seen Terry hang his coats in there. The thick carpet muffled his footsteps as he limped along the short corridor to the second door. It was slightly ajar and he slipped inside.

The kid was asleep on her back, her hands up either side of her head. Her bedclothes were kicked to one side and he slid his hands beneath her easily and lifted her up. She stirred and he whispered 'Shh, it's only Daddy.' She snuggled into him and he grimaced as he limped out of the bedroom. He swung open the cupboard door next to her room and lowered her onto some folded dust sheets that were covered in paint. They'd have to do. Better than the cold floor, which might wake her. He toyed with the idea of tying the scarf around her mouth, but he needed that for Cathy's hands. He closed the door quietly and she didn't make a murmur.

As he stood silently contemplating his next move the telephone rang out. *Hell, don't wake the kid up, please.* Cathy shot out of the bedroom and grabbed the phone just as Lucy yelled out, 'Mammy!' Jack opened the cupboard door quietly and picked her up. 'Shhh,' he soothed. She'd cried out in her sleep – her eyes were still closed.

'Mam,' he heard Cathy say as he stood hidden just around the corner. 'You're kidding me. Yes, all my doors are locked. Where's Gianni?'

*

Johnny finally got through to Alice and told her Jack was on the loose in the area, that he'd caused the fire, and to phone Cathy right away. 'Keep all the doors locked and make sure Cathy's are as well. Tell her Gianni is on his way. The police are out searching nearby gardens. Yes the house is fine, love. It was the brick outbuilding. He'd been living rough in there, it would appear. I'll be with you as soon as I can.'

*

Alice rang her daughter and passed on the message. 'Make sure everywhere is locked up tight. Gianni is on his way. The police will pick Jack up tonight, I'm sure. I'll see you tomorrow, love.'

*

As Cathy dropped the phone back onto the cradle, she felt the hairs on the back of her neck prickling with fear. She wished Gianni would hurry up. She realised Lucy had gone quiet after crying 'Mammy'. She hurried round the corner – and ran straight into a grinning Jack, who had Lucy in his arms. Cathy started to scream but the noise died in her throat as she looked into his mad eyes.

'Please don't hurt my baby,' she gasped. 'Give her to me.'

Jack laughed in her face and she gagged at the stink of his foul breath. 'Now do as I tell you and the kid stays safe,' he said. 'I'm putting her back into the cupboard and you are going to give me something I've always wanted.' He lowered Lucy back onto the dust sheets and closed the door. He grabbed Cathy's arm. She couldn't move, felt frozen to the spot, but Jack frogmarched her into the bedroom and threw her onto the bed.

'No, please, leave me alone.' Cathy kicked out with her feet and nearly overbalanced him, but he was determined and lashed out at her face. Remembering Eloisa's awful injuries and what he was capable of, she lay still, willing Gianni to get home. If she screamed and made any noise it would frighten Lucy, and locked in the cupboard in the dark she would be terrified.

Jack tore at her nightdress and yanked it off. Cathy was naked underneath and she cringed at the look on his face. He knelt on the end of the bed and yanked her legs apart. She closed her eyes so that she didn't have to look at him. She heard his zip being undone and froze as he touched her intimately.

Then, suddenly, there was the noise of the front door being unlocked and Gianni was calling her name. There were other voices too and she screamed for all she was worth and pushed Jack as hard as she could. The bedroom door opened and Gianni dragged him off her and threw him on the floor. Cathy pulled the bedspread over herself as Gianni grabbed hold of her and held her tightly while she sobbed against him. Two police officers were yanking Jack upright when Lucy's terrified, muffled cries rent the air.

'Where is she?' Gianni yelled at Jack.

'He put her in the hall cupboard,' Cathy cried. 'It's dark and she'll be so scared.'

'Right you,' one of the officers said to Jack. 'Got you at last. Attempted rape and kidnapping of a minor to add to your list of crimes.'

'I didn't kidnap anyone,' Jack growled. 'The kid's in the cupboard.'

'Yes, but you removed her from her mother's care and imprisoned her against her will – to me that'll do as kidnapping. You're nicked, Jack Dawson. We'll take him down the station and another of our officers will be with you shortly to take statements. Mrs Romano, did he hurt you? Do you need to go to the hospital? Your face looks a bit swollen.'

'I'm okay,' Cathy said. 'I'm a nurse, I can see to myself.'

'I'm glad we got here in time. You just take care and tell the officer everything that happened here tonight.'

Gianni saw the officers out. They dragged Jack up the garden path and pushed him into the back of the police car. He went back in to Cathy, who was sitting on the bed white-faced, cuddling a sobbing Lucy. 'It's a good job those officers caught up with me on my walk home because I swear I would have killed him,' he said, sitting beside his girls. 'I'll ring your mam and tell her what's happened. Do you want her and Johnny to come round?'

Cathy shook her head. 'They need to be at home for the kids. I just want to be with you and Lucy after the next officer goes.'

Gianni held her tight. 'If you're sure. Thank God he's been caught. His reign of terror is now over. May he rot in hell.'

Chapter Twenty-Four

On Monday morning, Cathy tried hard to put the last few awful days to the back of her mind and welcomed both Sarah and Penelope to Woodlands. She told them to hang their coats on the hall stand and leave their cases by the bottom of the stairs for now, and took them through to the kitchen where everyone was enjoying a morning break. She introduced them to the others.

'Hello, girls. Come and sit yourselves down,' Marlene encouraged and pointed to two adjacent chairs around the large table. 'We have got a posh dining room for formal occasions, but I hope you don't mind having your tea and toast in the servants' quarters,' she joked, putting them at ease.

Sarah smiled. 'This is right posh compared to what I'm used to,' she said, taking her seat. 'I hardly ever get to sit at our table with so many of us.'

Marlene poured them mugs of strong tea. 'Help yourselves to sugar and milk, and there's jam in that pot if you want some on your toast.'

Sarah thanked her and Penelope, who seemed rather shy and nervous, nodded and gave a little half-smile.

Karen introduced herself and the others. 'You won't remember all our names at once, but we midwives have all got name badges. Mrs Harrison might let you call her Alice if you ask her nicely, because Millie our receptionist is also a Mrs Harrison and she will be looking after all your records and paperwork. We don't want you getting confused. After you've had your snack, Sandra here will show you where you will be sleeping, and then Millie and I will take one of you at a time into the office and book you in. Now just relax and I'll come back for you shortly.'

Cathy and Alice waited in the room that had been made from dividing two back rooms in half, and set aside as an examination and antenatal room. Ellie brought Sarah to them first and Alice pulled up a chair for her to sit on. Sarah was weighed and measured and Cathy took blood samples. Alice gave her a small pot and asked her to do a urine sample in the cloakroom next to the kitchen. When Sarah came back with her pot Alice tested her urine with a dipstick and declared all was well.

'When did you last see a doctor, Sarah?' Cathy asked.

'When I had tonsillitis two years ago,' Sarah replied.

'You haven't seen a doctor since you were confirmed pregnant?'

Sarah shrugged her shoulders. 'My mam said there was no need. She heard me chucking me breakfast up a couple of days on the run, asked me about me monthlies, and when I said I hadn't seen them for ages, she clattered me around me head and said I was stupid and whose was it.

'I told her it were Barry Taylor's from the youth club but I didn't want him to know because his girlfriend is a right nasty cow and she hates me. But me mam marched me round to his house and his dad kicked up a right fuss and said he should do the right thing. But his girlfriend Gloria said she'd kill me if I went anywhere near him again. So I've kept away and hidden at home. I lost me job at Tate & Lyle for not going in because Gloria also works there and Mam went mad and said I'd have to go away. And then her mate told her about this place opening soon and she came to see you Saturday and that's why I'm here. I can't keep it, because I got nowhere to take it when it's born. It'll be better with someone what can give it a nice home.'

Cathy nodded and chewed the end of her pen. 'If you are sure that's what you want to do, we can arrange the adoption for you and make sure your baby goes to a nice family. So what date was your last period?'

Sarah screwed up her face. 'July tenth I think.'

Cathy nodded and did a quick calculation. 'Hop on to the bed while I see if the fundal height measurements tie in approximately with that date.'

Sarah clambered up onto the bed with Alice's help and lifted her dress up past her waist. Cathy took a cloth tape measure and took a measurement from the top of her bump to just below her belly button, noting how skinny Sarah was apart from the bump. *Some good meals from Marlene's kitchen will soon fill her out a bit*, she thought. She smiled. 'I think that's all for now. Nurse Harrison will check your blood pressure before you go, but your due date is around April the seventeenth.'

Sarah thanked her and Alice helped her down and took her blood pressure.

'We'll see you in the dining room about twelve thirty,' Alice told her.

Sarah smiled and thanked her. 'Where do the nuns stay? Haven't seen any knocking about yet.'

'Nuns?' Alice said, looking puzzled. 'We don't have any nuns here, Sarah.'

Sarah frowned. 'My bessie mate said all mother-and-baby homes are run by nuns that make you do horrible chores all day long and say prayers and hail Marys all night to repent for your sins.'

Alice laughed at Sarah's worried face. 'Not at this one. There are no nuns. We are not run by the Catholic Church. We are independent. We'll never ask you to do chores apart from keeping your rooms tidy. But if you ever feel you want to give Marlene a hand in the kitchen or around the house, she won't object. She works very hard to keep us all fed and the house nice and clean and could probably use a hand from time to time. Plus she makes lovely cakes and doesn't mind sharing a slice or two.' Alice winked.

'I'll be happy to help her any time.'

Alice smiled. 'Right, you're free to go and unpack your things and have a little rest before dinnertime and I'll see to Penelope. See you later.' She held the door open and Sarah left as Ellie brought Penelope to them.

'Take a seat, Penelope; I'll be with you in a minute.' Alice changed the draw sheet on the bed.

Cathy smiled at the young girl and asked her the same questions she'd asked Sarah. Penelope was guarded with her answers and not as open, as though she found it hard to talk about her condition. There was no information forthcoming about her baby's father. She just mumbled that it was a boy she once knew but she had nothing to do with him now and she didn't want to keep the baby. She kept her head down and didn't meet Cathy's eye once during their conversation, and when Alice asked her for a urine sample she looked horrified, but obliged when told it was important and that they needed the sample to check for various conditions.

As Penelope left to use the cloakroom, Cathy turned to Alice. 'What do you make of that? She was really evasive about everything.'

'Maybe she's just a bit shy,' Alice said. 'Give her time. She'll come round. It's a horrible situation to come to terms with. She's been shunned by her family and presumably the lad that got her into trouble too, poor girl.' She stopped as Penelope came back into the room and handed her sample pot to Alice. 'Thank you, love. Just take a seat again. We're nearly done now and then you can go and unpack your stuff and have a bit of a rest before dinnertime.'

*

As everyone was tucking into Marlene's shepherd's pie Millie dashed to answer the phone. She popped her head back around the door. 'That was Cynthia Elliott's husband. She's gone into labour and he's bringing her in right away.'

Everyone cheered and Jean and Cathy jumped to their feet. They'd finished their meals and were waiting for pudding. 'We'll have ours later with a brew,' Jean said. 'Our first baby is on its way.' They dashed out of the kitchen to loud clapping.

In the sparkling new delivery suite Cathy got out the sterile packs they needed and placed them onto the trolley. She checked to make sure the gas and air cylinder was working and lowered the delivery bed to the right height for Mrs Elliott to climb on to.

'Feels real now, Cathy,' Jean said. 'Hope she's not too far on that we can't get her up the stairs.'

'Oh heck, so do I. But we did give them warning to come in at the first sign of labour. Better they are here relaxing on our beds where we can monitor them than at home until the last minute, and then arriving here in a panic. It would be nice if they'd come in a day or two before their due date, but I suppose if they've already got a little one at home it might be difficult.'

'I'll go and wait in the hall for her,' Jean said. 'See you shortly.'

Cynthia's husband Alan accompanied his wife into the hallway. 'She's not been having the pains long, Nurse,' he told Jean as she led them to the staircase. 'But like you told us, we've come right away.' He and Jean helped Cynthia up the stairs and Ellie carried her case, following behind them.

'This is your room, Cynthia,' Ellie said, opening the door of one of the single rooms.

'Err, I'd better get off,' Alan Elliott said, backing away to the top of the stairs. 'Leave you good ladies to it. Not really a man's place is it? We only get under your feet.' He took a hanky from his jacket pocket and wiped the beads of sweat from his brow. 'Will you phone me when it's all over, Nurse?' he directed at Ellie.

'Of course we will, Mr Elliott. Say goodbye to your wife then. You can go in the room with her.'

He nodded nervously and quickly ushered Cynthia inside. 'I'll see you later, love. Good luck.' He pecked her on the cheek and fled as fast as his legs would carry him.

Cynthia and Ellie laughed. 'He thinks it's ready to drop out,' Cynthia howled. 'Did you see his face, Nurse? White as your apron. Daft beggar that he is. You'd think this was our first but he can't stand the sight of blood. He nearly fainted when our little lad fell off his bike and cut his leg and needed stitches a few months ago.' She held on to her baby bump as she laughed loudly. 'Oh, I'm going to wet myself if I don't stop.' She looked towards the door where Cathy and Jean were struggling to keep a straight face.

'Come on, let me check you and see where we're up to,' Jean said as Ellie helped Cynthia onto her bed. 'We need to get serious now.' She chuckled as her patient gave another raucous laugh. 'How long is it since you felt your last contraction?' She palpated Cynthia's tummy. 'Baby's the right way up anyway, that's a good start.'

'My last pain was about ten minutes ago,' Cynthia replied. 'But it wasn't too painful, just that tightening feeling and a bit like period pains low down. At my last clinic appointment, they said the head was engaged so I knew I wouldn't have too much longer to go before the baby put in an appearance. Oh I do hope it's a girl this time, but as long as it's okay, that's all that really matters.'

Jean nodded. 'You'll love it no matter what. But I think we've a few hours to go yet before we welcome him or her into the world. One of our nurses will bring you up a cuppa and some magazines to look at while you rest. There's a little bell there on your bedside table. Just give it a ring if you feel things are moving along quickly and your pains become stronger and more frequent and we'll get you on the delivery table and do a quick internal check, but for now you can take it easy.'

'This is lovely,' Cynthia said, looking around her pretty blue-and-white decorated room. 'It's like being in a nice hotel on holiday rather than in labour. Much nicer than the hospital. Wait until I tell my friends. Two of them are expecting later this year.'

Jean smiled. 'That's what we like to hear. I'll be back shortly.' She left the room and called to Alice over the banister rail. 'Can you take Cynthia a cuppa in please, Alice, and something to read? *Woman's Weekly*, maybe.'

'On my way,' Alice called back.

*

By six o'clock that night, Woodlands Maternity Home was welcoming its first new arrival. Baby Elizabeth Jane Elliott arrived hale and hearty. Her mother lay back on the delivery bed, her beaming face red with exhaustion, as Cathy placed the sheet-swaddled bundle in her arms. 'Congratulations, she's beautiful.'

'I can't believe it's a girl,' Cynthia said. 'I'm really shocked. I'd chosen a name, just in case, but never thought I'd get to use it.'

'I'll get someone to give Alan a call,' Jean said, pulling off her delivery apron. 'Our first baby. That's something quite special for all of us. Congratulations, Cynthia.'

Jean hurried down to the kitchen, where everyone was eating their tea. They all looked up in anticipation as she burst into the room. 'We have a beautiful little girl,' she announced. A cheer went up and they all clapped.

Marlene dabbed at her eyes. 'What wonderful news. And are they both okay?'

'They're fine,' Jean said. 'I'm just going to let Cynthia's husband know.' As she dashed away, Penelope and Sarah exchanged shy grins.

Alice smiled at the pair. 'Exciting, isn't it?'

Sarah nodded. 'Will we be allowed to see the baby?'

'In time. We'll let Cynthia have a good rest first. We have a little nursery that new babies will be taken to so their mums can have an undisturbed sleep for the first few nights.'

After Cynthia's excited husband had paid a visit, and Sarah and Penelope had settled down for the night, Jean called the others to sit around the kitchen table. Marlene had gone home after telling them she'd left a cold supper in the fridge and they should just help themselves 'We need a proper duty rota drawing up,' she said. 'I know today has been exciting and busy and we wanted to be in on it, but we can't work full shifts and all night as well. We'll burn ourselves out in no time. We need two of us midwives on duty at a time, and Alice, and we also need to think about employing another auxiliary nurse who can be here when Alice is off duty.'

'My auxiliary colleague from the hospital would like a job here,' Alice said. 'She asked me to let her know if anything comes up. I can ring her when I get home. She works with the babies on the children's ward and she's good with them.'

'She sounds perfect, Alice,' Jean said. 'Give her a call then and ask her to pop in for a bit of an interview as soon as she can. You can work out your shift patterns between you.'

Cathy chewed her lip as Jean said that the four of them needed to get their heads together and work out who would do what shift and when. She'd prefer not to do nights if possible. But anything would have to do for now, until they really got under way. More staff would need to be brought in if things were going to get busier. She'd been there since first thing this morning and it was now almost eight o'clock. She felt light-headed with tiredness mixed with elation at the very successful first day.

Epilogue

April 1964

Penelope wriggled around on her bed, trying to get comfortable. The baby was never still. She put her hands on her stomach and could actually feel its feet sticking up near her ribs. She smiled, thinking how her estranged boyfriend James would say it was a boy and he'd be a footballer. She wished she knew where James was. All she did know was that he'd been sent to a boys' Borstal for six months after getting involved with a tough gang who robbed shops and then sold on the goods to make money. He'd wanted to leave the gang but they'd threatened him and told him he knew too much for his own good and they'd have to kill him to keep him quiet, and the fear had made him go along with them. He'd written to her, but her mother had laughed and thrown his letter onto a roaring fire and told Penelope to forget about him as she'd never see him again.

They'd met walking home from school one day, he from Quarry Bank school and she from a small, private girls' school nearby. He'd hurried around a corner and bumped smack into her. She'd dropped her bag and he'd picked it up and carried it to her house, leaving her at the gate with a wave. The following night he'd been waiting for her on the same corner and they'd met regularly after that and had fallen in love.

They'd been inseparable until he was sent away. He didn't even know she was pregnant as there'd been no time to tell him. He would think she didn't care because she hadn't replied to his letter, but she had no address to contact him. Fat tears rolled slowly down her cheeks. The midwives here were so kind and caring and she wondered if they would help her if she confided in them about the secret that she'd never told to anyone. Once she'd given birth and her baby was adopted it would be too late to do anything. She looked across at Sarah, who was snoring quietly, oblivious to Penelope's turmoil. The pain she felt when she thought of James was agony and tore at her heart every single day. There was a tap at the door and it opened slightly. Alice popped her head around.

'Tea and cake going spare in the kitchen,' she whispered so as not to wake Sarah.

Penelope struggled to her feet. 'I'm on my way.' She'd be like the side of a house with all the cake she'd eaten since arriving here. But it was so nice to feel loved and cared for, and the staff here at Woodlands always made them feel as though they were a part of the family. Many new mothers and babies had come and gone since she and Sarah had arrived on that cold February morning. Sarah's baby was due this month.

In the kitchen Cathy was taking her morning break and greeted Penelope with a grin.

'You okay, Pen? You looked a bit serious as you walked in the door then. Have a seat. Do you want to talk?'

Penelope nodded. 'Yes please, I think I do. But could we do it privately somewhere?'

Cathy nodded. 'Let's go in the lounge. It's empty at the moment.' Penelope followed Cathy and they sat side by side on the sofa. 'Go ahead. Anything you say to the staff here is confidential and we won't tell your parents. You know that don't you?'

Penelope nodded and told Cathy the tale of how she came to be in Woodlands Maternity Home and how she now wanted James to know where she was and to let him know about their baby, but that she had no idea how to get in touch with him.

Cathy nodded. 'We may be able to help with that. I'll write down some details and see if Millie can start the ball rolling. Leave it with me and we'll see what we can do. If it's what you want, then that's what matters. Right, I'll bring you a notepad and pen and if you can give us as many details as you know about James, his birthdate, home address, that sort of thing. He may well be back home by now and for all you know it's possible he's tried to get in touch again.'

'Well there's no chance my parents will tell him where I am. They'll have sent him packing. My mother is a right snob and she said he's not the right class of boy for me.' She rolled her eyes, smiled and patted her baby bump. 'I guess I've well and truly blotted my copybook class-wise now, anyway.'

*

Cathy told the others at break about what she and Penelope had talked about. 'I hope we can find James for her. Millie's on the case already. We might have a successful pairing there for one of our young mums and if they want to make a life together then we can help them to do that. James sounds a decent enough lad, just one who was easily led astray by the gang he got involved with. Borstal may have straightened him out, with a bit of luck.'

Millie popped her head around the door. 'Mrs Roper is on her way in. Pains started an hour ago and she's just managed to get hold of her hubby at work. He's gone home to collect her. And Miss Hannah Shaw is being brought in by her mother later this afternoon. She's booked in long-term, not due for three months but according to her mother the neighbours are starting to notice.' Millie shook her head. 'I ask you. What are some people like?'

'Indeed,' Cathy replied, jumping to her feet. 'We've two due to go into labour over the next few days, so it's going to be another busy week and Sarah may start very soon too.' She frowned and clutched the edge of the table. 'Oooh, I feel a bit dizzy.' She took a deep breath.

'That's with jumping up too quickly,' Ellie said. 'Take it easy.'

By teatime, Millie had located James, who was now living back with his parents in Allerton. The news was conveyed to Penelope, who was told she could write to him. He hadn't been told any details of her condition or her whereabouts just yet, but had sounded overjoyed according to Millie, who'd pretended she was a friend of Penelope's passing on a message. 'I thought it best to keep it informal at this stage seeing as we didn't need to contact any of the authorities to locate him,' Millie told Penelope.

'I'll write to him tonight. Has anyone got a stamp? I'll pop out to the postbox at the end of the road when I've finished. Stretch my legs a bit and then I'll know for sure it's on the way. It is okay to put this address on for him to write back, isn't it?'

'Of course,' Millie said. 'I've got stamps in the office and if he wants to visit you here, maybe on a Saturday afternoon, then that's fine too. We can give you somewhere private to talk. Will you tell him about the baby in your letter?'

Penelope nodded. 'Yes, I don't want him just turning up and then me presenting him with this.' She pointed to her bump. 'If he doesn't want to know then he needn't reply and that will tell me how he feels.'

'It's worth a shot,' Millie said.

*

On her day off the following morning, Cathy walked away from the doctors' surgery feeling her smile stretching her face. She couldn't wait to see Gianni's face when she told him the good news. She hoped all would go well and she wouldn't miscarry again, although she'd been assured that there was no reason she couldn't carry a baby to full term this time. Her mam was off today too, so she'd call in and see her before picking Lucy up from school, but she wasn't saying anything until she'd told Gianni. They'd been trying for a baby since before Christmas and she'd been getting worried when the months passed and there was no sign.

It was very early days, she was only about eight weeks, but she'd suffered her usual nausea and just had a feeling, and when Luca said Maria was seeing babies in the crystal ball she'd seen it as a good omen. She would work until she no longer could, and then take her maternity break. Gianni had started up a small business at home, using his draughtsman skills to design built-in storage furniture and kitchens, and he had told her they'd look after the children between them. He'd had a few interested clients and once his design was approved, Johnny and Jimmy would carry out the construction and fitting work, with Gianni overseeing the final stages. It was a new addition to the renovation work they did and was proving popular.

Cathy let herself in at the front door. Her mam was pegging washing out on the line in the back garden. 'Hiya, Mam,' she called.

Alice came bustling in with an empty basket. 'Great day for drying the washing. Have a seat and I'll make us a brew. We drink enough tea in this neighbourhood to sink a battleship.'

Cathy laughed and sat down at the table. 'Just thought I'd call in on my way to pick up Lucy. Shall I get Roddy for you and take him back to ours for tea?'

'Oh, love, that would be such a help. I can get on with cleaning upstairs then. I never seem to get a minute since we opened Woodlands.'

'I know the feeling. But at least Gianni is home a lot and he can stick the washing out for me or put a casserole in the oven for our tea. He's a big help.'

'He's a good lad. But then Sadie brought him up the right way. So I'd expect nothing less from him.' Alice looked across to the mantelpiece at a framed sketch that Gianni had given her last year of Sadie, Millie and herself. He'd copied it from an old war-years photo they'd had taken. Friends forever; even though Sadie was no longer here, she was never forgotten and often brought up in their conversations.

'He's definitely a one-off,' Cathy said. 'And I'm so glad he's *my* one-off. How's our Sandra enjoying her training? I've not seen her for ages. Can't seem to catch her in these days.'

'She's loving it. She's never here. If she's not at the hospital she's round the corner at Ben's house or at the Cavern with her mates.' Alice rolled her eyes. 'Young love, eh?' She laughed. 'Oh to be a teenager again.'

'Just as long as Ben's not too much of a distraction,' Cathy said. 'Keep reminding her what happened to me!'

'Oh I do,' Alice said, trying to frown at Cathy, but smiling. 'All the time.'

Cathy left her mam's and knocked on Debbie's door to see if she was ready to walk to school to meet Jonathon.

'I am. Come on in, I'll just strap Catherine into the pram. I'm meeting myself coming backwards today,' Debbie said. 'I've not stopped since I got up.'

Cathy laughed and tickled her namesake under the chin.

'I've still not got around to getting her christened,' Debbie said. 'She'll be going to school at this rate. But with Johnny and Jimmy doing loads of work for us, everywhere is a mess and the garden is full of junk. It'll be next year before I can invite anyone in for a buffet.'

'You can have the buffet at ours,' Cathy said, 'or better still, at Woodlands. We could have a garden party if the weather is nice. Just let me check with the others tomorrow and I'll let you know. The garden is lovely right now, Freddie's worked hard and there's a swing and a sandpit for any kiddy visitors. It's ideal really.'

'Oh, Cathy, that would be brilliant. Thank you so much. As soon as you can let me know I'll book the church and vicar. They do christenings on the last Sunday of the month. So end of April will be lovely.'

*

As Cathy was asking the others if they'd object to the garden being used for Catherine's christening, the postman arrived. Millie called out to Penelope that there was a letter for her and she jumped to her feet, her chair crashing to the floor as she shot into the hall.

'It's got to be from James,' Ellie whispered. 'Fingers crossed everything will work out all right.'

'Wish I could write to Barry,' Sarah said wistfully. 'But Gloria would make mincemeat of us both if I did that.'

Alice patted her hand. 'Gloria sounds a right one if you ask me. Barry needs to grow a pair. He's entitled to his own life and to make his own decisions. If you are having any doubts about letting your baby go, then don't do it. You can stay here while you get on your feet and then we'll help you to find a job and a place to live. You mustn't feel bullied by this Gloria.'

*

The others all agreed that it would be a lovely idea to host a garden party for Catherine's christening at the end of April. Cathy rang Debbie from the hall phone and told her the good news. She and Gianni had last night decided they would wait another week or two before announcing their new baby news to everyone else. Cathy had told him she didn't like to tempt fate too early, she was still scared she might lose the baby and they'd agreed the end of April would be a good time. He'd been thrilled to bits and had hugged her until she squealed to be let go. She knew he'd enjoy a son to share his love of engines. Fingers crossed she could give him one this time.

*

By the time everyone arrived back from the church, where baby Catherine had behaved impeccably, Marlene had a sumptuous spread laid out on trestle tables. Bunting was tied on the trees, courtesy of Freddie's wife, who had made it from odd bits of fabric and ribbons she'd had in her work box for years. The sky was blue with fluffy white clouds and although it was still spring, no one needed a coat outdoors. Lucy, Jonathon and Rodney were arguing over who should have first go on the swing; Lucy won the argument by stating that ladies should always be first.

Cathy stood on the back doorstep and looked out at the people milling around in the garden. She felt contented, loved and happy, and above all else, safe. Even the outbuilding where Jack had hidden didn't spook her like she'd thought it might do. Everyone who had meant something to her from the past was here. Her godparents, Marlene, Freddie and Millie. Her lovely mam, Debbie, her lifelong best friend, and Davy, who she'd known since her first working day, Karen, Ellie and Jean, her nursing colleagues who were like sisters to her. Her younger siblings, her much-loved husband and daughter, and Jimmy and Johnny, who had helped to make Woodlands such a successful venture. She felt a little tug on her heartstrings as she wished Granny Lomax and Sadie could be here too. But she was sure they were with them in spirit. It was good to see the young mums-to-be enjoying themselves, and Penelope and James were talking in earnest at the bottom of the garden. Penelope had asked if she could invite him today as it was the only day he got off work from his new job and was the first time they had met for months. Her face had lit up as he walked into the hall and they'd not stopped talking since. Things were looking good on that score at least.

Doctor Kelso was here and he hadn't taken his eyes off Ellie all day; she in turn had smiled more than Cathy had ever seen her do before. A sure sign that her friend was healing inside and learning to trust again. After Davy had made a short speech and thanked everyone for their help and kindness in making today happen at last, Gianni got to his feet and, taking Cathy by the hand, he said, 'I'd like to make a little speech too if that's okay? First of all, I'd like to congratulate everyone at Woodlands for the success of this very worthwhile project. It goes from strength to strength as the weeks go by. The girls have worked so hard and the dedication they show to all their patients is reflected in the visitors' book and many letters of thanks on the pinboard in the hall.'

Everyone clapped, and then Gianni took a deep breath. 'Now, I know they are booked up for many months ahead, but if possible, could you just squeeze one more delivery in later this year for my lovely wife?' Cathy burst out laughing as everyone looked at them with puzzled expressions. Gianni continued with a big smile on his face, 'Cathy and I would like to announce that we are expecting a second baby Romano in late November.'

As a loud cheer went up and glasses were raised, Gianni pulled Cathy into his arms. 'I love you, Mrs Romano,' he whispered. 'Here's to us and ours and our wonderful new future.'

A Letter from Pam Howes

I want to say a huge thank you for choosing to read *The Midwives of Lark Lane*. If you did enjoy it, and want to keep up to date with all my latest releases, just sign up at the following link. Your email address will never be shared and you can unsubscribe at any time.

www.bookouture.com/pam-howes

To my loyal band of regular readers who bought and reviewed *The Nurses of Lark Lane*, thank you for waiting patiently for the fourth in the series. I hope you'll enjoy catching up with Alice, Cathy and the midwives. Your support is most welcome and very much appreciated. As always a big thank you to Beverley Ann Hopper and Sandra Blower and the members of their FB group Book Lovers, and Deryl Easton and the members of her FB group The NotRights. Love you all for the support you show me.

A huge thank you to team Bookouture, especially my lovely editorial team, Maisie and Martina, for your support and guidance and always being there – you're the best – and thanks also to the rest of the fabulous staff. Thanks also to my wonderful copy-editor Jacqui and excellent proofreader Loma.

And last, but most definitely not least, thank you to our wonderful media girls, Kim Nash and Noelle Holten, for everything you do for us. And thanks also to the gang in the Bookouture Author's Lounge for always being there. As always, I'm so proud to be one of you.

I hope you loved *The Midwives of Lark Lane* and if you did I would be very grateful if you could write a review. I'd love to hear what you think, and it makes such a difference helping new readers to discover one of my books for the first time. I love hearing from my readers – you can get in touch on my Facebook page, through Twitter, Goodreads or my website.

Thanks,
Pam Howes

Pam Howes Books

@PamHowes1

Acknowledgements

As always, my man, my daughters, son-in-law, grandchildren and their wives and partners. Thank you for just being you. I love you all very much. Thanks to my lovely friends for your support and friendship. A big thanks once more to my friends and beta readers, Brenda Thomasson and Julie Simpson. Thanks to the members of Stockport Rock'n'Roll Society for becoming readers as well as great friends. And love to Jackie and Derek Quinn and Jill McDonald, my lovely fellow R'n'R admins. And last but by no means least, a huge thank you to all the wonderful bloggers and reviewers who have supported my Mersey Trilogy and all four books in the Lark Lane series. It's truly appreciated.

Made in the USA
Middletown, DE
16 July 2020